MURDER BY DESIGN

MURDER BY DESIGN

a novel

BETSY BRANNON GREEN

Covenant Communications, Inc.

Cover image: *Painters Palette and Brushes* © FlamingPumpkin, courtesy of iStockphoto.com

Cover design © 2010 by Covenant Communications, Inc.

Published by Covenant Communications, Inc.
American Fork, Utah

Printed in the United States of America
First Printing: October 2010

16 15 14 13 12 11 10   10 9 8 7 6 5 4 3 2 1

ISBN: 978-1-60861-099-0

To my grandfather Julian Adair Brannon—
92 years young and still going strong!

CHAPTER ONE

THE DAY STARTED OUT BAD and went downhill from there. By the time we discovered the body, I wasn't even surprised.

My name is Kennedy Killingsworth, and I'm the librarian in Midway, Georgia (the dullest place on earth). I have lived in Midway all my life and currently reside in an apartment above the office for the Midway Store and Save—a self-storage facility and one of Midway's few thriving businesses. In exchange for my apartment, I collect rents for the owner, Mr. Sheffield.

My parents are upstanding citizens in the community and attend the Midway Baptist Church. Both my sisters are married and no longer live in Midway. Madison demonstrated only moderate good sense by making the nearby city of Albany her permanent residence. She and her husband, Jared, have four children (Mollie is a newborn and Maggie is barely two; Major is a demon at six and Miles at four isn't far behind him). Reagan wisely lives more than an hour away in Macon. She and her husband, Chase, have one daughter, Dallas (who has not shown any demonic tendencies to date).

I solidified my position as black sheep of the family when I divorced my husband, Cade. I am constantly reminded by family and friends that I'm the only Killingsworth in recorded history to put asunder what God has joined together. But while I thought we were happily married, a few months ago Cade had a romantic reunion at the local drive-in with an old high school girlfriend. Unfortunately I was an eyewitness (along with both of my sisters and a significant number of Midway's small population). Having come face-to-face (literally) with Cade's unfaithfulness, I felt that divorce was my only option.

And if my life weren't already complicated enough, it's possible that I'm falling in love with Luke Scoggins, a really cute ex-Marine who is also a member of Midway's most disreputable family. Luke and I have known each other since the third grade but didn't become friends until a couple of months ago when while trying to solve his uncle's murder I discovered that his father was the guilty party. It would have been understandable if Luke had decided to end our association after this. But instead he had maintained regular contact with me—even though he moved to Indiana to pursue his education.

The Saturday in question was the last one in May, which was designated by some former generation of Midway residents as Decoration Day. Each year everyone with relatives buried in the town's cemetery gathers on the last Saturday in May to clear away weeds and plant fresh flowers around the headstones of their ancestors.

I'm not crazy about dead people. I hate dirt and bugs and sweating in the hot sun. And I absolutely detest eating a meal while perched on the mounds of earth that cover the final resting places of the dearly departed. And barbaric though it sounds, that's exactly what we do as soon as the cemetery beautification is over. But Decoration Day is an occasion like Christmas and Easter, where attendance is not optional.

I was awakened from a wonderful dream just after one o'clock that morning. In my dream I was taking a bath in a stream deep within a dense forest. The fragrance of flora and fauna, combined with the clean smell of soap, was mesmerizing, intoxicating. I didn't want to wake up, so when I heard my name, I resisted—clinging to sleep and my beautiful dream. But the voice, though soft, was insistent, and gradually the flower-filled forest disappeared.

I opened my eyes to see a figure dressed all in black kneeling by my bed. He pressed a hand against my mouth to prevent a scream. Then he whispered, "I'll move my hand if you promise to be quiet."

I took a deep breath of his woodsy, soapy cologne and pledged my cooperation with a stiff nod. As soon as his fingers left my lips, I hissed, "You nearly scared me to death!"

He laughed softly under his breath. "Sorry." But he didn't look the least bit penitent.

I had met Sloan a couple of months before when he arrived in Midway as part of the construction crew that was going to help Drake

Langston remake Midway. During our brief association he had kissed me and saved my life. He's gorgeous and yet a little terrifying. When he left Midway along with his employer, I had hoped that he was a part of my past so I wouldn't have to sort through the conflicting emotions he evoked in me. But since he was now in my bedroom, obviously this was not the case.

For a few seconds his incredible blue eyes held mine in a somewhat helpless, nearly hypnotic gaze. Finally I pulled mine away and looked toward the open window. "How did you get in here?"

"Your security is laughable. A four-year-old could break into this apartment."

"The question is *why* would anyone, especially a four-year-old, *want* to break into my apartment?"

The teasing smile left his face and he sighed. "I'm in trouble, and I need your help."

I won't say I was surprised. In my life trouble always seems to be just around the corner. I pushed myself into a sitting position. "Okay, go wait for me in the living room while I put on some clothes. Then we'll talk about your problems."

Sloan stood in one fluid motion—graceful like a cat. "No one can know I'm here," he said. "So don't turn on any lights."

I tucked the edge of the quilt under my chin and nodded.

With a smile he closed the bedroom door.

I waited for a few seconds, giving him time to walk down the hall. Then I stood and pulled off my nightgown. Fumbling in the dark, I found a pair of jeans and a T-shirt. Then I tiptoed into the living room. Sloan was standing by the window, looking at the empty parking lot below. When he saw me he let the curtain drop into place and then waved at the couch.

"Let's sit down."

I accepted his invitation to sit on my own couch. Once I was settled on one end, he took the other.

"Now tell me what kind of trouble you're in," I commanded.

"It's complicated," he prefaced.

I gave him a smirk. "Talk slow and use little bitty words—hopefully I'll be able to follow."

He smiled, but the humor didn't quite reach his eyes. "I guess I should begin by telling you that I'm an undercover agent for the FBI."

Nothing he could have said would have astounded me more. However, in spite of my surprise, I didn't doubt that he was telling the truth. I don't know why I believed Sloan completely. Maybe it was because he had saved my life. Or maybe I just didn't think it was possible for anyone so handsome to be a liar.

"Really?"

This time his eyes smiled along with his mouth, but only for a second. "Yes. For almost ten years now."

"So all the time you were working for Drake, really you were . . ." I realized too late that there was no nice way to say it.

"Spying on him?" Sloan finished for me. "Collecting evidence against my friend and employer? Yes, that's basically what I do for a living." He sounded bitter.

I wasn't sure I wanted to know, but I had to ask. "Did you find anything?"

"No. Drake's financing strategies are creative, and he may not use government programs exactly as they were intended, but he does help people. There's a string of towns all across the southeastern United States to prove that. And considering the way the government manages its money, I don't know how anyone can complain about Drake."

"Apparently they can't," I replied. "That's why they are ending the investigation."

He nodded. "When I heard the official investigation was being closed, I figured I'd be told to turn in my resignation to Drake. But my supervisor said they wanted me to stay and keep an eye on him a little longer. So now I'm spying on someone who isn't even officially under investigation. I didn't think things could get worse, but they did."

"Is that how you got into trouble?"

He ran the fingers of his right hand through his silky, shoulder-length black hair. "No, I found a completely unrelated way to do that. I don't want to give you too many details, because then you could get in trouble too."

I nodded and he continued.

"Awhile back I stumbled onto something. I took some pictures and did a little checking. Once I had enough evidence to justify an investigation, I wrote up a report and sent it to my supervisor at the field office in Atlanta. I expected to hear back immediately, but weeks went by with nothing. Finally I called my supervisor, and he said he never got any report from me. No pictures, nothing."

"Maybe it got lost in the mail or something."

"That was my first thought. So I told him I would resend it. But when I got home, my apartment had been broken into. My laptop and camera were stolen along with all my files."

"Maybe whoever the report was about was trying to keep the FBI from investigating."

"That was my second thought—until I got to Drake's offices to use one of their computers and saw that all my e-mails had been deleted. That means that whoever was trying to stop my report was inside the Bureau."

"Do you know who?"

He frowned. "I have a pretty good idea. But proving it is going to be a problem."

"Without your laptop and camera?" I guessed.

"It's worse than that." He paused to heave a sigh. "While I was at the office searching vainly for my old e-mails, a federal marshal showed up with a warrant for my arrest."

"On what charges?"

"Tax evasion," Sloan replied.

Like most Americans, I have a healthy fear of the IRS. "That's serious."

"I pay my taxes on time every year, and there is nothing even remotely questionable about my returns."

"Then you just need to call the IRS and show them your records," I advised.

"I would love to do that," he agreed. "But without my laptop or personal files, it's going to take time to reconstruct my financial information for the past few years. Besides, it's not necessarily a matter of what's true and what's not. When the government is out to get you, they have ways of working around the whole 'innocent until proven guilty' thing."

I didn't have any trouble believing this either. "Well, at least they weren't successful in arresting you."

"No, Drake told the marshal that he didn't know where I was, and the guy left. Then Drake offered his legal department to help me fight the IRS, but I couldn't accept."

"Because if Drake's lawyers do any digging, they'll find out you're an agent who has been spying on him."

Sloan nodded miserably. "And I can't go to the police for help . . ."

"Because there's an outstanding warrant for your arrest." I thought for a minute. "Maybe if you explain all this to your boss at the FBI, he can help you straighten it out."

Sloan stood and started pacing around my tiny living room. "My supervisor is probably the one who framed me! My apartment is being watched, so I can't go back there. The IRS froze my assets so I can't access my bank accounts or use a credit card. I can't rent a car or buy a plane ticket because that requires showing my driver's license."

I mentally inventoried my bank account and said, "I've got two hundred dollars that I can loan you."

He stopped walking long enough to lean down and stroke my cheek. "Thanks, but money isn't my problem. I always keep cash in case of an emergency."

I felt relieved—partly because I couldn't really spare two hundred bucks and partly because I was glad Sloan was a good enough FBI agent to plan ahead. "So what are you going to do?"

Sloan clenched his fists and whispered fiercely, "I'm going to catch my enemy at his own game. If he wanted to silence me, he should have just killed me. Because I will go to any length to clear my name—even if it costs me my life or costs him his."

I shivered. "What do you want me to do?"

He pulled a tiny plastic case from his pocket. "This is the photo disc from my camera. It has the incriminating pictures on it."

I stared at the disc.

"I need you to hide it for me."

I swallowed the lump of fear that formed in my throat and nodded. "Okay."

He smiled. "I've been very careful to cover my tracks, and we don't have an established relationship with each other, so as long as you don't tell anyone you have it, I don't think anyone will think to look here. But if someone comes for it, you give it to them," he said firmly. "It's not worth *your* life."

This went without saying. "Where are you going to hide it?"

He stood and walked the length of the room. Finally he walked over to the Tiffany-style lamp on the table beside the couch.

"This looks old."

I waved around us. "Like everything else in here, it is."

"Does it still work?"

I shook my head. "No, it's too old to be dependable but not old enough to be valuable."

"It's actually good that it doesn't work," he said as he lifted the shade and attached the disc underneath. "Heat might loosen the adhesive on this." He put the lamp back in its place. Because of the multicolored plastic pattern on the shade, the disc blended in perfectly, making it nearly impossible to find unless you knew it was there. He walked back to the couch and sat a little closer to me this time. "That should be a safe place."

He hadn't asked for additional help, but I was worried about him and wanted to find a way to get him out of trouble. "I know you don't trust anyone inside the FBI, but there's an agent in Haggerty, Mark Iverson. I've met him, and he seems honest and, well, maybe he could help you."

He shrugged. "I know Iverson, and I think I could trust him. I'm not sure he has the connections necessary to really help me, and if I involve him, I'm putting him in danger. So it's not something I can decide without careful consideration."

I hadn't thought of this. "Now what?"

"Now I need a place to sleep. I've been up for forty-eight hours, and I'm rapidly reaching the point where I can't think straight. And if I can't think, my enemies will catch up with me. I was hoping you'd let me stay here tonight."

I nodded. "That's not a problem."

The relief showed on his exhausted face.

I stood and collected a pillow and a light blanket from the hall closet. When I returned, he was stretched out on my couch.

He reached for the bedding. "I should be comfortable here."

I shook my head. "No way." I walked over and opened the door that led down to Mr. Sheffield's office below my apartment. I pointed at the dark stairs. "You'll be spending the night down there, and this door will be locked."

Some of the tension left his face, and he gave me one of his smart-aleck smiles. "That lock wouldn't slow me down if I really wanted to come in here."

"Well, then maybe the .45 I keep in my nightstand drawer will."

He laughed. "You won't shoot me!"

This was true. "No, but that won't even be an issue, because I trust you to stay downstairs tonight."

He took the blanket and pillow from my arms. "Your trust is very important to me. So I will sleep downstairs—not because I have to but because you want me to."

I felt a little breathless (that happens often when Sloan is around). After such a declaration it seemed distrustful to make him sleep downstairs. But I was afraid that allowing him to sleep on my couch instead of the one in Mr. Sheffield's office would send the wrong message. So rather than change the arrangements, I just watched him descend the stairs.

Once he reached the landing below, I locked the door and went into my bedroom. I locked that door too and the window as well—although this meant that by morning I might die of heat exhaustion. At least I wouldn't have to worry about burglarizing four-year-olds or FBI agents sneaking into my room for the rest of the night.

Then I curled up on the bed and stared at the ceiling—worrying about Sloan. And even though I felt guilty for it, I had to wonder if by helping him I might be endangering myself and possibly even my family. My life was never simple. Often boring—but never simple.

***

I didn't think I'd be able to sleep anymore after Sloan's dramatic, early-morning arrival and the disclosures that followed. But I did fall asleep, giving Sloan the opportunity to wake me up again a few hours later by pounding on the door separating my apartment from the office below.

I was still wearing the jeans and T-shirt I'd put on in the wee hours of the morning so I didn't have to worry about getting dressed. And it was still dark so I had to feel my way down the short hallway. Then I yanked open the door. Sloan was standing on the top step and still looked exhausted. He walked to the couch and deposited his bedding there, all neatly folded.

"Why are you up so early?" I whispered. "You didn't get any sleep at all."

"I got a little," he replied. "But I need to leave here under the cover of darkness, so it's time for me to go."

The polite thing to do was argue, but the safe thing to do was agree. So I said, "Be careful!"

He nodded and took a step toward the door. Then he stopped and pulled me into his arms. "Thanks for everything, and don't worry about me. I can take care of myself." After pressing a quick kiss to my forehead, he opened my front door and slipped out.

I walked to the window and watched as he descended the stairs. Seconds later he was swallowed up by the night. Relieved and sad at the same time, I pressed my fingers to my temple where a headache was starting to form. The last thing I needed on Decoration Day was a migraine, so I walked into the kitchen and took some medication. Then I stretched out on the couch—certain that I wouldn't be able to fall asleep again.

I woke up two hours later. I had slept through my alarm and now had almost no time to get ready for work. I dragged myself from the couch, feeling tired and groggy. Since I had closed all my windows as a security precaution, my apartment was stifling. So I turned on the window air conditioner in the living room, even though it was fifty years old and didn't work much better than the Tiffany-style lamp hiding Sloan's photo disc.

Then I checked my cell phone, but as further evidence that it was going to be a bad day, there was no customary good-morning message from my . . . boyfriend . . . the aforementioned, and often maligned, Luke Scoggins.

I assumed the worst. It had always been just a matter of time before Luke met a cute college girl and forgot all about me. I had to smile at the irony. I'd been worried about whether or not to mention Sloan's visit to Luke. I didn't want to endanger Sloan, but I didn't want to keep something from Luke. But if he was breaking up with me, it would be a nonissue.

Disappointed more than I had a right to be over what I assumed was the end of a short-term, limited relationship with a man whose life I had nearly ruined, I forced myself to get ready for work. After a shower I felt only marginally better. I checked my phone again—still no message from Luke. Annoyed with myself, I walked to my closet and surveyed the clothes hanging there. My wardrobe consisted almost entirely of clothes given to me by my sister, Reagan. Consequently, getting dressed always felt a lot like putting on a costume.

I needed an outfit that would be professional enough for the time I had to spend at the library that morning but cool enough to keep me from dying of heatstroke while at the cemetery in the afternoon. Finally I decided to compromise on a pale green broomstick skirt and a white peasant-type blouse. The outfit was too casual for the library and too dressy for the cemetery—which in my life qualifies as a perfect compromise.

While drying my hair, I frowned at my reflection. My sister Madison "surprised" me with a free makeover the day before, which had included an appointment with a much sought-after stylist at her expensive hair boutique. I asked for subtle highlights that would give me that "just got back from the beach" look. What I got was thick blonde streaks that contrasted too much with my natural hair color, making me look striped rather than sun-kissed.

My plan, upon seeing the less-than-hoped-for results, was to buy a box of Miss Clairol and return to my drab but not obnoxious, light brownish hair color. But since I forgot to go to the store the night before, I would be forced to face the world in this condition. Annoyed with my faulty memory, I applied my makeup quickly to reduce the amount of time I had to look at my hair then hurried out to my truck to continue my worse-than-usual day.

Traditionally Decoration Day starts with a brunch at my parents' house, so that is where I should have been headed. Brunch on Decoration Day was a substantial meal—since it had to last us through hours of gardening until the late lunch my mother served around two o'clock. This year I had excused myself from this part of the annual ritual by scheduling myself to work at the library. So I stopped by the Jiffy Mart and bought myself a double-decker chocolate MoonPie and an ice-cold Diet Pepsi.

I climbed back in my truck at five minutes before nine o'clock, which meant I wouldn't be late for the library, baring unforeseen difficulty. However, in my life difficulty abounds. This time it presented itself in the form of black smoke billowing out of my 1972 Chevy Cheyenne C10 about half a mile down the road.

I pulled onto the shoulder, got out of the truck, and propped open the hood. After a few minutes of futile examination, I admitted to myself that I couldn't determine the cause of the smoke. So I called my father. Then while waiting for him to come, I glared at my truck and fumed about the injustices of life.

And I fervently hoped that my ex-husband, Deputy Sheriff Cade Burrell, would not learn about my humiliating circumstances and feel duty-bound to rescue me. Being indebted to anyone was bad, but having to *thank* Cade, especially on this already terrible day, would be too much.

Fortunately, Daddy arrived before anyone else. And proving that he was wise as well as dependable, he didn't mention my hair. "Morning, Kennedy."

"It's a morning, all right," I muttered. I pressed a grateful kiss on his cheek. Then I watched him look under the hood. When I couldn't stand the suspense any longer I asked, "What do you think?"

Daddy let the old truck's hood slam shut and shook his head. "I think we're going to have to take it to Maxwell's."

My father is an amateur car expert, so if the problem was too big for him, it was bad. And Maxwell's is a shop in Albany that specializes in rebuilding engines. Repairs of this magnitude would be very expensive and very possibly beyond my means—in which case I would have to sell my old truck to someone who could afford to fix it and then buy something that runs. I was stunned with grief at the prospect.

"I'll see if Terrance Cook can tow it in before he goes to the cemetery," Daddy continued, his voice lowered to show respect for my truck's critical condition. "And then we'll wait to hear what the fellows at Maxwell's have to say about it. In the meantime you can drive Luke's Torino."

Luke inherited the Torino from his dead uncle. He left it with me instead of driving it to Indiana to keep from putting a lot of miles on it (and thus reducing its value). But I considered the Torino parked in my father's workshop much more than a car-sitting job. It was a promise that Luke would return to me. Of course this theory had been thrown into question by the absence of his regular good-morning text.

I knew that there was possibly a reasonable explanation for Luke's failure to contact me that morning. And I also knew he wouldn't mind if I drove the Torino in a pinch. But I'm a car lover (especially an *old* car lover) and therefore hated to be responsible for any unnecessary devaluation. I could have asked my mother to borrow her new Mazda. But the last time she'd loaned me her car, I'd returned it full of bullet holes. And as a result I'd received countless lectures on a variety of subjects ranging from ladylike behavior to car care. I couldn't risk that again, so putting miles on the Torino was the best choice—especially since there was a chance that Luke was dumping me.

We abandoned my truck and rode in dejected silence back to my parents' house. Once there, I walked straight to my father's workshop, where the car keys were stored. I grabbed the ones for the Torino and marched back outside.

My father followed me step for step. When I opened the car door he said, "As long as you're here, why don't you come on in and eat some breakfast?"

"Sorry, Daddy," I said. "I'm already going to be late getting to the library. Mother understands that I have to work."

He nodded, although he didn't look like he believed it.

I did feel a little guilty that Daddy was going to have to face my mother alone and explain why I left without saying a word or eating a bite. But after all, he did marry her and was used to giving explanations. I slid behind the wheel of the old car. Since it was already hot and the Torino had no air conditioning, I rolled down the front windows. Once I had a little air moving through the car's interior, I turned the key in the ignition and was pleased when the old engine roared to life. Then, with a wave at my father, I pulled onto the street and resumed my journey toward the Midway Library.

I couldn't have driven more than fifty feet before my mother called my cell phone.

"Kennedy, are you leaving without breakfast?"

I hate it when she knows the answer to a question but asks it anyway. "I can't. I'm already late, thanks to my truck problems."

"Your daddy said the truck repairs will be expensive, so I told him to start looking around for a nice used car you could buy." Mother had always hated my truck.

"I'll wait to see what the guys at Maxwell's say about my truck before I start car shopping."

"And I don't understand why you didn't close the library so everyone could be with their family on Decoration Day," Mother continued as if I hadn't spoken.

I took a deep breath and fought exasperation. "The county doesn't recognize Decoration Day as a holiday, Mother. The library has to stay open. I've arranged my hours around my school schedule so you know I always work on Saturday."

"But you're finished with classes until fall."

"It wouldn't be fair for me to change my hours during the summer and then change them back when I'm ready to start school again in the fall."

"I wasn't asking for the whole summer," Mother said. "I was just asking for Decoration Day."

My mother loves family gatherings, and I love my mother, so I tried to soften my tone. "I know, but everyone wants Decoration Day off. You wouldn't want me to force someone to work in my place, would you?"

"I guess not." She didn't sound positive. "Just come to the cemetery as soon as you can."

I promised without enthusiasm and continued toward the library. The weather was not only oppressively hot, but also humid. So by the time I parked the Torino in the employees' lot I was sweating as well as late.

Miss Ida Jean—my parents' annoying neighbor—was waiting for me right outside the front entrance. "I can just about set my clock by you," she said as she followed me inside the blessedly cool confines of the library. "You're always fifteen minutes late."

This is not true. Sometimes I am more than fifteen minutes late. But arguing with Miss Ida Jean is pointless so I just kept walking.

"I don't mean to complain," Miss Ida Jean lied through her ill-fitting dentures. "But if you post a sign that says the library opens at a certain time, then that's when it should open."

"Carmella opened the library right at nine o'clock," I said, although Miss Ida Jean was very well aware of this fact.

"But I came to see *you*," she informed me, "not Carmella."

This was news bad enough to rival being dumped by Luke, Sloan's imminent arrest, and my truck problems. I turned and frowned. "You knew I'd be at the cemetery this afternoon. Why didn't you just wait and talk to me then?"

"It's urgent," Miss Ida Jean claimed. Then she squinted and pointed at my head. "Are you going prematurely gray?"

I gritted my teeth. "No, it's just blonde highlights."

"I don't like it," Miss Ida Jean said as if I'd asked for her opinion.

Since I didn't like it either, there wasn't much I could say to this. So I reminded her of her purpose in coming to the library that morning—besides to aggravate me. "You said you needed to see me? *Urgently?*"

"Oh yes! I wanted to tell you that Robby is getting out of prison next Wednesday."

Miss Ida Jean's son had been incarcerated at the state penitentiary for as long as I could remember, so this was big news. I wasn't exactly sure what to say under these circumstances but settled for, "You must be very happy."

"I am," she confirmed. "He's completely rehabilitated and anxious to be a contributing member of society."

I figured time would tell about that, so I murmured a noncommittal, "Mmmm."

"But he's been away for a long time," Miss Ida Jean went on, "and he's not sure how people will feel about him coming home."

Since Robby's name and his location were never mentioned in polite company, many Midway residents probably didn't even remember that Miss Ida Jean had a son. And it was unlikely that the ones who did remember him would be glad to see him return. Obviously I couldn't say *that*, so I just nodded and said, "Mmmm," again.

Miss Ida Jean got to her point. "I was thinking how nice it would be if the whole town welcomed him home. We could use yellow ribbon to tie bows all along Main Street so he'll pass them on his way to the bus station. Just like in that old song."

"Song?"

Miss Ida Jean sang a few bars, interspersed frequently with humming where she couldn't remember the words. Her off-key singing, punctuated with an occasional warble and combined with the perpetual spit string between her lips, took my lifelong morbid fascination to new heights. And I'll admit I let her go on longer than I should have.

Finally I came to my senses and held up a hand to stop her. "I get the idea." I couldn't help but think how odd it was that Miss Ida Jean—who does nothing for anyone else—thought that when her son returned from prison the town should go out of its way to welcome him. But that was just Miss Ida Jean. "Where will we get that much ribbon?"

"We could ask the Haggerty Mortuary," Miss Ida Jean suggested—and the word *we* was not lost on me. "Or maybe Cecille at Floral Occasions would donate some."

"If we can find some ribbon, I guess we could ask people to tie bows down Main Street."

Miss Ida Jean clapped her bony little hands. "I know Robby will be so pleased!" But not one to be easily satisfied, she added, "And we could have a party with cake and punch and invite the whole town!"

I don't like Miss Ida Jean, and I didn't appreciate her making demands on my limited time and resources. But her son had been in jail forever so I decided to be nice. "I'll ask Mother to organize something at the Baptist Family Life Center."

Miss Ida Jean frowned. "Robby never was one for religion, and after having spent so much time in prison, I don't think he'd be comfortable at a church."

I was losing patience with Miss Ida Jean. "If you don't have it there, where can you have it?"

"I was thinking we could have the party here." She waved to encompass the newly renovated First National Bank building which now housed the Midway Library.

While it was my intention to use the new library for community functions, I hadn't expected to start with a welcome-home-from-jail party for Robby Baxley. But, then, as I've mentioned, life is always throwing me curves.

"You can use the library." I walked behind the circulation desk. "But you'll still need the church ladies for refreshments."

Instead of showing a little gratitude, Miss Ida Jean stayed right on my heels, asking for more. "You know how awkward people feel when I talk about Robby—everyone but you, that is. So I think it will be best if you arrange the refreshments with your mother."

The last thing I wanted was to get involved with Miss Ida Jean or her recently rehabilitated son. But since this seemed like the only way I was going to get rid of her, I said, "I'll talk to Mother."

Miss Ida Jean gave me a big smile—which with her saliva condition was not a pretty sight—but she didn't leave as I had hoped. Instead she followed me behind the circulation desk, in flagrant disregard for library policy. She watched while I checked in with my assistant director, Carmella, who informed me that Miss Ida Jean was our only patron so far.

I sighed. A few months ago, when Drake Langston was trying to put Midway on the map, this new library had been a big part of his vision. Based on his plans to increase the number of tax-paying residents in the Midway city limits, the county library board agreed to extend our hours of operation, raise my salary, and increase our staff. But after Drake left town suddenly (with most of his dreams for Midway unrealized), the library board reconsidered. My salary was now basically what it had been when the Midway Library was in a double-wide trailer across from the city pool. Our hours of operation had actually been reduced, and I was running our beautiful new facility with one assistant, two part-timers, and four volunteers.

After telling Carmella to call me in my office if she was suddenly swamped by patrons, I headed toward the back of the building. I didn't realize Miss Ida Jean was still following me until she said, "Isn't that something about Cade and Hannah-Leigh Coley-Smith getting engaged?"

That stopped me in my tracks.

My family, like everyone else in town, felt I should adopt the "boys will be boys" attitude and overlook Cade's "misconduct" in the back of his Rodeo at the drive-in with Missy Lamar. Even after the divorce was final, they kept waiting for me to take him back—as if the legal dissolution was temporary . . . my way of punishing Cade for his bad behavior. They never expected me to actually mean it. But I did (and do).

For months Cade tenaciously tried to win me back. Finally I convinced him that while I could forgive him, I could never trust him again. Therefore our marriage was over, finished, another boring little part of Midway history. I even encouraged him to date, and when he started seeing Hannah-Leigh on a steady basis, I was honestly relieved to have his attention directed elsewhere. And I was completely certain that our marriage was over. But hearing Miss Ida Jean announce his engagement was still a shock.

I turned to her and clarified, "They're *engaged?*"

"Well, practically." She was so excited that she was the one to tell me the news that her beady little eyes were shining. "Margaret Thibodaux said she saw them at a Kay Jewelers in Albany yesterday looking at rings. She asked them if they'd set the date, and they said not *yet!*"

That did sound pretty official. And even though I resented the fact that Miss Ida Jean was taking such pleasure in breaking the news to me, I was thankful to find out about this unexpected development in the semi-privacy of the library. It would have been much worse to hear it for the first time at the Midway Cemetery with the whole town watching.

"Well, I wish them the best," I said, which was mostly true. "Now, if you'll excuse me, Miss Ida Jean, I need to do some important library business." This was completely untrue. I just wanted to be alone to think about Cade and his upcoming remarriage and what effect, if any, it would have on my life. So I stepped into my office and closed the door.

Miss Ida Jean promptly knocked. "You won't forget to tell your mother about a party for Robby, will you?"

"I won't forget," I replied without opening the door. I listened until I heard the sound of her retreating footsteps. Then I collapsed with relief into the dainty leather chair behind the antique desk and rubbed my temples.

Even though Cade had cheated on me and ruined our marriage, he was going to move on while I was still stuck in lonely limbo. Like most things about my life, it wasn't fair.

I checked my phone, hoping for a text from Luke to reassure myself that I wasn't a total loser. There was nothing. So I decided to take the bold approach and text him first. I sent a cute, friendly, nonaggressive message and then waited for his reply.

While I was staring at the tiny screen on my phone, willing Luke to answer, there was another knock on my door. Assuming it was Miss Ida Jean, back with more demands or painful disclosures, I hollered, "I said I'd tell my mother about Robby!"

The door eased open a few inches, and a tall, elderly woman peeked in. "Miss Killingsworth?"

Embarrassed, I stood. "Oh, yes, I'm sorry. Please come in."

The door opened wider, and my visitor came into the office. I studied her as she approached my desk. In addition to being tall, she was thin, and the length of her neck was exaggerated because she kept her chin raised in an unnatural way. Her dress was probably expensive, but even to my unfashionable eyes it looked outdated, and she smelled vaguely of mothballs.

She settled herself into one of the chairs in front of my desk and said, "My name is George Ann Simmons, and I live in Haggerty. Your grandmother Killingsworth was a friend of mine."

This was the Southern way of saying, "I'm about to ask you a favor, and you're obligated by family connections to help me."

I gave her one of my fake nice smiles and lied. "It's nice to meet you."

She gave me a condescending nod and informed me, "My father was the mayor of Haggerty for years and was quite influential in building up this area."

This was the Southern way of saying, "I'm about to ask you a favor, and since I'm part of an important family, you have to help me." The combination of the two coercion methods was powerful and a little alarming.

I could have said that my grandmother had never mentioned her or pointed out that our "area" was not really all that *built up*. But either remark would get me in trouble with my mother. So instead I downgraded my facial expression from fake smile to merely attentive and asked, "What do you need, Miss George Ann?"

Her chin moved a little higher. "I understand that you solved the mystery of Foster Scoggins's murder."

They say that pride comes before the fall, and I'm living proof. This sudden turn in the conversation caught me by surprise, and

I didn't realize it was a trap until too late. Foster's murder, the subsequent investigation, and ultimate arrest of the guilty parties were highlights in my otherwise dull life. So I demurely replied, "I assisted the sheriff's department and the FBI."

"I read about it in the papers," she said. "You are to be commended."

"Thank you." While I was basking in the glow of this compliment, Miss George Ann moved in for the kill.

"And based on your success, I believe you are qualified to investigate a case for me."

My eyebrows rose of their own accord. "There's been another murder?"

She waved this question aside impatiently. "Of course not, but a crime has been committed."

I have no legal authority, and I knew I shouldn't get involved in anything even remotely related to a crime. Not again. But I'm a very curious person (and as I mentioned, I've grown up in the dullest place on earth). So I stepped further into her trap. "What kind of crime?"

"I own several parcels of land around Dougherty County," Miss George Ann prefaced with her air of self-importance. "I rent them out, providing me with a steady and considerable income."

I work two jobs to provide myself with a tenuous and insubstantial income, so my expression became almost a grimace after this announcement.

"The only parcel I can't seem to rent is a small farm off Highway 46. It doesn't have enough acreage to make leasing it for crops profitable in today's economy. I talked to a developer about the possibility of building a new subdivision on the land, but he said the property was too far from town to make it attractive to prospective homeowners."

I nodded, even though I had no interest in Miss George Ann's real estate holdings.

"So it's been vacant since before my father died, but there has never been a problem with vandalism." She scooted to the edge of her chair before adding, "Until now! I drove out there yesterday to check on things, as I do at least once a quarter, and found that nearly one whole side of the barn is gone."

This was odd enough to draw a little of my attention. "Gone?"

"Cut off with a saw," she confirmed. "Someone has stolen the wood, and I want to find out who it was!"

"Then you need to talk to the police—not me."

"I spoke to Chief Jones, and he was most unhelpful. He said my farm is out of the Haggerty city limits and therefore not in his jurisdiction."

I took a deep breath and willed myself to be patient. "If your farm isn't in the Haggerty Police jurisdiction, you should talk to Sheriff Bonham. He's responsible for the rural areas."

"I'm perfectly aware of what Sheriff Bonham is responsible for—although he apparently isn't. He said he couldn't invest police man-hours searching for some old boards. He even had the gall to say I should just not worry about it." Her eyes widened as if this were the most ridiculous statement in the world. "Not worry about being *robbed*." She shook her head. "I don't understand why the sheriff would stand by and let property be vandalized without reprisal!"

"Then you should talk to Miss Eugenia," I advised. "She's the crime-solving expert, not me."

Miss George Ann pursed her lips, making herself even less attractive (which honestly I wouldn't have thought possible). "Eugenia and I are in the midst of a disagreement, and I won't give her the satisfaction of asking for her help."

I was more interested in the feud than the stolen wood, but I didn't want to extend Miss George Ann's visit by asking any questions. I preferred to call Miss Eugenia and get her side of the story. So I said, "I'd really like to help you, but I'm pretty busy with college classes and my work here at the library, and I have a second job collecting rents for Mr. Sheffield at the Midway Store and Save . . ."

Miss George Ann narrowed her eyes at me. "I'm sure you parents would expect you to help me in this matter."

And I knew she was right. She was not a part of my family, and it made no sense that I had to help her just because she knew my grandmother. However, in the South that's how it works. If I didn't do exactly as she asked, she would tell my mother. Then my mother would be upset, and I'd get a lecture on good manners and end up having to help her anyway. So to avoid all the drama, I nodded.

"Okay. I'll drive out to your farm and look around. But I warn you that I have no experience at this type of thing, so I can't promise that I'll find the thief."

Miss George Ann looked satisfied if not completely pleased by my agreement to provide limited assistance. "I'd like it to be done immediately before any more property damage occurs."

For the first time in my life I was glad for the inescapable graveside picnics on the last Saturday in May. "Since this is Decoration Day, I have to go straight to the cemetery when the library closes," I told her with a sweet, I-care-about-my-ancestors smile.

Miss George Ann didn't seem to notice my lack of sincerity. "Immediately after you finish at the cemetery will do."

My mouth actually dropped open at her audacity. But before I could tell her exactly what I thought, she pulled a small envelope from her purse, which I foolishly assumed contained gas money (it seemed like the least she could do).

She dispelled this misconception by saying, "Here are directions to the farm. I've written my phone number along the bottom so you can call me and report your findings."

I put the envelope in my purse and walked Miss George Ann to the front entrance, partly to be polite but mostly to hurry her departure. Then I went back to my office feeling a little discouraged. I checked to see if Luke had sent me a text message. Nothing.

Baffled, I looked through our texts from the past week, searching for something I might have said to offend him or clues that he was about to end our relationship. Again nothing.

Even though it was impossible, I started to wonder if Luke somehow knew that Sloan had come to my apartment during the night and had drawn the wrong conclusions. I didn't feel guilty about Sloan's visit, since I knew I had done nothing wrong. But having Luke mad at me was better than having him uninterested, so I almost liked this theory.

Finally I decided that it was foolish to jump to dire conclusions. It was equally silly to sit in my office and wonder why Luke had failed to send me a good-morning text for the first time in over two months. I was a twenty-first-century woman (even if I did live in a town stuck in the dark ages). So I dialed Luke's cell number. While listening to the phone ring in my ear, I mentally composed a light, cheerful greeting. When his voice mail answered, I left a light, cheerful message. Then I closed the phone and frowned. Still nothing was settled.

To distract myself I opened the envelope Miss George Ann had given me. Then with the assistance of Google Earth, I found an aerial picture of the farm in question. I could see a house and the barn. Even in the blurry, long-distance photos, I could tell that both structures were in a bad state of repair. The surrounding fields were overgrown, and the entire property was encircled by trees, which eventually gave way to grasslands dotted with a couple small lakes. The little farm was charming in a sad, dilapidated sort of way. It was also miles from any semblance of civilization, and I could see why no developer would want to build houses there.

The farm's closest neighbor was half a mile to the west. It was even worse than Miss George Ann's property—just a trailer and a couple of storage sheds. From my vantage point it was impossible to tell whether or not the trailer was occupied. I swung the mouse over to the south. There I found a few fields planted in an odd, patchwork pattern next to what was left of an old plant. Through some quick Internet research, I learned that it had once been a milk bottling plant and had gone out of business in 1957.

I printed off a map so I could question the neighbors in hopes that one of them had seen signs of old wood larceny. Honestly I didn't expect to find the guilty party. I was just doing my duty for my grandmother's friend. The most I thought I might accomplish was to prevent future vandalism by alerting the culprit (or culprits) that they were under scrutiny.

And I'll admit that even though Miss George Ann was twisting my arm, I was mildly excited about the opportunity to investigate something again. Especially since at this point it seemed like a simple, harmless case of wood theft. And by the time we found the body, it was too late. I was already irrevocably involved.

CHAPTER TWO

WE HAD NO PATRONS—THANKS to Decoration Day—so I decided to leave Carmella in charge of the empty library and get my investigation of Miss George Ann's farm out of the way. As I walked to the Torino, I called Miss Eugenia, hoping she'd agree to ride along with me. I did this partly to annoy Miss George Ann but mostly because I had no idea how to conduct a proper investigation—even one of something as inconsequential as missing barn wood.

I rushed Miss Eugenia through the obligatory small talk about my family—particularly my sister Madison and her horrible children. Miss Eugenia knows them well since, like Madison, she attends church with the Mormons. It's hard to think of nice things to say about Madison's kids, making this ritual uncomfortable for both of us. Once these niceties were blessedly over, I told her about my visit from Miss George Ann.

Miss Eugenia was gratifyingly appalled. "She seriously asked you to find out who stole some boards from a barn on a farm that no one uses?"

"She did," I confirmed.

"And she didn't offer to pay you?"

"Not one cent," I was delighted to inform her.

"That is beyond imagination, even for George Ann."

"And she said she wouldn't give you the satisfaction of asking for your help because the two of you are having a disagreement."

"Well!" Miss Eugenia's voice trembled with indignation.

"But I have to help her because she and my grandmother Killingsworth were friends."

"The way I remember it, your grandmother didn't like George Ann any better than the rest of us did."

"I trust your memory, but if I call Miss George Ann a liar, my mother will be upset." This may have been the understatement of the century. "So I'm going to look around her farm and see if I can figure out who stole her wood. And if I don't find anything, at least I can tell her I tried."

"That probably is the best way to handle it," Miss Eugenia conceded. "Sometimes good manners can be such a nuisance."

My thoughts exactly. "I'm headed out to the farm now, and I was hoping you'd come along."

"George Ann will be furious."

"I certainly hope so!"

Miss Eugenia cackled into the phone. "I'd love to come."

"I'll pick you up in ten minutes."

After ending the call with Miss Eugenia, I climbed into the Torino and headed for Haggerty. My mother called before I reached the Midway city limit.

"I just spoke with Carmella, and she said you left the library early," she announced a little breathlessly. "The timing is perfect. I've almost got our brunch ready."

"I did leave the library," I replied carefully, "But I'm not coming to eat brunch. I left work for a little while to do a favor for Miss George Ann Simmons. She said she was friends with Grandmother Killingsworth."

"She said that? I don't remember them being close," Mother said. Then she asked, "And what kind of favor does she want?"

"Since I helped investigate Foster Scoggins's murder, she wants me to see if I can find out who has been stealing wood off an old barn on some property she owns."

"Why that's just silly," Mother replied. She'd hated my involvement with Foster's murder investigation more than she hated my truck. "You're not qualified to investigate anything."

"I tried to tell her that, but she insisted."

"Of course, if she needs help, I guess you have to do what you can," Mother wavered.

If I'd had the time or the energy for a lecture on good manners, I would have begged her to explain why I had to help a stranger we don't even like.

"But I hope it won't take long. We need your help at the cemetery." I wasn't much of a gardener, so this was most likely untrue. My mother just wanted me there.

"I'll hurry," I promised. Then I decided to get another matter of business taken care of. "And Miss Ida Jean wants the town to throw a welcome-home party for her son Robby at the library on Wednesday evening. Can you and the church ladies provide the refreshments?"

"Yes," Mother replied. "Ida Jean is here right now, about to eat brunch with us. She told me that you wanted to host a celebration for Robby and would need my help. That was awfully thoughtful of you."

I was furious with Miss Ida Jean. If she was going to ask my mother to help, why had she come by the library and wasted my time? And why did she make it sound like the party was all my idea? I had to grit my teeth to keep from saying something I'd regret. Miss Ida Jean is so annoying.

"Did she also mention that she wants everyone on Main Street to tie yellow ribbons along his path so he'll know we're glad to have him back as a member of our community?"

"She told me," Mother confirmed. "I've already called Cecille at the florist shop and she's agreed to donate the ribbon. I've got ladies coming over on Tuesday morning to help me tie the bows. Then Madison has volunteered Major's Cub Scout den to pass them out on Tuesday afternoon. That will give everyone plenty of time to get their bows displayed before Robby's bus arrives at five o'clock on Wednesday evening," Mother said as if he'd been spending a few years abroad.

"You've already got the whole thing set up." My mother isn't perfect—except when it comes to logistics. "We don't have enough tables and chairs at the library, so we'll need to borrow some from the church."

Mother was way ahead of me. "I've already spoken to the preacher."

"And the refreshments can be light—maybe a cake and some punch."

"I know what kind of refreshments we'll need," Mother replied, and I was only too happy leave this to her judgment. "Now hurry and look for that lost wood so you can get to the cemetery."

I closed my phone just as I pulled to a stop in front of Miss Eugenia's house. Once she was settled in the passenger seat of the Torino, she narrowed her eyes at me. "Well, that's an interesting hairdo."

I rolled my eyes. "This is what happens when you let Madison do you a favor. I'm planning to color over it as soon as I can find time to run by the drugstore."

"Is that why you look so grim?"

I shook my striped hair. "No, I'm grim because of Miss Ida Jean Baxley." I explained the way I'd been shamelessly used, and when I reached the end of my narration, Miss Eugenia laughed.

"You have to give Ida Jean credit," she said. "She knows how to get things done."

I didn't want to give Miss Ida Jean credit for anything. "I'm tired of being the one she pushes into doing things for her."

"It's the Southern way," Miss Eugenia pointed out. "Ida Jean paid her dues in the past. Someday you'll be old, and you can push around a future generation."

I'll admit, this did make me feel a little better. So I left the topic of Miss Ida Jean and her lifetime campaign to make me miserable. Instead I asked, "What are you and Miss George Ann fighting about?"

"I wouldn't call it a fight, exactly," Miss Eugenia replied. "About a year ago she tricked me into being in the bell choir at the Baptist church. I feel that my obligation has been satisfied, so I quit."

"But she thinks you're still obligated?"

Miss Eugenia nodded. "Apparently in her mind it was an agreement that can end only at my death, which might be soon if I have to keep listening to those tone-deaf women banging bells. But honestly I'm in no hurry to make up with George Ann. If she's mad at you, she avoids you, and anyone would realize that's a good thing."

"It's not good for me," I pointed out. "Because you're in a fight with her, she's got me looking for her stolen wood."

Miss Eugenia laughed again. "But I'm going with you and she'll be furious when she finds out."

I had to be satisfied with that.

I followed Miss George Ann's directions to County Road 46, but I wasn't sure which of the many intersecting turnoffs led to her farm. Since there was a limit to my mother's patience regarding Decoration Day participation, I didn't want to waste time trying all the possibilities. I had resigned myself to calling Miss George Ann for clarification when we passed a small store.

The sign above the door identified the establishment as Meyer's Grocery. Under the name was a list of services that included fishing licenses, limited legal services, live bait, and faxing for one dollar per page. A wooden table displaying a variety of fresh fruits and vegetables was set up near the entrance.

"I think I'll stop here and ask for directions," I told Miss Eugenia.

"I don't know if it will do you any good," she informed me. "Mr. Meyer runs the place all by himself, and he's only open limited hours. And even if he's there, he might not know how to get to George Ann's farm. He just moved here a year or so ago after retiring from a law firm in New York."

I didn't even bother to ask how she knew so many details about the man's life. Instead I pulled the Torino to a stop in front of the store and said, "It's worth a try. And if nothing else, we can get us something to drink. I'm about to die of thirst."

We walked inside the dim interior and found the owner standing by the door. Mr. Meyer was a short, heavyset man of around sixty. He had a large nose that was peeling with multiple sunburns. He was wearing hip boots and a floppy hat decorated with fishing lures. In his left hand he held a cane pole, and in his right was a set of keys.

"I'm closing up for the day," he informed us brusquely.

I glanced at my watch. It was 10:35. "So early?"

He nodded and held his ground, essentially blocking our entrance. "That's the advantage of being the owner. I can close whenever I want."

"We won't keep you long," Miss Eugenia assured him. "We just need some directions to the old Simmons farm." She handed him the map I'd printed off the Internet and Miss George Ann's directions.

"And a couple of cold Pepsis," I added, looking around.

He stared at us for a few seconds—presumably deciding whether to help us or throw us out. Finally he stepped aside and pointed to a cooler behind the cash register. "Pepsis are there."

Cautiously I moved toward the cooler and extracted two ice-cold cans.

"And you're only about a mile from the Simmons place," he continued. "Just go back the way you came, and when you see an old sign advertising boiled peanuts, turn left. That road winds a bit, but you'll end up at the farm."

"Thank you very much." I put the Pepsis and a five-dollar bill on the counter. Then, feeling cheerful with the prospect of a refreshing drink, I said, "It's a nice day for fishing."

"Every day is good for fishing," Mr. Meyer replied. He deposited my five dollars in the cash register and handed me a single bill as change.

Two dollars each for a can of Pepsi was nothing short of back-road robbery, and I would have complained if I hadn't been so thirsty.

Mr. Meyer pointed at the map. "The old Simmons place—are you planning to buy it?"

I opened my Pepsi and took a sip. "No."

"We're just trying to figure out who has been stealing the wood from the side of George Ann's barn," Miss Eugenia said. "Any ideas?"

"No." He walked over to the door and held it open for us. Once we were outside, he locked the door to his store and took off walking across a field without another look in our direction.

"Well, he certainly isn't what I'd call friendly," I said to Miss Eugenia as we got into the Torino.

"But he did give us directions," she pointed out.

"Let's just hope they're right," I muttered.

The directions were exactly right, and a few minutes later we parked on the packed earth that separated the dilapidated farmhouse and the barn.

Miss Eugenia leaned forward, clutched the dashboard, and whispered, "I remember this place."

"You've been here before?" I'll admit I was a little annoyed that she hadn't recognized this fact sooner and remembered how to get there, thus eliminating our need to stop at Mr. Meyer's store.

"It was years ago," she continued. "George Ann's father let all the teenagers from the Baptist church to come out here and pick up pecans to sell as a fundraiser. Then when we were finished, he had the caretaker who lived here take us on a hayride."

I didn't even try to hide my amazement. "Wow."

She narrowed her eyes at me. "Hard as it is to believe, I was at one time a teenager."

I laughed. "That isn't what surprised me. Based on my encounter with Miss George Ann, I'm surprised that her father would be kind enough to give the church kids a chance to earn money and then throw a party for them."

"Actually he threw parties fairly often. It was the only way he could be sure George Ann would have a social life. She was as unpleasant then as she is now. But old Mr. Simmons was a very nice man and generous. George Ann was his only child and she was born later in his life. Like many doting parents he spoiled her and, well, you see the result."

"I've seen it," I assured her.

We climbed out of the car and I started toward the barn. Inexplicably, Miss Eugenia went toward the house instead. Reluctantly I followed.

"After the hayride we gathered in the house for hot chocolate. While we were singing by the fire, my husband—who was just my boyfriend at the time—stole a kiss. It was so romantic, and the farmhouse was quite charming."

I looked at the grim surroundings. "I'll have to take your word for it."

Miss Eugenia didn't smile. Instead she looked down at the rotting nuts that carpeted the ground. "It looks like nobody has picked up pecans here in years."

"It's been a while," I agreed.

"It's sad to see it deserted and in such bad repair." Her voice quavered. "It makes me feel old."

Of course, Miss Eugenia is old, but I didn't want her to dwell on that depressing thought. So I tried to distract her by pointing at the barn. "Let's go check out that stolen wood."

Miss Eugenia dragged her eyes away from the house and walked with me to the barn. The entire edifice was listing to the right and looked structurally unsound. "We'd better stand out here," I suggested. "Going inside could be dangerous."

"I don't know why in the world George Ann is upset that someone is stealing her wood. This place needs to be torn down anyway, so whoever took the wood is just saving her some trouble."

"I think it's partly the principle of the matter," I said. "She doesn't like being robbed. And she claims that this old wood is valuable."

"Humph! If you ask me, I think she just wants to cause a fuss."

We walked around to the far side of the barn, and, as Miss George Ann had reported, nearly one entire side was gone. The wood seemed to have been removed in an orderly, systematic way.

"It looks like they intend to just keep on going around the barn until all the wood is gone," Miss Eugenia remarked. "There must be a market for it, or they wouldn't go to the trouble to take it down so carefully." She pointed at several sets of tire marks that crisscrossed the barn's dirt floor. "Whoever took the wood has been here more than once and several times when the ground was muddy."

"It doesn't make sense." Solving the mystery seemed hopeless, and I was hot.

"Not to us, because we don't have all the facts," Miss Eugenia contradicted. "But no one would come out here and repeatedly remove pieces of wood from George Ann's barn unless there was a good reason to do so."

She shielded her eyes with her hand and looked into the distance. I stood beside her and followed the direction of her gaze. The trailer I'd seen on the Internet was barely visible to our left. To the right we could see the old milk plant. And in between were the oddly planted fields that resembled a patchwork quilt.

"How will we figure out who took the wood and why?" I asked.

Miss Eugenia dropped her hand from her eyes and headed for the car. "We'll go talk to the neighbors."

We used the map I'd printed to find the road that led up to the old bottling plant. When we were only about a hundred yards away, the road branched and a metal gate blocked our progress toward what was left of the milk plant. I parked in the road since there wasn't much chance of being a traffic hazard out in the middle of nowhere. And from there we studied the old building.

"It was built by Mr. Oscar Holloman," Miss Eugenia informed me. The misty, remembering-the-happy-times look was back in her eyes. "He used the most modern technology available at the time. He was very proud of it and used to allow school groups to come out for field trips to tour their facilities."

I have a pretty good imagination, but it was hard even for me to imagine the plant as state of the art. The paint had peeled off the cinderblock walls. Plywood covered the broken windows, and shards of glass littered what had once been a gravel parking lot.

Miss Eugenia stared at the old building, that sad look still in her eyes. "After old Mr. Holloman died, his children closed it down. They said it wasn't profitable enough. They didn't seem to realize it was a monument to their father and a service to the community. They had no interest in providing inexpensive milk to all the folks around here unless they could make a lot of money."

"Sometimes tough business decisions have to be made."

Miss Eugenia nodded. "I guess. Well, let's go find out if anyone lives in that trailer."

We turned right when we reached the main dirt road that connected Miss George Ann's farm to the old milk plant. As we came around a curve, we almost had a collision with a battered little Toyota truck. The driver was a young man about twenty, and I could tell he was as surprised to see us as we were to see him. We both slammed on our brakes and skidded on the loose dirt before shuddering to synchronized stops.

I was trying to catch my breath when the young man got out of his truck and rushed over to make sure we were okay.

"I'm sorry," he apologized. "I wasn't paying attention, but there's never anyone driving along here!"

I was about to point out that even if you don't expect oncoming traffic, you should still stay on the correct side of the road. But Miss Eugenia spoke first.

"We're fine," she assured him. "What's your name?"

The young man had obviously been expecting a lecture—or worse. So at Miss Eugenia's words, his shoulders relaxed and he said, "Tripp Hughes."

"Do you come out here often?" Miss Eugenia persisted.

"Yes," Tripp confirmed. "I'm a student at Heatherly College, and we're doing a senior project. We've planted various crops and we're testing fertilizers. The class members who are part of the project take turns coming out here to record data about the growth, temperature, moisture, and stuff like that."

I remembered the patchwork fields. "Why do you divide your fields into small sections?"

"So we can test several different crops at once."

"Do you know if anyone lives in that old trailer?" Miss Eugenia waved to our left.

Tripp—apparently glad that we weren't dead or pressing charges against him for reckless driving—was anxious to be of assistance. "An artist guy lives there. I've seen him a few times at Mr. Meyer's store."

Miss Eugenia nodded and then pointed toward Miss George Ann's farm. "There's a deserted farm over that way and someone has been stealing boards from the barn. You wouldn't know anything about that, would you?"

"No, ma'am," Tripp answered, but a telltale blush rose in his cheeks, which made me wonder if he was telling the truth. "I just come out here when it's my turn and write down the crop data. Then I head back to school."

Miss Eugenia didn't seem suspicious of his response, which surprised me. She's suspicious of everyone. "I'd like to know more about your project," she told Tripp. "What is your professor's name?"

"Mr. Shepherd," the boy replied promptly. "But if you really want to know more about the project, you should go to our website. We set it up as part of our grade, and it tells about the concept behind our project and details of the execution."

Miss Eugenia nodded. "That sounds mighty interesting. How would I find this website?"

"Do you have something I can write on?" Tripp asked.

I handed him the directions to Miss George Ann's farm and a ballpoint pen. He scribbled a string of letters, numbers, slashes, and dots. Then he handed the paper and pen back to me.

"There's a place for you to leave comments," he said. "I'll get extra credit if you mention my name and say I told you about the project."

"I'll be glad to mention you," Miss Eugenia promised. "Now you can go, but drive carefully."

With a wave, Tripp climbed back into his truck and proceeded past us at a more sedate rate of speed.

"So what do you think?" I asked as we waited for the cloud of dust Tripp had created to settle.

"He's lying," Miss Eugenia replied matter-of-factly. "The question is about what?"

* * *

By the time we pulled into the overgrown yard in front of the rusted trailer, I was no longer excited about the opportunity to investigate a crime. I was hot and covered in road dust, and even an afternoon at the cemetery was starting to sound appealing. Miss Eugenia, on the other hand, seemed to have forgotten her earlier melancholy and climbed from the old Torino like a woman on a mission.

While Miss Eugenia walked up to the trailer and rapped on the front door, I studied the yard. It was littered with beer containers of all types, sizes, and brands. There was also an impressive number of empty paint cans scattered around—oil-based, latex, interior, exterior, and even some deck stain. Lined up along the edge of the trailer were eleven abstract "portraits" (and I'm using that term loosely, if you didn't notice the quotation marks). They were all about three feet tall and two feet wide. The "canvas" consisted of weathered boards fastened tightly together. I moved closer to get a better look while Miss Eugenia continued to beat on the trailer's metal door.

The wood was old, and the "artist" (yet another loose interpretation) hadn't bothered to remove the rusty nails from the boards before gluing them together. Some slats even had little bits of hay still embedded in them. There was a lean-to beside the trailer with more boards stacked underneath. A makeshift worktable (consisting of two beer kegs and a mildewed piece of plywood) was set up near the woodpile. An old handsaw with several missing teeth was leaning against it. My heart pounded a little faster when I realized there was a good chance we had just located Miss George Ann's missing wood.

I motioned to Miss Eugenia.

She glanced at the wood, nodded, and then resumed her knocking.

I studied the artwork more closely. Several colors of paint had been applied in multiple layers using a variety of stroke sizes. The paintings lacked grace, vision, or artistic merit of any kind that I could see. The initials "JD" had been scratched into the right-hand corner with a sharp tool.

Abandoning her efforts to get anyone to answer the trailer door, Miss Eugenia joined me.

"Have you ever seen anything like this?" I whispered.

"They're terrible," she said, putting my thoughts into words. She pointed to the splintered edges of the wood. "The artist didn't invest much time in preparation." Her finger moved to the little globs of yellow that marred the wood surface. "He didn't even wipe the glue that came through the cracks. The colors are garish, the technique is juvenile, and the painting itself . . ."

Before she could pass her final uncomplimentary judgment, the trailer door swung open, and a thin man with long, gray hair and a wild look in his eyes hollered, "Hey, what are you doing?"

Hoping he hadn't heard our reactions to his paintings, I stepped forward and said, "Hello! My name is Kennedy Killingsworth, and this is my friend Miss Eugenia Atkins."

He nodded warily. "Name's Jarrard Dupree."

I gave him one of my you-can-trust-me smiles. "It's nice to meet you, Mr. Dupree."

Apparently my smile worked. Some of the tension left his face and he said, "Call me JD."

I turned my smile up a notch and accepted his invitation (even though addressing an elderly man with such casualness went against my mother's version of proper etiquette).

"JD," I said, "some wood is missing from a nearby barn owned by Miss George Ann Simmons, and we're trying to find out what happened to it."

I was going to wait and let him make the connection between the wood stacked under his lean-to and the boards missing from the barn, but Miss Eugenia didn't waste the time. "Wood just like this pile you've got here." She pointed to the side of his trailer.

Mr. Dupree looked in confusion from us to his woodpile and back at us again. "You mean this wood was stolen?"

Stolen seemed like such a strong word. "Well, the wood was taken without the owner's permission," I amended.

"You didn't pull it off George Ann's barn?" Miss Eugenia asked.

"No. I bought this wood," Mr. Dupree replied. "A fellow came by about a month ago with it piled in the back of his pickup truck.

He offered it to me at a good price, and I bought it. Gave him fifty dollars cash."

Miss Eugenia squinted her eyes. I couldn't tell if she didn't believe him or if the sun was just bothering her. "If you'll give us his name, we'll have a talk with him."

Mr. Dupree scratched his head. "Now that's a bit of a problem because I didn't get a name."

"Could you describe him?" Miss Eugenia continued the interrogation.

"He was just an average guy."

"How old?" Miss Eugenia persisted.

"Maybe around thirty."

"Tall or short—dark hair or light?" Miss Eugenia prompted.

Mr. Dupree looked sheepish. "Sorry but I don't remember. He only came the one time, and that's been a few weeks back."

"I wonder how he knew you needed wood for your . . ." I searched for an accurate yet honest word. I finally came up with "projects."

"Don't guess he did know," Mr. Dupree replied. "He was trying to sell the boards as firewood."

"Did you ask him to bring you more?"

He shrugged. "Naw, I figured when this ran out I'd just go back to using scrap wood from the landfill. My neighbor, Mr. Mcyer, takes me there whenever I need more."

"So you haven't always painted on these glued-together wooden planks?" Miss Eugenia asked, and I cringed. Fortunately, Mr. Dupree didn't take offense.

"No, I paint on whatever I can get my hands on—planks, scrap wood, even pieces of sheet metal."

I was trying to imagine how much worse the paintings looked on metal when Mr. Dupree continued. "I paid for this wood fair and square, but I don't want trouble. So if that fellow took it from a barn without permission, I'll be glad to pay the owner for it."

I was delighted by his cooperative attitude and saw an end to my investigation in sight. "That's very nice of you to offer. We'll talk to Miss George Ann and see if we can work out an arrangement that is fair to everyone."

His eyes skimmed me and then studied Miss Eugenia before he asked, "Are you two policewomen?"

I managed to keep from laughing out loud but just barely. "Oh no!"

Obviously Miss Eugenia was amused as well, because she was smiling when she said, "My only qualification as an investigator is a curious nature."

"Miss Eugenia is too modest," I corrected. "She has helped the local police and even the FBI with some cases."

"And Kennedy helped to solve a murder recently," Miss Eugenia told him.

"But we're not here in any official capacity," I felt obligated to add.

Mr. Dupree didn't seem concerned by our lack of authority to investigate barn wood theft. He looked at me and asked, "So what do you do—officially?"

"I'm the director of the Midway Library."

His expression became sort of dreamy. "I love books but never get to read anymore."

"Well, you should come to the Midway Library," I invited. "We're not too far away, and we have plenty of books."

He hung his head. "I've had a couple of DUIs, so they took my license away. I can't drive to Midway or anywhere."

All the beer containers scattered around his yard took on new meaning. "How do you get groceries and," I toed a rusty can, "things?"

"Mr. Meyer brings me groceries from his store."

"That's awfully nice of Mr. Meyer," I said with a speculative glance at Miss Eugenia.

She shrugged as Mr. Dupree replied, "He's a good friend. We fish together a lot."

"Well," I said, returning to the original subject, "if you can't drive into town, I could put you on a bookmobile route. But you'll have to be a library patron first."

Mr. Dupree seemed very interested in this. "How do I become a patron?"

"You fill out an application for a library card."

Mr. Dupree's hopeful expression faded. "That means driving into Midway, which I can't do."

I was happy to provide a solution to this problem. "Actually, I have a blank application in my purse."

Miss Eugenia raised an eyebrow. "You carry library applications around with you?"

I nodded, not the least embarrassed. "Since our funding is tied to our patron base—and we desperately need money—I'm always trying to drum up new patrons." I walked over to the Torino, reached into my purse through the open window, and removed one of the applications I keep in the side pocket. Then I handed it to Mr. Dupree. "Just fill it out and mail it back in to the address on the bottom."

He accepted the application with near reverence. "I hate to be a bother."

"It's no bother. You'll be doing me a favor," I replied magnanimously. "More patrons mean more funds, which means I can buy new books."

Mr. Dupree nodded. "Then I'll apply, but the mailman only comes by here when he has a delivery, and I don't get much mail. Would you mind if I fill it out now and let you take it back for me?"

Miss Eugenia had walked over to study the paintings again, so I got out the same pen I'd loaned to Tripp the college student and handed it to Mr. Dupree. He completed the application quickly and gave it back.

I tucked the application into my purse. "I'll send this in on Monday, and you should be getting a visit from the bookmobile soon."

"I just don't know how I can thank you enough." He really did seem happy. "I didn't think I'd ever have a library card again."

Miss Eugenia rejoined us. "When did you start painting, Mr. Dupree?"

"Call me JD, please," he insisted. "And I've been painting for about a year."

I contributed a little small talk. "This remote location is perfect for an artist . . . free from distractions."

"It's quiet," JD agreed vaguely. "And I've lived here so long I can't imagine going anywhere else. I'm saving my money so I can build myself a genuine log cabin here on my land." He pulled a well-worn brochure from his pocket.

I looked at his ragged clothes and figured the chances of his ever having enough money to build a log cabin, genuine or otherwise, were slim to none. But I smiled and said, "How nice."

Miss Eugenia seemed content to stand around and chitchat all day, but my presence was required at the cemetery so I said, "Well,

I guess we'd better go. We'll let Miss George Ann know about the wood, and then we'll be back in contact with you."

Mr. Dupree frowned, and I thought he had reconsidered his offer to pay for the wood a second time. But instead he turned to his recently finished paintings and said, "Before you go, I'd like to give you one of my paintings for the library."

Miss Eugenia and I were rendered simultaneously speechless by this.

"You could sell it and use the money to buy books and things."

The idea that his paintings could be sold for money was preposterous. But my mother had spent years teaching me good manners, and her hard work finally paid off when without thinking I said, "That is very kind of you, Mr. Dupree."

"JD," he reminded me as he rushed over to stand beside the portraits on display beside his rusted trailer. "Which one do you like best?"

"I really can't choose the best one." Now that was the truth. They were all equally bad.

Thankfully he misunderstood me. "Pick one or I'll have to do it for you."

I decided this was the best course of action. "You do it, then. I can't decide."

He studied the pictures for a few seconds and then smiled. "You're right. I can't choose either. I'm going to give you all of them."

Even my mother's extensive etiquette training had not prepared me for this situation. Obviously we couldn't take all his awful paintings. But I had no idea how to graciously refuse.

Miss Eugenia had been taught the same rules of Southern etiquette, and so I wasn't surprised when she nodded and said, "Thank you, JD."

He smiled. "When you get back to the library, you should call the newspaper and tell them you're having an auction at the library. Tell them to come out and take pictures of my paintings and print up a nice article in the paper about all the books you'll be able to buy with the money you make."

"You want your art to be recognized and appreciated by the community?" Miss Eugenia guessed.

JD shook his head. "No, I don't care about recognition. But if I show the newspaper article to the judge at my next hearing, it might convince him that I'm an upstanding citizen. And he might consider giving me my driver's license back."

Miss Eugenia chuckled. "That's not a bad plan. When is your hearing with the judge?"

"Next Thursday."

Miss Eugenia put a finger to her lips and considered this. "There's a big party planned at the library for Wednesday evening. The whole town of Midway is invited, and there will be free food. If we have the auction immediately afterward, we'll inherit their crowd and improve our chances of selling the paintings." She must have realized that this didn't sound very complimentary, so she added, "For the best prices."

"You want to have the auction this Wednesday?" I repeated.

Miss Eugenia nodded. "That way when JD goes to his hearing on Thursday, he can tell the judge all about it."

JD looked excited. "And if we get it in the Thursday paper, I can show him the article."

"It's perfect," Miss Eugenia decreed.

"I guess we can schedule the auction for next Wednesday night after the party for Robby," I said.

"Kennedy will make sure there is plenty of press coverage," Miss Eugenia further volunteered.

"I can't thank you enough," JD told us.

"We're the ones who owe you thanks for giving us such a . . . gift," I said, thinking that the library's social calendar was filling up fast. We hadn't had a single event since Drake Langston completed his renovation, and now we had two scheduled on the same day. "I'll set it all up. And I'll even arrange for someone to come get you so you can attend the auction."

JD shook his head. "No, it's better if I'm not there. I'll just read about it in the newspaper."

I wanted to insist, but Miss Eugenia silenced me with a little shake of her head. She leaned close to me and whispered, "Imagine how embarrassing it would be for him if no one buys the paintings." Then she turned back to JD and pointed at the paintings leaning against his trailer. "Well, help us load them in Kennedy's car."

I whispered back to Miss Eugenia, "We can't possibly take *all* his paintings!"

JD heard me and said, "Please take them. I can make more."

I couldn't argue with that since he could undoubtedly make pictures of similar quality in about fifteen minutes. So I said, "One painting is generous, but all this," I waved to encompass his portrait inventory, "well, it's just too much."

JD's expression clouded, and I knew I'd said the wrong thing.

Miss Eugenia stepped in to save the situation. "It *is* overly generous," she agreed, "and very much appreciated."

JD smiled and started picking up the paintings. "Let's put them in your car."

Reluctantly I opened the trunk, and he stacked most of them neatly inside. The rest he put in the backseat. Just as he placed the last one in, we heard the sounds of someone approaching. We all turned to see Mr. Meyer from the nearby convenience store walking over the hill toward us.

Once Mr. Meyer got close enough, he said, "I was going to invite you to go fishing with me, JD." He let his gaze move slowly from Miss Eugenia to me. "But I see you have company."

"Let me introduce you!" JD offered.

"That won't be necessary," Mr. Meyer said. "We've already met. I just didn't expect them to be here."

Miss Eugenia narrowed her eyes at him. "We stopped by to ask JD about George Ann's stolen wood and look what we found." She pointed at the stack of barn slats under the lean-to. "Since you obviously know JD and his work well, you could have told us that he had the wood when we asked you an hour ago."

"You asked me if I knew who *stole* the wood—not where it was," Mr. Meyer said in the annoying way lawyers have of picking apart a sentence and then putting it back together to suit themselves. "And I knew JD didn't steal it."

I was just about to make a scathing reply to this when JD stepped between us.

"That doesn't matter now," he said. "I told these ladies that I'll pay the owner for the wood since I did purchase stolen property—even though I didn't know it at the time. And as long as you're here, I need your legal services."

Mr. Meyer frowned. "What kind of legal services?"

JD pointed at the Torino, which was brimming with terrible paintings. "I'm giving this batch to the Midway Library, and I want to be sure that there isn't any question about ownership when Ms. Killingsworth sells them at the auction next Wednesday night."

"Call me Kennedy, please," I begged. It was bad enough that I was calling him JD—but worse if he wasn't calling me by my first name.

Both men ignored this. "Can you write up some kind of legal paper saying I transferred ownership to them?" JD asked Mr. Meyer earnestly.

Coming from a man who purchased wood from a stranger, this seemed like a cautious suggestion. But before I could frame a question that wouldn't sound rude, Mr. Meyer turned and spoke to me.

"You're taking *all* his paintings?" His expression had gone from merely unfriendly to downright hostile.

He acted like we were robbing Mr. Dupree, and I was highly insulted. "We aren't *taking* anything!" I assured him. "In fact, I've spent the last several minutes trying to talk JD out of his overly generous gift. Maybe you'll have more success."

"Nobody is going to talk me out of this," JD insisted. "All I need is for you to write out something to prove it's legal."

Mr. Meyer walked over to stand close to JD. Then in low tones he asked, "Are you sure about this?"

"I'm sure," he whispered back like a belligerent two-year-old. "They're my paintings, and I can give them away if I want."

"It's going to take time to replace them." Mr. Meyer waved at the boards stacked up in the car.

JD shrugged. "I got plenty of time."

Mr. Meyer fixed the artist with a stern gaze. "If you're determined to do this, get me a piece of paper so I can write out a statement for you to sign."

Jarrard Dupree returned to his trailer in search of paper. Miss Eugenia and I stood awkwardly with Mr. Meyer, who obviously thought we had coerced the artist in some way and didn't even try to hide his disdain for us. I was trying to think of a way to convince him of our innocence, but Miss Eugenia was still working the case.

"JD said he didn't know the man who sold this stolen wood to him," she said.

"If that's what he says, then it's the truth," Mr. Meyer replied.

"He said the man just stopped by out of the blue and offered it to him for a good price," Miss Eugenia mused. "But since the wood was stolen—even though JD didn't know it—he's willing to compensate George Ann. Is that the wise thing for him to do—legally speaking?"

"I'm not a practicing attorney anymore," Mr. Meyer disclaimed.

"I'm just asking for your opinion," Miss Eugenia countered.

"Then I think that's the best way to handle it," Mr. Meyer said. "If you can get Miss Simmons to settle for a reasonable price—which is unlikely, based on my experience with her."

"George Ann's never been reasonable a day in her life," Miss Eugenia murmured.

"You've had dealings with Miss George Ann?" I asked.

Mr. Meyer nodded. "I tried to buy that farm with the broken-down barn she's making such a fuss about. But the price she quoted me was ridiculous."

I wanted to learn more about Miss George Ann's ridiculous offer, but before I could question Mr. Meyer further, JD rushed out of his trailer waving a slightly yellowed piece of loose-leaf paper.

"I couldn't find a pen!" he announced breathlessly.

So I retrieved my ballpoint from my purse and extended it toward Mr. Meyer. He looked at JD one last time. The artist nodded, his eyes fixed on the paper.

Mr. Meyer wrote out a few succinct sentences stating that the paintings were now the property of the Midway Library and named me as the legal agent authorized to approve future sales. Then he signed and dated it. He had JD, Miss Eugenia, and me do the same.

Once we were done, he reviewed the finished product and nodded. "That should hold up in a court of law if necessary."

I resisted the urge to roll my eyes. What were the chances of anyone taking us to court over the ownership of eleven terrible paintings?

"Thank you for your help, Mr. Meyer," Miss Eugenia said in a conciliatory tone. "And thank you, JD, for donating the paintings."

JD blushed. "I'm glad I could help the library."

He watched as I closed the Torino's trunk and back door, hiding his artwork from view. "You need to keep the paintings in a safe place until the auction."

I appreciated JD's generosity and his kindness and his willingness to pay Miss George Ann for her wood so this silly case could have a happy ending. But honestly, I was getting a little tired of his visions of grandeur. He certainly hadn't been safeguarding the paintings when we arrived.

Of course, I didn't say that. Instead I thanked Mr. Dupree again and promised to lock the paintings up in my office at the library until the auction. "And I'll get you on the bookmobile route as soon as possible," I added as I waved I good-bye. I included Mr. Meyer in my wave even though he was still staring at us like we were criminals. I tried not to let it bother me, but it did.

Then I climbed into the Torino and Miss Eugenia did the same. Seconds later we were on our way down the dusty dirt road that would eventually lead us back to civilization.

Once we were back out on the highway, I turned to Miss Eugenia and said, "Well, that turned out pretty well. We found Miss George Ann's wood and a new patron for the library."

"And got a bunch of horrible paintings to auction off at Robby Baxley's welcome-home party on Wednesday," Miss Eugenia added.

I frowned. "Did you think it was odd that Mr. Dupree doesn't want to be present at the auction? He wants press coverage to impress the judge—so you'd think he'd want to be in the pictures!"

"Maybe on some level he knows they're not any good and is afraid that no one will buy them," Miss Eugenia said thoughtfully. "Being at the auction to witness that would be humiliating."

"True," I admitted. "And I certainly don't want to embarrass him. So instead of actually holding an auction, I could just talk to the local newspapers and ask them to do an article about JD's generous donation. He can show the article to the judge at his hearing, and that should be good enough."

Miss Eugenia shook her head. "No, I think we need to have the auction just as we promised. And I'm sure we'll make some money for the library."

I was amazed. "You think people will really buy those awful paintings?"

"I know they will," she responded. "As long as we invite the right people—ones with money who need tax write-offs!"

I laughed. "You are a genius."

"We might even be able to trick George Ann into buying one," Miss Eugenia said with a smile. "Or we could give her one to pay her for the stolen wood so that JD wouldn't have to come up with any additional cash."

I loved this idea. "Now *that's* what I call a good solution!"

"So we'll have the auction next Wednesday night," she said. "I'll spread the word in Haggerty."

"I'll tell my mother," I said. "That will take care of Midway. And I'll contact the local news folks."

"The refreshments your mother is already planning for the welcome-home party will probably be sufficient, but tell her about the auction just in case she wants to make a little extra."

I nodded, thinking I was really keeping my mother and the church ladies busy.

"If you're really going to store the paintings in your office at the library until the auction, you might want to see about having an exterminator come in and spray them. That barn wood is bound to be full of termites and who knows what else."

I shuddered. "I'll spray them."

"Now you'd better call and tell Miss George Ann the good news."

I pulled my cell phone from my purse and checked first to see if there was a text from Luke. The tiny screen was blank. No regular good-morning greeting was certainly bad, but his failure to respond to my text and subsequent phone message seemed even more ominous. I tried to tell myself that I didn't care, but honestly I felt like crying.

"Is something wrong?" Miss Eugenia asked.

I pasted on a fake smile. "No," I lied. "Of course not," I added to convince myself. Then I dialed Miss George Ann's number and turned up the volume so Miss Eugenia could hear the conversation too.

When Miss George Ann answered, I said, "I have good news!"

"You found the thief who stole my barn wood?" she asked.

"Well, I didn't find the thief, but I did find the wood," I responded. "A stranger sold it to Mr. Jarrard Dupree, who lives in the trailer across the woods from your property. He paints pictures, and he was using the wood as his canvas. He didn't know the wood was stolen, but he's willing to pay you for it. Or if you'd prefer, you can have one of his paintings as payment. He donated several to the library, and we're going to have an auction next Wednesday night to raise money."

"Tell her it's going to be a big auction with lots of press coverage," Miss Eugenia whispered. "And that we expect to get hefty tax-deductible donations for each painting."

I relayed this information.

"Well that's all fine and good," Miss George Ann replied. "But I don't need a painting. I need a barn. Otherwise my property doesn't qualify as a farm."

I frowned at my phone. "But Mr. Dupree only paid fifty dollars for the barn wood. That won't be enough to repair your barn."

"I don't care what Mr. Dupree paid that thief," Miss George Ann said. "He is in possession of stolen property, and the removal of that wood damaged the structural integrity of my barn. Unless he wants a lawsuit, he'll pay whatever the repairs cost."

For the second time in less than an hour, I was at a complete loss for words. I turned to Miss Eugenia for help.

She grabbed the phone and said, "Listen to me, George Ann Simmons. Mr. Dupree has a fancy New York lawyer, and you'd better be careful about using words like *lawsuit* when you're talking to him. You come to the auction on Wednesday and pick out a painting. That's the only repayment you're going to get for that old wood. And since it's only a matter of time before the barn collapses on itself, I suggest you work out a deal with Mr. Dupree to sell him the rest of the wood."

Miss Eugenia handed me back the phone. I pressed it to my ear and said, "Hello."

There was a brief silence, and then Miss George Ann said, "I thought I made it clear that Eugenia was not to be involved in this investigation."

"She isn't involved, exactly," I hedged. "She just came along for the ride."

There was another pause before Miss George Ann finally said, "My barn wood is none of Eugenia's business, and I don't appreciate her insulting tone of voice. However, I will come to the library auction, and I suppose I can accept a painting as payment." She added this as if she were doing us a favor.

"I think that's very sensible. And I'm glad I was able to help a friend of my grandmother Killingsworth." Mostly I was relieved to be done with her, but since our association was about to conclude, I was feeling generous.

"But you didn't find the thief," Miss George Ann pointed out.

"We may never know who stole the wood," I explained. "Mr. Dupree didn't get his name and can't describe him. So unless he tries to sell more wood to Mr. Dupree, we won't be able to catch him."

"But I asked you to help me bring the thief to justice," Miss George Ann said doggedly. "That was our agreement."

We didn't have a formal "agreement," and I didn't receive any compensation, so I couldn't believe that Miss George Ann was trying to hold me to some imaginary fine print.

"I did the best I could," I said a little testily. "But if you're not satisfied with my investigation, you feel free to hire a professional and see if they can do better. Now I'm about to be late for Decoration Day, so I'm going to have to let you go." I added a quick, "Good-bye." Then I closed the phone.

I turned to Miss Eugenia and said, "Can you believe she still wants me to keep looking for the thief even though we found her wood?"

Miss Eugenia laughed. "I can believe it, all right. George Ann redefines *audacity*."

I still couldn't really believe it had happened. "You'd think she'd thank me instead of complaining about the quality of my work and pressuring me to continue the investigation. It would be impossible to find out who stole that wood!"

"Actually, I'm pretty sure we know who stole the wood."

I was shocked. "We do?"

Miss Eugenia laughed. "It was either JD himself or someone else acting in his behalf."

"JD?" I repeated. "But he seemed so sincere when he said he didn't do it."

"His story about someone coming up with a truckload of wood and offering it to him was a little far-fetched. Who would drive up to that trailer and think that they could sell anything to the owner?"

"You do have a point there."

"And JD was too quick to offer to pay for the wood. A truly innocent man would have waited until the police forced him to pay or return the wood. And we saw multiple sets of tire prints at the barn. The wood was taken over the course of weeks—maybe months. It wasn't a one-time deal."

"But JD doesn't even have a car."

"Not one that we know of," Miss Eugenia conceded. "So I figure it was probably Tripp and his fellow students who are growing crops with experimental fertilizer out by the old milk bottling plant. College kids are always on the lookout for a way to make an extra dollar. Besides, I saw little pieces of wood in the back of Tripp's truck"

I was stunned. I hadn't noticed any of these clues. "If you doubted their stories, why didn't you accuse them?"

"Because I don't think they meant any harm. JD needed wood to paint on; the boys saw the old, broken-down barn and offered him the wood. JD is willing to pay for what he used. And I certainly don't want to give George Ann any satisfaction."

I was still marveling at Miss Eugenia's deductive reasoning when we pulled up in front of her house. "I can see how you were able to help the FBI crack cases."

She laughed as she climbed out of the Torino. "My sister's birthday is coming up, and she loves to own unique things she can show off to people. So would you sell me one of JD's paintings in advance of the auction?"

"You don't have to buy one!" I said. "You can have one for all the help you've given me."

Miss Eugenia shook her head. "Nonsense. I'll give you a hundred dollars."

This seemed like an exorbitant amount, and I was about to argue, but she held up a hand to stop me.

"It's basically a donation for the library, and I have to buy my sister something anyway."

I had known Miss Eugenia long enough to realize that arguing with her was a waste of time. So I climbed out of the car and opened the trunk. "Well, then I accept. Which one would you like?"

"They're all about the same," Miss Eugenia said. "I'll just take the one on top. If you'll bring it in for me, I'll get your money."

I lifted the top painting from the stack in the trunk and carried it into the house for Miss Eugenia. She had me put it in a back closet so that her sister wouldn't see it before her birthday. Then she gave me a hundred dollars in cash.

"I'll write you a receipt when I get back to the library," I promised.

"No hurry. I'll just get it from you the next time I'm in Midway, which will be next Wednesday at the auction." She turned to me with a sly expression. "And of course I'll come early enough to attend Robby Baxley's welcome-home party as well."

I rolled my eyes. "You should come. Events like that don't happen every day."

Miss Eugenia's laughter was still ringing in my ears as I walked back out to the Torino. And I had to admit that my bad day had taken a turn for the better. Thanks to Miss Eugenia I had solved a mystery and raised a nice sum of money for the library with the prospect of more ahead.

***

The little investigative excursion took longer than I expected and by the time I got back to Midway, my faithful assistant, Carmella, had closed the library. I unlocked the back door and lugged JD's paintings—one at a time—into my office. I stacked them in the corner furthest from my desk and then found some Raid in the utility closet. I didn't want to damage the paintings themselves, so I just sprayed all around them, hoping to exterminate any bugs living in the old wood.

I tucked Miss Eugenia's hundred-dollar bill in the receipt book I kept in a desk drawer. Left with no more excuses, I headed for the cemetery.

CHAPTER THREE

I GROANED WHEN I SAW cars already lining Main Street blocks from the cemetery—indicating that this year there was a particularly large crowd of grave decorators. But rather than join those who parked on the outskirts, I drove on with unreasonable optimism past several available spots and continued through the black wrought-iron columns that mark the cemetery entrance.

The Midway Cemetery is situated on arguably the best piece of land in Dougherty County. It's very green with a few gently rolling hills and is enclosed by a manicured hedge that—according to local lore—was planted during the Civil War. Daddy says it's a shame to waste such beautiful land on people who can't appreciate it. I rarely disagree with my father, but if there really isn't a heaven (and for years now, I've had my doubts), then where you're buried is important. And spending eternity in the Midway Cemetery wouldn't be a terrible thing.

The cemetery is divided into four sections with a huge limestone statue of an angel at the point where the sections meet. The northeast section is the "old" part with ornate headstones and a mausoleum—where people who have been cremated are buried above ground in little drawers that resemble post office boxes. All the plots and drawers in this section are being used, so no one else can be buried there. I've always found this whole area vaguely terrifying. As a child I always ran past the mausoleum. As an adult I don't run, I just walk very fast.

The cemetery's interior roads were clogged with vehicles. There were trunks full of plants, backhoes, and even one cement truck. Just as I was about to give up hope of finding a place to park, a florist van pulled out of a prime parking spot, and I eased the Torino into it—thinking to myself that sometimes optimism pays off. Then I got out of the car and trudged through the cemetery in search of my family.

As I walked by people, they called out greetings, and I responded politely. And I tried to say something complimentary about everyone's decorating—whether I liked what they had done or not.

No one actually calls Decoration Day a *contest*, but there is the unspoken spirit of competition. My mother admits to feeling the pressure but contends that decorating graves requires understatement to remain within the bounds of good taste. There was a life-size statue of Elvis going up on the southeast quadrant—proving that everyone didn't share my mother's sense of cemetery decorum.

The Killingsworths are buried near the statue in the middle with some folks in the old northeast section and some in the newer northwest section. When I reached the gathering spot, I learned that Madison and her family would be joining us after she finished nursing her new baby. And Reagan had bravely left her husband and their daughter, Dallas, at home in Macon. My mother's grim expression eloquently conveyed her feelings about this decision.

"You weren't the only family member who decided to skip brunch this year," Mother said tightly.

"Chase had some work he had to finish, so I left Dallas with him," Reagan explained for my benefit. "They'll be here before time to take our annual family photo."

I expected Mother to take comfort in this knowledge since the picture of us all gathered around the graves is very important to her. But Reagan's mention of the picture only seemed to upset her more. She pulled a lace handkerchief from her pocket and dabbed at her eyes. "It just doesn't seem like too much to ask that I have all of my family together for brunch on Decoration Day."

It also didn't seem like the crime of the century to miss brunch on Decoration Day, and I was just about to point this out when my father intervened. "Let's discuss this later. People are starting to stare."

There was nothing Mother hated more than making a public scene, so she gave her nose a swipe with the hanky and returned it to her pocket.

I saw Luke's eight-year-old niece, Heaven, who was living with my parents until a permanent foster home could be found for her. She held a rake, a pair of hedge clippers, and a trowel. She has delinquent tendencies, so I considered these items in her possession a show of questionable wisdom on my mother's part. I figured it was only a matter of time before she lost interest in grave gardening and tried to dig up a corpse.

"You'd better keep your eyes on Heaven," I whispered to my mother. "Especially since she's armed."

Mother frowned at me. "Don't be absurd, Kennedy. Heaven never gives me a bit of trouble. I was worried that being here so soon after her uncle Foster's death might upset her, but she insisted on coming."

Heaven's eyes met mine, and there was challenge in her gaze. She had seen more than her share of tragedy and in the process had learned to hide her emotions well. So it was hard for me to imagine the circumstances under which she would be truly "upset." But Foster Scoggins's grave a few feet away did make me feel a little sorry for her. I gave her what I hoped was a reassuring smile.

She stuck her tongue out at me and then said, "What's wrong with your hair?"

My goodwill evaporated. I couldn't think of a response that was adequately scathing but wouldn't get me in trouble with my mother, so I stuck my tongue out too.

At this moment my oldest sister drove up in her shiny new Escalade and parked on the sidewalk (an infraction of both the cemetery rules and good common sense). I turned away from Heaven, angry with her and with myself, and watched Madison extract her newborn, Mollie, from a car seat. Madison climbed the small hill to where we stood, leaving her husband, Jared, to bring the other three children, a comfortable camp chair, and a playpen.

Mother waited for all of them to join us before distributing our assignments. Each sheet listed the graves we were responsible for beautifying—complete with a little sketch showing exactly what was to be planted and where.

"I divided the graves equally," Mother said. Then she shot Reagan an annoyed look. "But since Chase isn't here, someone is going to have to double up."

"If we all work a little harder, everything will still get done," Daddy said, obviously anxious to avoid another public display. "We have Heaven to help us this year, and I think Major's old enough for an assignment too."

Major is Madison's oldest son, and I think he might be the devil himself. At my father's announcement, he sidled up to Heaven with a look of adoration. Heaven had instantly recognized Major as a kindred spirit, and since their initial introduction he'd been her evil protégé.

"Gardening tools, plants, fertilizer, and topsoil are all in the back of our truck," Mother said. "Major, you and Heaven work with Grandpa. Miles, you can help me." Mother paused with a frown. "Madison, I guess someone will have to do your assignment too so you can watch Maggie and Mollie."

I've been uninterested in kids all my life, but lately that has changed. And I definitely prefer babies to gardening. So I extracted Mollie from Madison's arms. "Since I need to improve my childcare skills, I'll take the girls, and Madison can do my assignment." I pointed to a big oak tree a few yards away. "Jared, will you set me up in the shade?" Then before anyone could object, I took Maggie's hand and started walking toward the tree.

For the next two hours I sat in relative comfort and ate graham crackers from Madison's diaper bag while the residents of Midway made cemetery improvements. Maggie was in her playpen, munching happily on goldfish crackers, and Mollie was cuddled against my chest, sound asleep. Heaven and Major were working diligently beside my father, and as of yet I'd seen no signs of an exhumed skeleton.

But all good things do, eventually, come to an end. The baby woke up hungry, and Madison came over to collect her. When she said she thought she'd go to our parents' home to feed the baby, I knew we wouldn't see Madison again until all the grave decorating was done. She hates gardening as much as I do and hates being hot and sweaty even more.

She did offer to take Maggie with her as well, but without a baby to tend I'd have no excuse to avoid my mother and her assignments. So I told Madison to leave Maggie and then, in an effort to look too busy to decorate graves, I offered to take the two-year-old on a walk. She was delighted by this.

As I lifted Maggie from the playpen, she grabbed my white peasant blouse with both of her goldfish-coated hands, leaving behind two unsightly orange spots. I did the best I could to clean up with baby wipes, but my best wasn't very good. Rather than eradicate the stains, I had managed to create two larger orange smears.

I had just given up on improving my appearance and returned the wipes to Maggie's diaper bag when someone called Cade's name. I turned in time to see my ex-husband walk into the cemetery with the lovely Hannah-Leigh Coley-Smith at his side.

Even though Hannah-Leigh is about my age, she and I could not be more different. I barely managed to get an associates degree at the local junior college while Hannah-Leigh graduated with honors from Vanderbilt. I wear hand-me-downs from my sisters while Hannah-Leigh is always impeccably dressed in the latest style (I felt sure she'd never found herself with goldfish-stained clothing at the cemetery on Decoration Day). She is never at a loss for the right thing to say while I rarely say the right thing. I avoid church whenever possible, but Hannah-Leigh is deeply religious. (She finds a way to work the Lord into almost every sentence.) Hannah-Leigh is even semi-famous. She's the weekend news anchor for one of our local television stations. So if you compare the two of us, she beats me in every category.

I watched them work their way through the crowd, holding hands and exchanging the occasional loving glance. I felt alone and very conspicuous there under the oak tree—especially with those orange spots on my shirt. I lifted Maggie, wishing she was bigger so she could hide me. Then we began our walk by heading for the far side of the cemetery in an attempt to put as much distance between myself and the happy couple as possible.

I had about two minutes of peace (if you don't count Maggie's attempt to eat potentially poisonous berries from the century-old hedge) before Cade joined us. He didn't even have the decency to wipe the ridiculously happy smile off his face.

"Hey, Kennedy," he greeted as if I were his kid sister instead of his ex-wife.

"Hey, Cade," I returned with much less enthusiasm.

He pointed at the baby. "Is that Madison's kid?"

I nodded. "Maggie."

"I'm two," Maggie provided. Then she held up a couple of orange fingers in case Cade needed clarification.

Cade's grin widened. "Well, how about that?"

I was done with small talk. "So are you and Hannah-Leigh really engaged?"

His expression took on a dreamy quality. "Not officially," he said—which meant yes.

"Margaret Thibodaux saw you at the jewelry store in Albany and has been sharing that with everyone she knows," I told him. "So if you were planning to keep it a secret, you're out of luck."

The knowledge that his privacy had been invaded didn't dim Cade's goofy smile. "I don't guess it matters," he said. I noticed the direction of his gaze and turned to see Hannah-Leigh being escorted around the cemetery by Cade's mother.

I watched Mrs. Burrell put her arm protectively around Hannah-Leigh as they walked from one family group to another and felt betrayed all over again. The Burrells had been very kind to me after Cade's drive-in affair and our subsequent divorce. While I knew they expected—like the rest of Midway—that I would eventually forgive Cade and take him back, they never openly accused me of breaking up our marriage (*unlike* the rest of Midway). So although I was no longer legally their daughter-in-law, I hadn't felt divorced from Cade's parents. But now suddenly I did.

Cade startled me from these painful thoughts by saying, "You were right."

Those were words that had rarely passed his lips, so they caught my attention. "Right how?"

"When you said that the two of us weren't meant for each other."

What I said was that he wasn't the kind of man to stay committed to one woman, so I would never be able to trust him and therefore had to divorce him. But before I could correct him, he was talking again.

"I tried to cling to the past," he said. "I didn't want to accept that our marriage was a mistake. But you forced me to see the truth, and now, well, I never imagined I could be as happy as I am with Hannah-Leigh."

His words hit me like physical blows. Our marriage was a mistake? He'd *never* been happy with me? Was he seriously saying that our marriage didn't work out because we weren't "meant" for each other—not because he'd broken his vows?

Maggie wriggled, and thanks to Cade's astonishing remarks, my arms didn't have the strength to hold her. So she slid down my body and plopped onto the ground. She grinned up at me, pleased about the unexpected freedom.

Completely oblivious to my state of mind, Cade continued to sing Hannah-Leigh's praises. "She's my soul mate." Belatedly realizing that I might take exception to his words, he glanced over at me and hastily added, "Nothing against you."

I nodded automatically, but his happiness with Hannah-Leigh did feel like an indictment against me. If he could be happy with her—and not be tempted to cheat—maybe it was me, after all. Maybe it was my lack that caused his misbehavior and ended in our divorce. The only painful emotion I had not felt in my relationship with Cade was guilt. Until now.

His mother called to him, and he was already walking away from me before he looked over and said, "Gotta go!"

After Cade left me to join his mother and Hannah-Leigh, I felt isolated and more alone than ever before. I sensed the furtive glances from people anxious to gauge my reaction to Cade and Hannah-Leigh and their obvious infatuation with each other. I felt their private judgments and even worse—their unwelcome sympathy.

Maggie grabbed my skirt to pull herself up out of the dirt, and when she released me she left two little dirty handprints behind on the pale green fabric. Humiliated even to my limits, I was about to pick up Maggie and run for my life when a late-model gray Malibu pulled through the cemetery entrance. I watched as the car meandered through the congested cemetery lanes and finally parked as close to the Killingsworth section as you can get without driving up on the sidewalk like Madison.

I watched in astonishment as the door opened and Luke Scoggins climbed out. His hair was a little longer than it had been the last time I saw him—less military and more attractive. He was perfectly dressed for a day at the cemetery, wearing a light blue polo shirt, khaki pants, and leather loafers. His eyes sought mine, and he gave me a big smile. Then my cell phone vibrated. I pulled it out of my skirt pocket and looked at the screen.

His message was only one word. "Surprise."

He pulled two potted planters brimming with beautiful mums out of the Malibu's backseat. Then he ambled toward me. He took his time, speaking politely to everyone he passed. But he glanced over at me and Maggie often, so that no one would have doubts about his ultimate destination.

He paused by Foster's grave and deposited one potted plant on each side of the headstone. Then he crossed the final few yards to join me by the hedge.

He gave me a quick hug and said, "Hey."

"Hey, yourself." I replied a little breathlessly. "Why didn't you tell me you were coming?"

"That would have ruined the surprise."

"I hate surprises," I told him.

"That just makes it more fun."

I was too happy to see him to be mad. I knew all of Midway was watching, and I stood a little straighter. Even though Luke and I had made no definite commitments to each other for the future, his mere presence dispelled the notion that I was unwanted.

I lifted Maggie and introduced her to Luke.

He shook one of her chubby little hands and didn't seem to mind that they were covered with slobber, goldfish crumbs, and dirt. "Hello, Maggie. I see you inherited the Killingsworth beauty."

The baby looked about as bad as I did, so I knew he was teasing us both. I waved a hand to encompass the orange stains on my blouse and the dirt prints on my skirt. "We're both a little worse for the wear."

"Food and dirt can't diminish true beauty." He directed his comments directly to Maggie, which made them funny instead of awkward. Then he turned to me. "And I love your new hair."

"No, you don't." I tucked a striped lock behind my ear as Daddy walked over.

When Luke saw my father, he stood a little straighter and said, "Good afternoon, sir."

Daddy nodded. "Hey, Luke. It's good to have you home."

"It's good to be here, sir," Luke responded.

Daddy turned to me. "Your mother sent me to get the baby."

I'm usually pretty good at reading my mother's signals, but I wasn't sure if this meant she wanted to give Luke and me some time alone together or if she wanted us to come decorate graves. I decided to assume the worst.

"Well, if you're taking over babysitting duty, I guess I'd better start grave gardening."

Daddy shook his head. "No, we're about done with that. You two just visit while your mother gets our picnic spread out. She'll call you when we're ready to eat."

"Wow," I said after Daddy and Maggie left us.

"What?"

"My mother never excuses anyone from decoration duty," I explained. "She really must be crazy about you."

Luke grinned. "One Killingsworth girl down and one to go."

"What about my sisters?"

"Since they're married, they aren't technically Killingsworths anymore. So I figure I'll concentrate all my charm on you."

I rolled my eyes.

Luke laughed and looked around the cemetery. "This is nice—everyone getting together to fix up their family graves."

I've already expressed my feelings about Decoration Day, so I won't be repetitious. But I did say, "I don't ever remember seeing you here before."

"I've never had a reason to attend Decoration Day before. Uncle Foster is the first Scoggins to be buried in the Midway Cemetery."

I narrowed my eyes at him. "Where are all the other Scogginses buried?"

Luke shrugged. "Out behind the salvage yard."

I wasn't sure if he was teasing me or not. "Is that legal?"

"I guess, although my family never worried too much about the law." He looked back over at his uncle's grave. "Since this is my first time, I wasn't sure what to bring. Some of the families are doing pretty elaborate decorating. I hope my mums are okay."

I nodded with confidence. "They'll let you get by with that for your first year, but next year you'll be expected to plant something."

I saw the relief in his eyes and realized that public opinion was important to him—even if he pretended otherwise.

He pointed toward the road and said, "Is the old Torino running good?"

I hung my head in shame. "I know this looks like I'm carelessly putting miles on it, but really I don't drive it all the time . . ."

He held up a hand to stop me. "I'm glad you're driving it. That's what cars are for."

"Well I wouldn't be driving it if my truck hadn't broken down this morning," I told him. "Daddy thinks it's the engine."

"Oh." Luke had been raised in a salvage yard, and he understood the significance of engine problems. "I'm sorry."

I sighed. "Me too. So anyway, that's why I'm using the Torino. But since you're in town, you should drive your own car. I can borrow my mother's."

"I've already rented that Malibu for the time I'll be here, so I don't need the Torino."

"How long will that will be?"

"I leave early Thursday morning."

That was longer than I expected, but I knew that Thursday would arrive too quickly, and soon we would be saying good-bye again.

Luke frowned, and I thought that he, too, was thinking of our impending re-separation. But then he asked, "Why were you hiding over here by the hedges instead of decorating graves with the rest of your family?"

"I wasn't really hiding. I was taking Maggie for a walk."

Luke just raised an eyebrow and waited expectantly.

"Okay, I was sort of hiding." I looked away so he couldn't see my eyes. "Cade is here with his new girlfriend, Hannah-Leigh Coley-Smith. She's the weekend news anchor from Channel 3 whom we met a couple of months ago when Heaven did her Scoggins Family Exposé."

Luke nodded. "I remember her."

"Well, they are about to get engaged."

Luke let my words hang in the air for a few seconds. Finally he asked, "Is that a bad thing?"

"No, or yes, or I mean I don't guess it is," I stammered. Then I turned back to face him. "It's not that I want him back or anything."

"I'm glad to hear that."

I tried to explain how I felt. "Cade ruined our marriage, but I'm the one being left behind while he moves on with his 'soul mate.' He even went so far as to say that we weren't meant for each other—insinuating that was why we had to get divorced."

"And you think the two of you *were* meant for each other?"

I grabbed his shirt and pulled him close. "Do you think it's my fault my marriage failed?"

He reached up and covered my fist with one warm hand. "I think there's no excuse for Cade's drive-in encounter with Missy Lamar."

I felt instantly better (Luke has that effect on me a lot). "Even if he was unhappy in our marriage?"

"If he was unhappy, he should have told you so," Luke said firmly. "But that's all in the past now. You're divorced, and you should be glad that Cade is moving on. That leaves you free to look to your own future."

I let my eyes skim over him. My future was looking pretty good at the moment.

He leaned close, and I'm pretty sure he was about to kiss me. Then the romantic moment was ruined when mother called for us to come over and join the picnic dinner she was serving on the graves of dead Killingsworths. I don't know why, but for some reason Luke accepted the invitation.

CHAPTER FOUR

As Luke and I walked toward the little gathering of Killingsworths, I noted that Reagan's family had arrived. Madison had returned with Mollie, and Miss Ida Jean had horned in on our picnic as she did every year. So when we joined them, the gang was all there.

We gathered for the annual picture, and I saw Mother take in the stains on my clothes with a look of horror, but before she could comment, Jared held out a hand to Luke and said, "I don't think we've met."

This breach of her normally impeccable manners jolted my mother out of her grief over my appearance. She quickly introduced Luke to Jared then to Chase and finally to Madison's children. While presenting Luke to Major, she made the mistake of mentioning that Luke was a former Marine who had served in Iraq.

Major, the little brat, immediately fixed Luke with a piercing look and asked, "So did you kill anybody?"

I didn't know a lot about Luke's military service, except that he hated it. So I held my breath, waiting for the answer.

"I did my best to keep people from getting killed," Luke replied deftly. "I was part of a team that disassembled roadside bombs."

That sounded very dangerous, and I couldn't control a shudder, but Major was fascinated.

"Wow."

"Enough of this war talk," Mother said as if she wasn't the one who started it. "Now, let's get the picture made so we can eat."

Mother and several other ladies employ the same photographer from Albany for Decoration Day every year. He's so old I figure he was probably taking pictures back when the hedges were just little sprouts. Mother tried to insist that Luke stand in the picture, but he politely refused. This was the right thing to do. Mother's very particular about her pictures.

Once the photographer had moved on to his next customer, Mother passed out sturdy paper plates reinforced by the same wicker holders we'd been using at Decoration Day picnics for as long as I could remember. Then she waved toward the folding table that held an impressive array of picnic foods.

"Everyone help yourselves," she invited.

Miss Ida Jean was first in line, followed closely by Madison. Heaven and her sidekick, Major, were next. The rest of us approached the food at a less frantic pace and loaded our plates with generous helpings of fried chicken, barbecue pork, potato salad, and glorified brownies.

Once we had our food, Luke led me to the blanket where Heaven was already seated. I would not have chosen this particular spot to eat, but I figured the Scogginses wanted to stick together. To make matters worse, Madison settled her crew on the blanket beside us. But the kids were hungry so they concentrated on eating instead of whining, which made our graveyard meal less of an ordeal than I had expected.

We ate in pleasant silence for a few minutes, and then Reagan asked, "What's going on with Cade and Hannah-Leigh Coley-Smith?"

"They can barely take their eyes off each other," Madison contributed.

"They're nearly engaged," Miss Ida Jean said. "They've already picked out rings."

All eyes turned to me.

I shrugged. "He says she's his soul mate."

"Soul mate indeed," my mother said disdainfully.

Miss Ida Jean decided to say something in Hannah-Leigh's defense. "I always like watching her on the weekend news."

Everyone ignored this.

"Don't you think she's a little overdressed for Decoration Day?" Reagan contributed.

I sneaked a glance at the Burrell section of the cemetery. Hannah-Leigh was wearing a bright pink business suit with high-heeled shoes that matched perfectly. "It's dressy," I agreed.

"But not what I'd call over-the-top," Madison said.

"No, she's within the bounds of what's acceptable for Decoration Day," Mother agreed, although she sounded disappointed.

"There's a dress code for Decoration Day?" Luke asked in obvious amazement.

My father laughed. "Son, according to my wife there is a dress code for everything."

Mother took the teasing well. "Oh, for heaven sakes."

"Well, all I have to say is if Hannah-Leigh seriously plans to marry Cade, she better not ever let him out of her sight," Madison added. "Otherwise he'll be cheating on her too."

I knew this was intended to make me feel better, so even though it didn't, I gave her a weak smile. Then I surprised everyone, including myself, by saying, "If they get married, I hope they'll be happy together."

I saw my family exchange speculative glances and knew they were wondering if my casual attitude toward Cade's impending matrimony was a result of a serious relationship with Luke. But before anyone could ask the question, Major and Miles got into a wrestling match and had to be disciplined or what passed for discipline in Madison's household. Heaven smirked through the whole process, leading me to wonder if she had instigated the entire incident.

Apparently Luke thought so too, because I saw him lean close and whisper something to his niece, and her expression changed from amused to resentful.

Then a voice called out to greet us. "Good morning, Killingsworths!"

We looked up to see Miss George Ann Simmons walking over to join us. I had to work hard to control a groan.

The presence of a lady required all the men to stand. Once the polite greetings were out of the way, my mother asked, "What brings you to the Midway Cemetery today? I didn't realize that you have relatives buried here."

"I don't," she said with a somewhat condescending smile. Then she raised the little pot of nearly dead pansies she was carrying. "I brought some flowers to put on one of the unidentified graves."

"The Midway Baptist Church handles that every year so that nobody's grave goes undecorated," Mother told her. "But that was very thoughtful."

Miss George Ann nodded. "I feel that as a Christian I have an obligation to do whatever I can for others."

"I wish more people shared your attitude," Mother said. "It would be a better world."

My sisters murmured politely in agreement. I couldn't bring myself to say anything, and I noticed that my father and the other men remained silent on the issue as well.

"Obviously you have done a good job of raising your children," Miss George Ann continued. "I cannot tell you how much I appreciate the help Kennedy is giving me. An elderly woman like myself would be defenseless against vandals otherwise."

My mother beamed with pride, and I realized I had severely underestimated Miss George Ann. She intended for me to continue my investigation, and she was there with her droopy pansies to enlist my own family against me.

My father asked, "What is Kennedy helping you with?"

"Someone has been stealing the wood from a barn I own, and Kennedy is helping me to bring the culprit to justice."

I was rarely responsible for making my mother proud, and I hated to wipe the smile from her face, but really I had no choice. "Miss George Ann is giving me too much credit. Miss Eugenia is responsible for finding the wood that was stolen, and identifying the person who stole it is well beyond my capabilities—even if I had the time to dedicate to it"

"I know it's a big imposition," Miss George Ann continued sweetly, "but since Kennedy has been taught about Christian duty and has a talent for solving mysteries, I've asked her to continue her investigation. I believe that with persistence she'll be able to find the culprit before he completely destroys my barn."

In my mother's world, good manners rule. So she said, "I'm sure Kennedy can find some time to help you, especially since she has a break from her college classes in the summer."

I was trying to think of a response that wouldn't result in a public scene when Luke spoke.

His tone was respectful and his face the picture of kindness when he said, "If you've confirmed that a robbery took place at your barn, it's a police matter, ma'am. Kennedy could be charged with obstruction of justice if she interferes, and I know you wouldn't want to get her arrested."

My mother gasped, and Miss George Ann pressed her already thin lips together. I had to work hard to prevent a smile. I didn't know if Luke's remarks were legally correct, but I knew it was exactly the *right* thing to say. Refusing to help an old lady was bad—but getting thrown in jail was way worse.

Mother shook her head. "Oh dear, Kennedy can't put herself on the wrong side of the law."

Miss George Ann wasn't going to give up without a fight. "The sheriff refuses to monitor the illegal activities on my farm," she said as if she was actually renting the place and needed the income. "It's not right for someone to take advantage of an older lady by destroying her property. I was really counting on Kennedy's help."

My mother bit her lip, and I could tell she was wavering. Then Luke stepped in again.

"We're sorry about your barn," Luke said. "But I'm sure you realize that it wouldn't be safe for Kennedy to drive out to a remote farm by herself, especially if there's a possibility that criminals might be there."

My mother paled, and I knew the discussion was over. "Kennedy, under no circumstances will you go out to that farm alone—especially since we know that it's a place where criminals congregate."

Miss George Ann glared at Luke. "Of course I wouldn't put Kennedy's safety at risk."

"I'll be home for the next few days," Luke said. "Since Kennedy has been forbidden by her mother to ever go to your farm alone, while I'm here I'll be glad to go by there with her. And if we see evidence of any illegal activity, we'll report it."

Miss George Ann narrowed her eyes at him, but she nodded. "Very well."

Mother looked relieved. "Oh, I'm so glad we have that settled to everyone's satisfaction. Now, Miss George Ann, won't you eat with us?"

Miss George Ann shook her head. "No, thank you. I need to be going." With that she clutched her nearly dead pansies and stalked toward the entrance.

The next few minutes were awkward thanks to Miss George Ann and her stupid barn. But finally Daddy turned to Luke and asked him about school.

"So how do you like Purdue?"

"It's amazing," Luke replied. "Just a little too far from home. That's one of the reasons I came home this weekend." He glanced toward his uncle's grave. "Besides Decoration Day. This morning I met with some folks at Georgia Tech. If they can match my scholarship, I'm going to transfer there next semester."

My heart was pounding. "You're going to switch schools—to Georgia Tech?"

He smiled. "I'm going to try."

"Kennedy goes to school in Albany," Mother said. "Maybe you could go there too."

Instead of saying, *"Purdue is one of the best schools in the country,"* Luke modestly replied, "My major isn't offered at a lot of colleges, so I don't think Albany will be an option. But if I go to school in Atlanta, I could come home on weekends. My brother, Nick, wants to keep the salvage yard going, so I figure I can give him a hand."

My heart pounded even harder, and I'll admit that it wasn't a completely happy sensation. I was comfortable with the long-distance relationship I had with Luke. And I looked forward to a closer one eventually. But I wasn't sure that I was ready now.

"When will you know for sure about school?" I asked him.

"They said they'd have an answer for me on Monday," Luke said.

While I digested this information, I heard Mother compliment Luke on his choice of flowers for Foster's grave. "Mums are hearty, colorful, and tasteful," she told him. "The perfect choice for the first year."

Luke looked very pleased. "Thanks."

"Now next May you might want to go with a little bush and some bedding plants to provide the grave with color year round," Mother instructed him.

"Or just marry Kennedy!" Madison said outrageously. "Then you'll be part of our family, and Mother can include your uncle in *her* grave-decorating plans."

A short, stunned silence followed this remark. I knew everyone was waiting for me to say something funny and play off Madison's insensitive joke. But my relationship with Luke was undefined, and the circumstances were changing. I didn't want to act like a marriage between us was ridiculous. But neither did I want to rush things by acting overly anxious. I was desperately searching for the perfect response and kept coming up blank. Then for the first time in my life, I was actually glad Miss Ida Jean was in our midst.

"Did you all hear that Kennedy is throwing a big welcome-home party for my son, Robby, at the library on Wednesday?" she asked.

This news was sensational enough to divert all the unwanted attention from me. Thankful that I no longer had to respond to Madison's semi-proposal in Luke's behalf, I said, "The whole town is invited."

Madison was frowning at Miss Ida Jean. "Your son is coming . . . home?"

Miss Ida Jean nodded. "On Wednesday."

"Well," Reagan said, obviously at a loss for words. "I guess you're excited after such a long . . . absence."

"I didn't even know you had a son," Chase commented, which earned him glares from my mother and sisters.

"I am excited," Miss Ida Jean confirmed. "Iris helped me clean out my spare bedroom, and Brother Jackson painted it for me."

I was wondering why it seemed that Miss Ida Jean's good fortune always resulted in extra work for the people around her when my mother picked up the conversation.

"We are going to have a lovely welcome-home party." Then she went on to describe the various refreshments that were planned and the efforts being made to publicize the event. "It's important to get the word out," she continued. "So we'd appreciate it if you would all tell anyone you see who might know Robby."

Everyone promised to do so with varying degrees of enthusiasm.

I nodded vaguely, wishing I could just leave. I needed someplace quiet to think. I knew I was going to have to say something to Luke about his possible move back to Georgia. My family seemed to think if that happened, we'd be officially "dating," a "couple," and soon to be seen looking at rings at the mall in Albany like Cade and Hannah-

Leigh. But I didn't know how Luke felt. Heck, I didn't even know how *I* felt. I hated the uncertainty.

While my mind was in turmoil, Luke stood. "The food was delicious, Miss Iris," he told my mother. "And I hate to leave so soon, but I'd like to go ahead and check out Miss George Ann's farm before it gets dark. I figure if I go by once a day until I leave next Thursday, I will have fulfilled my Christian duty."

My father snickered. "And then some."

But Mother just nodded. "We appreciate you taking care of that for us."

I wasn't anxious to be alone with Luke, since I still didn't know what to say about his possible school transfer. But he was obligated to Miss George Ann because of me, so I stood too. "I'll go with you so I can show you the way."

He grinned, apparently unconcerned by my family's assumption that he would soon be one of us. "Good, since I don't want to be lost on a bunch of country roads."

Madison stood and said it was time for them to go as well. "The kids get rowdy when they don't have their naps."

And her kids worse than normal is something that nobody wanted to see, so we all pitched in to get them packed up.

As Luke and I walked with Madison and her family to their Escalade, Major held one of Luke's hands and Miles held the other. Left without much of an option, Heaven walked beside me.

She cut her eyes over at me and said, "Are you and Uncle Luke going to get married?"

"He hasn't asked me," I replied carefully.

"But if he does, will you say yes?"

I decided to be completely honest. "I don't know."

She nodded, apparently satisfied with my answer.

We reached the car and Luke lifted the boys inside one at a time.

"Tell us some more soldier stories," Miles begged.

"Tell us how to take a bomb apart," Major added.

"Maybe another time," Luke said diplomatically as I strapped Mollie into her car seat.

Their fascination with Luke and his military career made me nervous. Both boys were already troublemakers, and I worried that by telling them war stories and bomb-disarming experiences, Luke might make matters worse. But there was no denying they admired him, and they certainly needed good role models.

After Madison pulled her Escalade off the cemetery sidewalk and headed for the exit, I saw both boys craning their necks to wave good-bye to Luke. In their eyes he was a hero, so I decided not to mention my concerns.

Luke invited Heaven to come along with us to Miss George Ann's farm, but the child wisely declined. We took her back to my parents and then cut through the older section of the cemetery in order to reach the area where our cars were parked. Out of habit my pace quickened when we reached the creepy old mausoleum.

Luke had to trot a few steps to catch up with me. "What? All of a sudden you're anxious to get to Miss George Ann's farm?"

I slowed down. "No. I always walk fast when I go by the mausoleum. Just in case."

"Just in case what?"

"In case one of the dead people laid to rest in there decides to come out and haunt me," I admitted. "Something about them being left out of the ground has always given me the creeps."

I expected him to laugh, but he frowned instead. "How can someone who has been cremated haunt people?"

I considered this. "Well, the fact that their body was burned to ashes does seem like it would limit their ability to torment the living. But I don't like to take chances."

He did laugh at this, and since we were past the mausoleum I smiled back.

"Thanks for helping me out with Miss George Ann, by the way. She has a lot of nerve, crashing my family's Decoration Day picnic to try to force me into doing things her way."

He shrugged. "I had to deal with a lot of people like her when I was in the Marines. No problem."

I was so wrapped up in Luke and worried about the cremated folks in the mausoleum and mad at Miss George Ann that I didn't see Cade and Hannah-Leigh until we were only a few steps away from them. She was looking perfect as usual and even had a camera crew behind her—like a backdrop.

I wanted to kick myself for being so distracted. But instead I pasted on a fake smile and said, "Hey. Is Heaven going to be on the Six O'clock News again?"

Hannah-Leigh's eyes moved up to my streaky hair and lingered just a second too long. Then she laughed. "Not unless her guardian signs a release form!"

"That will never happen," Luke assured her.

"Hannah-Leigh is doing a piece on Decoration Day," Cade told us. "She has a real talent for human interest stories."

This explained the nice suit Hannah-Leigh was wearing. She didn't overdress for Decoration Day or even come close. She was dressed for television.

"I like to do community service pieces when I can," the lovely Hannah-Leigh elaborated. "It's a way for me to give back to the people who have helped my career."

Cade's expression went from tender to adoring.

I couldn't bear to look and started to turn away, but then I got an idea.

"Speaking of community service," I said to Hannah-Leigh. "A local artist donated some paintings to the Midway Library, and we're auctioning them off next Wednesday evening. I'm going to notify the local newspapers, but it would be great if we could get some television coverage too."

"I'd love to help you," Hannah-Leigh said in a kind yet sad tone. "But our schedule is pretty tight, and I doubt if I can get a camera crew back out here by next Wednesday."

The guy with the camera shifted it from one shoulder to the other. "But hey, since we're here now, maybe we could come by the library right after we get through here. You could do a quick spot about the paintings before we head back to the station."

Hannah-Leigh's smile was a little less than genuine when she nodded and said, "Oh, that's a great idea." She checked her watch. "But we'll have to hurry if we're going to make the deadline for the Six O'clock News."

I was thrilled to get the free publicity, and knowing she didn't really want to do the spot made it all the better for me. "I'd really appreciate it."

Cade's eyes were shining with pride. "Kennedy, to conserve Hannah-Leigh's valuable time, why don't you go on to the library and get the paintings set up while they do the spot here?"

Many responses came to my mind, but since I wanted the weekend anchor's help, I kept them to myself.

Luke put a hand on my elbow and gently nudged me toward the cars. "Sounds like a plan to me. We'll be waiting for you at the library."

We hurried to our separate cars, climbed in, and drove to Main Street.

Since all the businesses downtown were closed, we parked right in front of the library, and I unlocked the main entrance. The dark interior seemed a little eerie, which I attributed to my afternoon spent at the cemetery. Once we had turned on the lights I felt better. I led Luke back to my office. While he examined the paintings, I searched my office for bugs that might have survived my extermination and migrated from the old wood to another part of the room.

Thankfully I didn't find any bugs, but when Luke was finished looking at the pictures, he shook his head. "I think it's going to be impossible to arrange these paintings in a way to attract buyers."

I laughed. "They're terrible, I know. But art is very much in the eye of the beholder. And we are particularly trying to target rich people who need tax deductions."

Luke didn't look convinced. "Just don't get your hopes up too high."

"I'm always prepared for disappointment," I assured him.

As we leaned the paintings against the wall, Luke said, "We should try to keep the same amount of space between each one."

When we were finished I examined them with a critical eye and finally nodded. "Our arrangement might not be exactly attractive, but it is neat."

He laughed as we heard the front door open and slam closed. Luke tilted his head toward the main entrance. "It sounds like our camera crew is here."

Seconds later Cade led Hannah-Leigh and the cameraman into the small office. I showed them the paintings, and Hannah-Leigh raised an eyebrow. "Is the artist a child? Because if so, that might be a good angle."

"No, the artist is not a child," I said through clenched teeth. Then I explained all about Mr. Dupree and how we wanted the auction to go.

She shrugged. "Okay. Well, maybe you and Mr. Scoggins could wait out in the hall to give us more room." Then she frowned. "Unless you want me to interview you about the auction." Her eyes returned briefly to my hair and then moved down to my stained clothes.

I stepped into the hallway and Luke followed me. "No, I'd like for you to do the spot alone."

She looked relieved. "Cade, honey, I need for you to leave this tiny office, too. You're blocking the light."

Cade gave her a sweet smile and joined us in the hall. Hannah-Leigh conferred briefly with her crew and struck a pose as the cameras started rolling. I have to admit she did a great job. By the time she was finished describing the auction, I could hardly wait to attend, even though I'd seen the horrible paintings up close.

"Come on, boys!" she commanded as she walked from my office. Cade fell in line behind the cameraman—apparently considering himself one of her "boys."

"We'll send this on to the station and get it on the Six O'clock News!" she promised me over her shoulder.

"Thanks!" I called back.

With a wave of her perfectly manicured hand, she was gone.

Luke and I restacked the paintings in the corner of my office. Then I pulled JD's library application out of my purse and explained to Luke about the artist's desire to receive regular visits from the bookmobile.

"I thought I'd go ahead and type up his temporary card, and we can deliver it when we go out to Miss George Ann's farm."

He nodded. "Sounds fine to me."

I prepared JD's library card and submitted a request for him to be added to a bookmobile route. Then I locked up the library, and we drove to my apartment so we could watch the news.

Sloan's bedding was still on the couch, but Luke didn't seem to notice. I moved it into my room. Then I gave him a MoonPie and a Pepsi before changing out of the skirt and blouse I'd been wearing all day. It felt so good to pull off my dirty clothes. I put on my most comfortable jeans and a T-shirt. Then I rinsed the old makeup off my face and pulled my striped hair back into a tight ponytail. I'm not sure it looked any better that way, but at least less of it was visible.

When I walked into the living room, Luke surveyed my attire. "So I guess there's no dress code for visiting a farm in search of stolen barn wood?" he teased.

"Oh, there's a dress code," I replied. "We should wear a trench coat and sunglasses, but since my mother's not here to enforce the code, I'm wearing this."

He smiled as I settled down beside him on the couch. Then I called Miss Eugenia to be sure she was watching the Six O'clock News. She was.

"I wish we had a phone number for JD so we could call and let him know," she said.

"He might not even have a TV," I pointed out as the segment on Decoration Day at the Midway Cemetery began. Staring at the screen, praying I wouldn't see my own disheveled image, I said, "I'll let you go so we can watch."

Blessedly I was not featured in the coverage of Decoration Day, but we had to sit through the weather and sports segments before they showed the spot about JD's paintings. Hannah-Leigh had positioned herself close to the camera, and her dominating presence cast the paintings into a vague and indistinct background. She gave all the information about the auction and even provided the library phone number for people with additional questions. It was perfect, and so was she.

Watching Hannah-Leigh, who someday soon would be Mrs. Cade Burrell, I couldn't help feeling like a victim of identity theft. As a result I was a little melancholy when the newscast ended. We walked outside, and it was still hot even though the sun was setting. Luke suggested that we take his rental car since the Torino didn't have air conditioning. I didn't argue.

Once we were driving down the highway, I decided to take the opportunity to find out more about the upcoming changes in his life and how they would affect me. Trying to sound casual, I asked, "So they'll let you know about your scholarship on Monday?"

"That's what they said," he confirmed. "I think they'll approve the transfer, but honestly it won't change things for me all that much. Atlanta is closer than Indiana, obviously."

I smiled but didn't meet his eyes. "Obviously."

"But being realistic, it's not close enough to come home more than one or two weekends a month. I want my brother to feel like I support his decision to keep the salvage yard going—if that's what he wants to do. But he will succeed or fail based on his own hard work—not what little I'm able to do for him."

I felt like a huge weight had been lifted from my shoulders. Apparently Luke wasn't accelerating the development of our relationship, after all.

Luke looked over at me and grinned. "What, you thought I was going to ask you to marry me just so I could get your mother to plan my cemetery decorations for next year?"

This was the easy, teasing relationship I was comfortable with. "I could see you were tempted! Nobody decorates graves like my mother."

He shook his head. "When and if we ever reach the point of discussing marriage, it won't have anything to do with your mother."

As usual he chose the perfect thing to say, and I sighed with contentment. The pressure I'd felt earlier was gone. When we said good night later, he would kiss me, but he wasn't demanding a lifetime commitment. Not yet.

He tipped his head toward the road. "So how do we get to the farm?"

I pulled the maps and Mr. Meyer's directions out of my purse. "If you can get to Meyer's Grocery Store on Highway 46, I can find the way from there. And if we're real lucky, the store will actually be open and we can buy a two-dollar Pepsi."

His cheek dimpled when he smiled. "I'll keep my fingers crossed."

The sun had gone down by the time we drove past Mr. Meyer's store, which had a big CLOSED sign on the door.

I looked out the window. "I hope it won't be too dark to even see the barn."

"It seems like robbers would prefer darkness to operate," Luke pointed out. "So maybe by waiting until now we've actually increased our chance of catching someone."

"I'm not sure I really want to catch them," I admitted. "I'm just going through the motions."

"Of your Christian duty," Luke teased.

"Exactly."

When we turned by the old sign advertising boiled peanuts, Luke frowned. "I've lived in the area all my life, but I don't think I've ever been out here."

I shook my head. "Me either—until this morning. I guess there's nothing here to attract visitors."

We passed acres of scraggly trees, unchecked kudzu, and the occasional abandoned vehicle. Finally we pulled onto the overgrown grass that separated the house and barn on Miss George Ann's farm. Luke turned off the car but left on the headlights. As he stared at the desolate landscape, he said, "It's beyond me why anyone, even Miss George Ann Simmons, would want to keep this place. If she had any sense, she'd just stop paying takes and let ownership revert to the county."

I had to laugh.

"I'm serious," he said. "She can't have any hope of ever using it."

"She told me she tried to sell it to a developer, hoping he'd build houses and make a little neighborhood here."

I saw Luke's eyebrows rise in the darkness. "She didn't strike me as an optimist, but I guess she must be."

"You don't see a lot of potential here?"

"This land is worthless," he said flatly. "And I should know about worthless real estate."

Since he'd been raised on at the salvage yard, I figured that did make him an expert.

"Unless she can find someone wanting to test nuclear bombs, it's not likely she'll ever sell it."

I was surprised by his vehemence. "You do hate this place!"

"Who could love it?"

"Actually, Mr. Meyer, who owns the grocery store on Highway 46 that is never open, said he tried to buy the farm from her when he moved here from New York. But she quoted him a ridiculous price."

Luke shook his head, obviously baffled. "Maybe it has sentimental value."

"Or maybe there's a treasure buried here!"

"Or maybe she's crazy."

I had to admit this was the most likely scenario. We got out of the rental car and walked toward the barn. I kept my eyes on our feet, hoping to avoid holes, poison ivy, and snakes. We stopped just outside the vandalized wall.

"It doesn't look like any more wood is missing," I commented.

Luke bravely stepped inside and squatted to examine the crisscross of tire marks left in the dry mud floor.

I stayed safely out from under the questionably stable structure. "Miss Eugenia said it looks like someone came here more than once to strip barn wood."

Luke nodded. "That's the way it looks to me, too."

"She thinks JD either stole the wood himself or paid someone else to come get it."

Luke stood back up and looked around. "That makes sense. Your artist needed wood to paint on, and this old abandoned barn is basically just a pile of wood. If it had belonged to anyone besides Miss George Ann Simmons, we wouldn't even know any wood was missing—or care that someone took it."

"Miss Eugenia said we don't have to tell Miss George Ann our suspicions," I said. "I feel a little guilty about that, but I'd feel worse if JD got thrown in prison for taking a few old boards."

"You shouldn't feel guilty," Luke said. "You haven't sworn an oath to bring criminals to justice. If the artist has offered to pay for the wood that was taken, it doesn't seem like a big deal to me."

A gentle breeze lifted the hair on my neck and I smiled. "Then I'm not going to worry about it anymore."

"And when I leave on Thursday—having fulfilled my promise to Miss George Ann—I won't worry about it anymore either."

He came out of the barn, and we started walking toward the car. I pointed out the spectacular sunset. "I guess that's the bright side of a hot spring day," I said.

"Let's take a closer look." He took my hand and led me up the hill behind the barn.

As we watched the sun sink below the horizon, I pointed to the milk bottling plant. I told him about Mr. Holloman who built a modern facility and provided inexpensive milk to local residents. "But after he died, his heirs closed the plant."

"You can't blame people for wanting to make a profit."

Then I pointed to the patchwork plots planted by the college students and told him it was a small experimental farm. "Isn't it beautiful the way they planted different crops to get the color variations?"

"I'm not sure they planned it that way," Luke said. "That might have just been a mistake."

"It's still beautiful."

"I wonder if they got permission from the owners to use that land," Luke said.

I shrugged. "It may belong to the county now. Mr. Holloman's heirs probably had the good sense to stop paying taxes on worthless land."

"They're just lucky they didn't plant their little experimental fields on Miss George Ann's farm," he said. "If she got so mad about some stolen wood, imagine how she'd react to unauthorized crops."

"That's the truth," I agreed. "If you want to know more about their project, they have a website. Miss Eugenia said she was going to check it out." Then I pointed at the corner of JD's trailer that we could see through the trees. "And that's where my new artist friend lives."

Luke pulled me close and smiled. "You know a lot about this ugly little corner of the world."

I laughed. "That's what happens when you spend time with Miss Eugenia. She knows everything about everyone."

Luke wrapped his arms tightly around me. "I don't want to talk about Miss Eugenia right now," he whispered. "In fact, I don't want to talk at all." His lips met mine in a sweet kiss that demanded nothing but promised much. When the kiss ended we stood in each other's arms and watched the sun set.

Finally I said, "We'd better take Mr. Dupree his library card before it gets too dark to find our way."

Reluctantly Luke agreed. He held my hand as we picked our way carefully back to the rental car. Just as he opened the passenger door for me, we heard the sirens nearby and coming closer—fast.

CHAPTER FIVE

ALARMED BY THE SIRENS, WE climbed into the car. Then Luke drove as fast as possible down the dirt road. Just before we reached the turnoff to Mr. Dupree's trailer, we saw the flashing lights. Two sheriff's department vehicles blocked the road, and I could see Cade standing beside one of them.

Luke pulled his rental to a stop, and Cade stalked toward us. His expression was stern until he recognized us. Then it changed to angry. He came around to my side, and once I was out of the car he demanded, "What are you doing here?"

I didn't like his tone, but in a spirit of cooperation I let it pass. "We promised Miss George Ann we'd look around her farm and try to figure out who stole wood from her barn."

"That's ridiculous," he said.

"It was Miss George Ann's idea—not mine."

Cade made a growling noise that meant he was both impatient and annoyed. Not that I cared.

"We were about to deliver a library card to Mr. Jarrard Dupree, the artist who donated all those paintings for our auction," I continued. "He filled out an application when I was here with Miss Eugenia this morning." I tried to look over his shoulder. "Now what happened?"

Cade glanced behind him with a scowl. "Jarrard Dupree won't be needing a library card. He was drunk and passed out in the road. Some college students leaving the experimental farm by the old bottling plant ran over him."

My mind struggled to process all this information at once. Mr. Dupree had been drinking. He'd passed out in the road. The college students had come out to care for their crops, and as they were leaving . . .

"I'm sorry, Kennedy," Luke said softly.

Tears filled my eyes, and I whispered, "Mr. Dupree is *dead*?"

Cade nodded. "And I'd like to know why every time a body turns up around here, they just finished filling out a library card application for you!"

Now Cade's tone had progressed to insulting, so I'd made up my mind not to answer him even before I saw Tripp. The college student who had nearly run me off the road that morning and another young man about the same age were standing by one of the sheriff's flashing vehicles. I raised my hand and called Tripp's name. Then I started to step around Cade, but he reached out an arm to stop me.

"Where do you think you are going?" he asked.

"I want to talk to Tripp." I pointed at the boy.

"And how do you know 'Tripp'?" Cade demanded.

"As part of our stolen wood investigation Miss Eugenia and I talked to several people this morning. Mr. Meyer, Tripp, and . . ." I lowered my voice in respect for the dead. "Mr. Dupree."

All Cade's yelling attracted attention from the others present, including Tripp, who rushed over to me like I was an old friend. "That artist guy who lived in the trailer is dead," he said miserably.

I gave him a quick and awkward side hug. "I heard."

Tripp wrung his trembling hands. "We were driving toward the highway, maybe a little too fast, but it's hard to get up much speed on these terrible roads with so many curves."

I nodded in agreement. The roads *are* bad and are full of blind turns.

"All of a sudden my truck hit a bump and we went flying!" Tripp paused to wipe his nose with the sleeve of his shirt. "We turned around as soon as we could find a wide enough place. And when we got back here we saw him." Tripp's voice cracked. "Just lying there on the road. We ran right over him!"

I couldn't think of anything to say that would be comforting, so I settled for a pat on his shoulder.

Tripp's distress escalated. "I can't believe we killed him!"

"It was an accident," I said, trying to calm him. "You couldn't have known he was in the road."

"I wasn't driving reckless this time," Tripp told me earnestly. "I swear!"

Sheriff Bonham drove up and parked his car on the side of the road. Then he joined our little group. We stood by and listened as Cade filled him in on the details. When he got to the part about my meeting with JD that morning, the sheriff asked me, "How did he seem when you saw him?"

"Fine," I replied. "Very nice. He gave me some paintings to auction off for the library."

"He wasn't drunk?" the sheriff clarified.

"No," I said. Then I felt obligated to add, "But that was hours ago."

"It doesn't take long to get drunk if you know what you're doing," Cade said.

The sheriff's frown deepened. "And JD was an expert."

At this point Cade made Tripp the college student repeat his story for Sheriff Bonham. Throughout this process the sheriff asked occasional questions and finally nodded. "Okay, I'm through with you. Let me talk to your friend."

Tripp led the sheriff over to the squad car where the other boy was waiting. Once they were gone, Cade turned back to me. He has many annoying characteristics, but one of the worst was his tendency to condescend. He gave me that don't-worry-your-pretty-little-head look and said, "You need to go home and forget all about investigating crimes."

"Where I go and what I do is none of your business," I retorted. "I can work on any case I want to."

This earned me a glare. "Do I need to remind you that I represent the law?"

"If you need to remind me, you must not be representing it very well!" I knew it was childish, but I couldn't help myself.

Cade took a deep breath and turned his eyes up toward heaven, as if dealing with me required the patience of a saint. Then he said slowly, "There's no 'case' to work here. Even if there was, you wouldn't be a part of it. And if you keep forcing your way into police investigations, it's only a matter of time before you become a victim yourself."

"I'm not forcing myself into anything," I insisted. "I was just delivering a library card."

Cade turned to Luke, which was a concession in and of itself. The two men had been enemies since high school. "If she won't listen to me, maybe you can talk some sense into her."

"Kennedy is perfectly capable of making sensible decisions on her own," Luke said. His voice was quiet but mildly menacing. "You're the one who consistently shows a lack of good judgment—like that embarrassing scene at the drive-in with Missy Lamar."

Cade's face turned red with fury. He took an aggressive step toward Luke and hissed, "You better watch yourself, Scoggins, or you'll end up in jail just like your daddy."

Rather than retreat, Luke moved closer until his nose was almost touching Cade's. "You're the one who better watch out, Burrell. I'm not a helpless kid anymore. The government spent a fortune teaching me how to defend myself. So unless you want to end up in the hospital—you and your *daddy* both—you'd better back off."

"Luke!" I cried. He ignored me so I tried, "Cade!" He ignored me too. If I couldn't stop them, I knew I had to find someone who could. So I turned and screamed, "Sheriff!"

"What is going on here?" Sheriff Bonham trotted over to us and sized up the situation instantly. "Move apart, both of you!" he commanded. His tone had me quivering with fear, and he wasn't even talking to me.

Luke and Cade each took a step backward but kept their eyes locked in silent combat.

"Now I want to know what happened." The sheriff looked at his deputy. "Cade?"

"Nothing, sir," Cade bit out.

Sheriff Bonham turned to Luke. "Scoggins?"

"Like he said, sir, not a thing."

The sheriff muttered something under his breath and then grabbed Cade by the arm. "You go over there and write down contact information for those two college kids in case I think of something else I want to ask them later."

After sending Luke one last venomous look, Cade said, "Yes, sir," and walked away.

Once he was gone, the sheriff turned to Luke. "If you want to have a happy future in Midway, son, you'd better learn to get along with the other residents—especially the law enforcement officers."

Luke nodded stiffly. "Yes, sir."

Sheriff Bonham regarded Luke for a few seconds. Then he tilted his head toward me. "Now why don't you take this young lady home?"

I hurried over to Luke's rental car—as anxious as I'd ever been to leave anywhere.

As Luke was getting in to the car, he looked over at Cade, and I saw Cade staring back. The message was clear. They would finish this later.

***

We rode back to Midway in silence, but when Luke parked in front of my apartment he turned and said, "Are you okay?"

I wasn't sure if he meant about Mr. Dupree's untimely death or his near-fight with Cade. And I didn't really want to talk about either incident. So I just nodded.

"Then would you like to eat breakfast with me at the Flying J tomorrow morning?"

It was our tradition so I nodded again. Then I added a condition. "But we'll need to meet early so I can get to church."

He raised both eyebrows. "The traditional services at the Baptist church again?"

I shook my head. "No, I've been attending meetings at the Mormon Church in Albany so I can help Madison with her kids. And believe me—she needs all the help she can get."

Luke didn't contradict me, but he did smile. "What time does her church start?"

"Nine o'clock," I muttered around a yawn. "So we should probably meet about seven thirty."

"No point in taking two cars to the Flying J," he said. "I'll just pick you up here at seven thirty."

"Fine with me."

Luke walked me to my door and waited for me to unlock it. Then we stood awkwardly on my front porch. I was tired and just wanted to go to bed. Besides, I could tell he was still mad at Cade, and I was still a little mad at both of them. So I didn't invite him inside.

Finally he leaned down and gave me a quick kiss on the cheek. "See you tomorrow." With a wave he descended the stairs and got back in his car.

I watched him drive away and then went inside my apartment. The door had barely closed behind me when the phone started ringing. It was my mother.

"Kennedy?" her worried voice came through the phone lines. "Are you okay? Cade called and said there was an accident out by Miss George Ann's farm and an elderly gentleman was killed!"

"It was the artist who donated the paintings for the library," I confirmed. "I just met him this morning, and now he's dead."

"Well, I'm sorry for the artist, but I don't like the idea of something like that happening so close to where you were," Mother said. "Cade thinks you should stay away from Miss George Ann's farm and I agree. In fact, I'm going to call her myself and tell her that your obligation to her has been fulfilled! With or without Luke, you're not going back."

This was, of course, what I had been hoping for since Miss George Ann had come to the library with her story about a vandalized barn and stolen wood. But I didn't want my mother fighting my battles, and I certainly didn't want Cade trying to control my actions through tattling.

So I said, "Thanks, Mother, but you don't need to call Miss George Ann. I'll talk to her myself." I was purposely vague so my mother would think I was taking her advice. However, in actuality I fully intended to keep checking on Miss George Ann's farm at least until Luke left on Thursday—and maybe beyond that. Nobody was going to tell me what to do. Especially not Cade Burrell.

"Well, okay, dear. I'll see you after church."

"I'll be there," I promised.

I was exhausted mentally and physically. I wanted to take a shower and eat a MoonPie and crawl into bed. But I didn't want Miss Eugenia to hear about JD's death from someone else. And since Cade was spreading the word—as evidenced by his call to my mother—I knew I didn't have much time to spare.

So I dialed Miss Eugenia's number, and she answered almost immediately.

"Hey, Miss Eugenia," I began. "This is Kennedy."

Instead of saying hello, she said, "Isn't it just awful about Mr. Dupree?"

I wasn't really surprised. Information travels at an alarming rate through small Southern towns. "It is awful," I agreed.

"Winston was at my house eating a piece of pound cake when he got the call," Miss Eugenia explained. "He said that college boy, Tripp Hughes, and another student ran over the poor man."

"Yes, but Mr. Dupree was passed out drunk on the dirt road when they hit him," I said in the boys' defense. "They never even saw him."

"Well, it's a shame all around."

That pretty much summed up the situation. "What about the auction?" I asked her. "I guess we should at least postpone it. Or maybe cancel it altogether."

"I think you should proceed just as planned with the auction," Miss Eugenia advised. "It would be hard to cancel it since it's been announced on TV."

"You don't think it will be disrespectful?"

"I believe JD would consider it a very fine memorial."

"Maybe I could keep one of his paintings and put it up in the library—to honor him and his donation."

"Yes, that's a nice thought," Miss Eugenia agreed. "If you can find the right spot to hang it—somewhere that won't scare away visitors or make children cry."

"I'll find the right spot. See you at church tomorrow."

After ending the call with Miss Eugenia, I took a long, hot shower. I brushed my teeth and pulled on a pair of cotton pajamas that were soft with age. Then bleary-eyed with fatigue, I was headed down the hall to my bedroom when I heard a soft knock on the door that led up from Mr. Sheffield's office below my apartment.

I tiptoed to the door and whispered, "Who is it?"

Sloan's voice whispered back, "It's me."

I pulled the door open and found him standing on the top step.

He grinned. "I see your hair is still striped."

I lifted a hand to my head. "I forgot to get any hair dye," I told him. "It was a busy day."

"It's starting to grow on me," Sloan claimed outrageously.

"Well I hate it and I'm changing it the first chance I get," I assured him.

Sloan walked into my tiny kitchen. "Do you have anything to eat? I'm starving."

I'm not much of a cook, but I made him some scrambled eggs and toast with my mother's homemade blackberry jelly. It didn't matter that the meal was simple. He ate it so fast he didn't even taste it. In the dim light I could see the dark circles under his eyes.

I stated the obvious. "You're tired."

He nodded. "I think I've worked out a plan that will clear my name and flush out the mole at the FBI. I'll put it into motion tomorrow. Do you mind if I sleep downstairs one more time?"

"Of course not." My stomach ached with anxiety. "What's your plan?"

He licked some stray jelly from his lips and smiled. "Any details I give you might put you in danger. So just keep my picture disc safe, and if something happens to me, take it to the FBI office in Atlanta."

"Oh, Sloan, are you going to do something dangerous?"

"I'll be fine," he assured me. "I only mentioned taking the disc to Atlanta as a precaution."

I felt a little better until he continued.

"But if you have to take it to Atlanta, don't give it to just anyone. Insist on giving it directly to the Special Agent in Charge. No one else."

I felt miserable again. "Okay."

He stood and stretched. "I'd love to keep visiting with you, but I've got to get some sleep."

"Me too," I said around a yawn. "It's been a long day, and tomorrow is starting early with a breakfast date at seven thirty."

He raised an eyebrow. "So you actually accept dates when other men ask you out?"

I gave him a weary smile. "Sometimes, if the right person asks."

"You and that Scoggins fellow are getting pretty chummy," he said as he stepped into the hall.

"Luke's a good guy," I answered. "But we're taking it slow. I don't want to make another mistake."

"Good thinking." He smiled. "I'll be gone when you wake up in the morning, and I won't bother you again."

The finality of his words made me sad. "You're no bother." I retrieved his bedding from my room and walked him to the door that led downstairs. "You'll come see me again when things are settled—so I'll know you're okay?"

He kissed me on the forehead and descended the stairs. It wasn't until later that I realized he never promised to come back. Ever.

***

I had a lot on my mind that night, and even though I was exhausted, I didn't expect to sleep. I was worried about Sloan—both his presence downstairs and his trouble with assorted government agencies. I was sad that JD was dead and that Tripp and his college friends would have to live the rest of their lives with it on their conscience. I was unsure about where my relationship with Luke was headed. I was a little depressed about Cade moving on into a new life with Hannah-Leigh. And I was terrified that at some point in the near future Cade and Luke would find an excuse to beat each other up.

But in spite of all this mental turmoil, the minute my head hit the pillow I fell into a deep, restful sleep.

I woke up at seven o'clock with barely enough time to get ready before Luke arrived to take me to breakfast. The first thing I did was look downstairs, but Sloan was gone and his bedding was stacked neatly on the top step.

After a shower I ironed a dress that I could wear on my date with Luke and that would also be appropriate for church. I was ready with four minutes to spare. So I sat on the couch and watched the sunrise, wondering where Sloan was and if he was in danger.

When Luke arrived, at precisely seven thirty, I stared at him in amazement. He was wearing the suit he'd worn to his uncle Foster's funeral.

"You look nice," I said as I joined him on the front porch. "Since suits are considerably above the normal dress code for the Flying J, I guess you're planning to attend church with me too."

He seemed a little embarrassed. "I guess it was kind of presumptuous of me, but I thought I would. That is, if you don't mind."

"I don't mind," I assured him. "But I warn you—Madison's kids are worse in church than they were at the cemetery yesterday."

Doubt clouded his eyes for a few seconds. Then he squared his shoulders and said, "I survived Iraq. I think I can take church with your sister's kids."

I laughed. "You're talking brave now, but we'll see if you've changed your tune by the time we get to my parents' house for dinner."

Luke looked a little uncomfortable. "I didn't mean to invite myself to your parents' house too."

"It's a package deal. If you come to church with me, you have to eat with my family afterward. My mother accepts no excuses."

He gave me a nice smile and opened the passenger door of his rental car for me. "In that case, I'll come."

Once we were settled in at the Flying J and had ordered our breakfast, we were able to relax and just talk. Since we communicated with each other daily, there wasn't a lot that we needed to catch up on. But after the physical separation of almost two months I was anxious to see if we still felt comfortable with each other. We did and I knew that our budding relationship had passed an important test.

We discussed his school and my school. We talked about the chances of his brother making a go of the salvage yard business without his uncle Foster's help. After the waitress brought our meal, Luke told me that Heaven's parents were going to remarry as soon as possible and apply for custody of their child immediately thereafter.

"I wonder how my mother will feel about that," I said. Heaven had lived with my parents since Foster Scoggins's death, and I knew my mother, particularly, was attached to the child.

"Just because Nick and Shasta remarry doesn't mean the judge will give them custody," Luke pointed out. "They've both been pretty terrible parents up to this point."

That was an understatement. Luke's ex-sister-in-law, Shasta Scoggins, had deserted her child to pursue a movie career. Luke's brother, Nick, who was Shasta's ex-husband, owned an eighteen-wheeler and was gone for months at a time delivering loads around the country. After Foster was killed and it was discovered that he'd left Heaven more than $100,000—both absentee parents had suddenly returned to Midway, anxious to raise their little girl.

It was obvious to everyone that they were just after the money and the family court judge had denied them custody. It was none of my business, but Heaven seemed happy with my parents, and I hated for her greedy parents to mess things up for her—again.

"If they do get custody, aren't you worried that they'll waste all of the money Foster left for Heaven?"

"As executor of Foster's estate, I have to approve all expenditures," Luke explained.

I sighed with relief. Heaven's future was in Luke's capable and responsible hands.

We left the Flying J at 8:15, and after a leisurely drive into Albany we arrived at the Mormon chapel. My phone rang as Luke was parking his rental car. It was my mother.

"Louise Lavender said she just saw you at the Flying J with a man," Mother said. "You told me you were going to church with Madison."

"I was at the Flying J a few minutes ago," I confessed. "And I was with a man. It was Luke. He took me out to breakfast. And now we're going to church with Madison, heaven help us all!"

"Oh, Kennedy, you're so dramatic," Mother said. "Tell Luke I said hi and bring him over for dinner after church."

"My mother says hi," I told him as I turned off my phone in preparation for entering the church. "And she said you'd better come for lunch afterward."

He watched me put my phone back in my purse. "Should I turn off my phone too?"

"It's good manners to at least put your phone on silent while you're at church," I replied. "And that's one rule of etiquette I actually like. This is the only hour all week long when I don't have to worry about my mother calling."

He smiled. "You're not going to get any sympathy from me. I think your mother is incredible."

My mother is incredible but also overwhelming. I knew it would be impossible to explain this to someone who had never experienced near-suffocating maternal affection. So I didn't even try.

We got out of the car, and as we walked toward the church I noticed that Luke seemed a little fidgety. This was a departure from his normal calm demeanor, so I asked, "Are you okay?"

He stopped and turned to face me. "Honestly I'm nervous about going to church. I've only been a few times in my whole life, and so I don't know the rules. I hate feeling unsure of myself, and I really hate making mistakes."

I put my hand on his arm and propelled him forward. "That's the beauty of going to church with Madison and her kids. They cause so much commotion nobody will notice what we do."

Luke actually seemed to find this thought comforting as I led the way through the side door and into the building. We crossed the foyer and were greeted by various congregation members. Some I remembered from my previous visits and some not. Everyone seemed curious about us, and once I told them I was Madison's sister, a little sympathetic.

Inside the chapel I walked to the third row from the back, which Madison and her family always claimed but never occupied until the very last moment. I scooted to the middle of the row and sat down. Luke settled beside me. Kate Iverson was at the organ and lifted one hand in a brief wave between musical chords.

We sat in peace for a few minutes, and then there was a disturbance at the door. I turned and saw Madison, holding the baby, burst into the chapel. Miles came in behind her, crying. He was followed closely by Major—who was undoubtedly the cause of his brother's tears. A weary-looking Jared brought up the rear, holding two-year-old Maggie.

"I hope you're ready for this," I whispered to Luke. "Because things are about to get ugly."

He nodded and I saw courage glinting in his eyes.

Madison collapsed on the pew beside Luke and passed Mollie to me. I pressed a kiss to the baby's soft cheek and then settled her on my chest. Miles sat between his parents while Major wiggled his way over and then stood looking at the insufficient space between Luke and myself.

Finally he said, "I want to sit there."

If I refused to let him sit between us, I would look childish or worse. So I slid to my right to make room for him and admitted to myself that Major had won the first round of the day. But as he settled himself in, I leaned close and whispered, "You'd better behave. Remember, Luke is a Marine and he knows how to hurt people—bad."

Luke seemed more alarmed by this pronouncement than Major, but I didn't regret my words since the child lapsed into uncustomary silence.

A man stood up and approached the microphone. He waited while Kate brought her organ playing to a harmonic conclusion and then announced that the meeting was about to begin. He welcomed everyone to church and asked that we excuse Bishop Iverson, who was out of town on business.

Major remained still as a statue, moving only enough to glance up at Luke occasionally. Mollie continued to sleep. So Luke and I were managing our half of the children just fine. Madison and Jared were not faring as well on their end of the pew. They wrestled with Miles and Maggie, trying in vain to keep them quiet. I knew they wondered how we were controlling Major, but since I didn't think they'd approve of my scare tactics, I just pretended not to notice the confused and envious looks they sent my way.

There was a family sitting in front of us who—like Madison and Jared—had four children. But there the similarity ended. The children were sitting quietly and required only occasional attention from their parents. The father was a strikingly handsome man who looked vaguely familiar. The mother was blonde and attractive in a natural kind of way.

The oldest daughter looked to be about ten and lovely. Beside her was a boy I estimated to be four. Then there was a baby about two and a newborn. I realized that the wife was on the same basic baby-schedule as Madison.

When the main church meeting ended, Jared and Madison took their kids to the children's church area in the back of the building where they would stay for the next two hours. Madison teaches the three-year-olds—an assignment that was unfathomable to me. She obviously couldn't control her own children—why would anyone want her to teach theirs?

I took Luke to the Sunday School class for people who are investigating Mormonism. I'd made it clear on my first visit that I wasn't interested in converting. And the boys in white shirts with name tags that designated them as "elders" (which I found ironic since neither one of them could possibly have been older than twenty) who taught the class seemed disappointed, since then they hadn't made any effort to force their religion on me.

The room was empty—so we took a seat on the front row and waited for the elders to come. Miss Eugenia came by and spoke to us while we waited.

"Have you heard anything else about JD's death?" she asked us.

I was surprised by the question. "What else is there to hear? He passed out on the road and was run over by some college kids."

Miss Eugenia frowned. "I don't think the police should be too quick to assume that the artist died accidently. He had walked back and forth from his trailer to Mr. Meyer's store countless times before and never got killed."

"If he was walking around drunk in the dark it was always just a matter of time," Luke said.

"But don't you think the timing is odd? JD had lived out there painting ugly pictures and drinking himself into a future case of liver disease for years. But yesterday he met us and applied for a library card. Then he gave you those paintings, and the auction was mentioned on TV. And the next thing you know he's dead."

"So what are you saying?"

"It just sounds fishy to me." Miss Eugenia raised her hand in a brief wave. "Well, I've got to go. Emily is giving a talk in Primary, and I don't want to miss it."

After Miss Eugenia left, I turned to Luke. "Do you think the police should check into Mr. Dupree's death?"

Luke shrugged. "I think everything is fishy to Miss Eugenia."

I laughed as the handsome man I noticed during sacrament meeting came into the room. The man said that the elders were fulfilling a different assignment that day and he would be our teacher. He said he was Jack Gamble and then asked us to introduce ourselves.

"I'm Kennedy Killingsworth from Midway, but I'm not a Mormon. My sister is Madison, and I just came to church with her because she can't handle her kids." I lifted Mollie slightly. "This is her baby."

Jack Gamble nodded and turned to Luke.

"Luke Scoggins," he said. "I'm not a Mormon either, and I'm only here because Kennedy is."

If Jack Gamble found it odd that I was bringing people to church when I wasn't even a member myself, he didn't say so. Instead he pulled up a chair and sat down in front of us.

"Well, since you're not investigating the Mormon Church and you're the only class members today, I don't have to give the assigned lesson. We can just talk about any questions you might have."

Now that sounded interesting. "I have a question," I said. "You look familiar to me, but I can't figure out why."

He smiled and if possible became even more gorgeous. "I just completed my first term as a state senator, so you might have seen me on television, being harassed by the press."

It was a humble sort of way to tell us that he was a person of some importance.

"We live in Atlanta during the school year and spend summers in Haggerty. So we'll be here for the next couple of months."

"I have another question."

He smiled again. "I'm ready."

"I had to threaten Major with bodily harm to keep him quiet during sacrament meeting. How did you teach your children to be so well behaved?"

"How do you know we don't threaten bodily harm?" he asked.

I gasped in amazement. "Do you?"

"Not often," Jack replied. "We just talk to them about reverence a lot and practice at home, and my wife, Beth, has bag full of quiet toys and books that the little ones can entertain themselves with."

"Well, I was very impressed," I told him.

Jack smiled again. "I'll tell her you think she's doing a good job."

"I have a question," Luke surprised me by saying. "Why don't you have a paid ministry in the Mormon Church?"

"I have some opinions as to why it was set up that way and why it works," Jack replied. "But that's all they are—my opinions. The most correct answer is because that's the way the Lord wants it to be. We believe that we are led by a prophet who is inspired by God."

I liked his straightforward, unapologetic answer, and I could tell that Luke did too. In fact, Luke liked it so much he was ready with another one in a matter of seconds. I leaned back in my chair and settled Mollie in my arms. Then I listened while Luke asked questions and Jack Gamble answered them.

They covered several religious topics and then moved on to global warming and who they thought would win the World Series. They tried to include me in the conversation several times, but I was content to listen and snuggle with Mollie.

The baby woke up just before the class ended, so I took her out and changed her diaper. When I returned the class was over and Luke was shaking hands with Jack Gamble. Kate Iverson stopped by briefly to say hello before she headed down to children's church to play the piano.

I introduced her to Luke and she admired Mollie.

"I noticed that you don't have a foster baby at the moment," I said.

Kate shook her head. "No, but we're supposed to be getting one at the end of the week. You'll have to come visit us when the baby arrives." She glanced back down at Mollie. "Although you do already have your arms full."

I laughed. "This one is just on loan. I'll try to come meet your new temporary baby."

Kate turned to Jack and gave him a friendly hug. "It's good to have you and your family back in town for the summer."

"Thanks," he said. "We're glad to be home."

At the Mormon Church during the third and final hour of their worship service they have separate classes for the men and the women. This had not been a problem in the past, even though Madison and Kate were busy in children's church because I could just sit by Miss Eugenia. But I didn't know what I was going to do with Luke. It turned out not to be a problem because they kept everyone together that Sunday and talked about ways to improve reverence in their meetings. I figured the simplest thing would be to ask Madison and her family to stay at home—but I kept this to myself.

When church ended we waited in the chapel until Madison came to find us. I returned Mollie to my sister and then walked with Luke out to his rental car.

"So what did you think about the Mormons?" I asked.

"The choir at your mother's church is better," Luke said. "And Baptists are definitely quieter."

"I can't argue with you there."

Luke smiled. "But everyone was friendly here, and I really enjoyed Jack Gamble's Sunday School class."

"You were just impressed because he's a state senator," I accused.

"Actually I was more impressed that he was so normal. A lot of important people take themselves too seriously."

"Jack Gamble did seem pretty normal," I agreed. "And he's handsome enough to be a movie star."

Luke shook his head. "I wouldn't know about that."

I laughed as I climbed into the car. "If we hurry, we can run by Miss George Ann's farm and then get to my mother's house before her dinner gets cold. Nothing puts her in a bad mood faster."

Luke demonstrated good navigational skills by driving to Miss George Ann's vandalized farm without consulting a map.

When we arrived at the farm, we got out and walked around what was becoming familiar territory. We went to the barn but saw no evidence of further vandalism.

"Now that Mr. Dupree is dead, there's probably no reason to steal the wood."

Luke nodded. "Yes, I can't imagine that they had many wood customers besides the artist." He ducked inside the barn and walked around, frowning. He stopped every once in a while to kick the old wood walls or scuff his foot along the dirt floor.

I was beginning to wonder if he, like Miss Eugenia, suspected something fishy. Then he abandoned his rotations and came over to stand in front of me. Sunlight coming through holes in the barn walls glinted off his hair, and dust particles, kicked up by his shoe-scuffing, danced around his head. My lips parted, and an appreciative little sigh escaped.

He didn't seem to notice and his expression was grim as he said, "I want to apologize for the way I acted toward Cade last night. I know that was uncomfortable for you and, well, I'm sorry."

I had been disturbed by the confrontation and I appreciated his apology. "Thank you," I said. "I understand that you have hard feelings against him because of the way he treated you in high school, but you're going to have to learn to control them. Cade is a very irritating person, and it's pretty much impossible to avoid him if you're in Midway. But he is my ex-husband, and he does represent the law."

Luke nodded. "I know." He stepped out of the barn and took my hand for the walk to the car. "I think we've seen enough here."

On the way back out to the highway we passed the old Toyota truck Tripp had been driving the day before headed the other way. Three young men, all about Tripp's age, were squeezed into the cab. They looked grim and didn't return my wave.

"I guess they are headed to those fields by the bottling plant to check on their crops," I mused. "I believe I've seen one of them every time I've come out to Miss George Ann's farm."

"They do seem very dedicated to their project."

"But I didn't expect to see them today," I said. "In fact it seems a little disrespectful to come back out here so soon after JD died."

"You'd think they wouldn't want to come out here since one of their own ran over him."

I wanted to defend Tripp and his fellow students, so I said, "If they don't come out here every day and take care of the plants and record the data, the whole project could be ruined."

Luke shrugged. "I guess."

When we arrived at my parents' house my mother met us at the door.

"Perfect timing," she said. "We're just sitting down at the table. Kennedy, take Luke's jacket and hang it up. "She pointed to the coat closet just in case I'd forgotten where it was. "Then you two join us in the dining room. Miss Ida Jean is here, but Reagan and her family couldn't make it. They're all sore and sunburned from the cemetery yesterday."

My mother walked out, and I leaned close to Luke. "If I had known those were acceptable excuses, I would have used them myself!"

Luke laughed. "I'm glad you didn't know. I've been looking forward to a good meal."

He shrugged out of his suit coat and handed it to me. I took a hanger from the closet and slipped it inside the jacket. The silky material was still warm from his body, and my stomach tightened a little. Then I turned back and watched him roll up his sleeves to expose his strong, tanned forearms, and my stomach tightened a little more.

We walked into the dining room and sat in the only two available chairs, which as my luck would have it, just happened to be on either side of Miss Ida Jean. Mother asked Jared to bless the food and then supervised as all the dishes were passed around, making sure each guest got plenty. Once everyone was served, she settled into her seat and asked Miss Ida Jean if she'd been able to arrange for the local high school band to play for Robby's homecoming party.

I turned to stare in astonishment. "You're having a marching band?"

"Oh yes, the band can come," Miss Ida Jean said with her mouth full of mashed potatoes.

I had to turn away.

"I wanted them to play the song about the yellow ribbon tied around the old oak tree, but the band director said they didn't have time to learn new music. So they're going to play the National Anthem and the school's fight song instead."

"Oh, I'm sure that will be very nice," Mother said absurdly.

It was all I could do to keep from rolling my eyes.

Then Madison said she had an announcement to make. Madison's announcements usually meant that there was another baby on the way—but since Mollie wasn't quite two months old, this was doubtful. So we all gave her our undivided attention.

She cleared her throat and said, "We've sold our house!"

That was pretty exciting news, and everyone immediately began talking at once.

"Who bought it?"

"When do you have to move?"

"Are you going to build again?"

"Where will you live?"

Madison held up a hand to stop the volley of questions. Then she answered them one at a time. "A family that's been transferred here from San Diego bought our house. We don't have to move out until the end of June, and we aren't going to build."

"We're going to try to find a house that meets our needs and is close to the pharmacy where I work," Jared contributed.

Madison nodded. "We're looking for something a little smaller and a lot cheaper. We want Jared to be able to reduce the number of hours he works so he can be at home more."

There was a stunned silence around the table. Madison had used the words *smaller* and *cheaper* when referring to a future purchase. It was a rare moment.

Madison broke the silence herself. "Once we decided to sell, our real estate agent didn't even have time to get a sign in our yard before we had an offer. The buyers sold a house in the expensive California housing market and have a lot of money they needed to invest in a house or they'll have to pay capital gains taxes or something." Madison waved her hand as if actually understanding property taxation was impossible. "So it's good that we sold our house, but now we have to find something else quick."

"Yes, a month isn't much time to find something as important as a house," Mother murmured. She was obviously still trying to figure out why Madison was suddenly being considerate of Jared's time as well as thrifty. I wondered what she'd think if she knew I was the one who suggested these changes.

Madison pulled me out of my reverie by calling my name. "Kennedy, the real estate agent wants to take us around to a couple of places this afternoon. Mother has choir practice, so would you be able to babysit?"

This sounded like as much fun as handful of hangnails. And I knew my mother would miss choir if necessary, but that seemed selfish since I didn't really have anything else to do. So I nodded. "Sure."

Madison, who loves getting her way, beamed at me. "I'll call you when I know what time I'll need you."

During dessert, the phone rang and my father answered it. Then he held it out to me. "It's Cade," he said with an awkward glance toward Luke.

I wasn't sure what to expect. Maybe Cade was calling to apologize about last night too. Maybe he was calling to fuss at me some more. So I answered hesitantly. "Hello."

"Hey, I'm at the sheriff's department and a guy stopped by here looking for you. He says he's an art broker from New York and wants to buy those paintings the dead artist guy gave you."

"JD's paintings?" I clarified as if I had donated artwork stacked all over the library.

"Jarrard Dupree," Cade confirmed. "He wants you to meet him at the library so he can see them. I thought maybe your dad could come with you. I'd go myself, but my shift is about to end and, well, I have plans."

I felt sure that his "plans" included Hannah-Leigh Coley-Smith. A couple of months before, Cade would have used any excuse to be with me. Now he didn't want to spare even a few minutes to protect me from a stranger. I silently reminded myself that my relationship with Cade was over. Then I took a little pleasure in saying, "Luke's here, eating dinner with us. I'll ask him to go with me to the library."

There was a brief silence on the other end of the line, and then Cade said, "Just so long as you won't be alone." His tone changed to soft and a little muffled, so I knew he was trying to keep the art broker from hearing him. "We don't know this guy from Adam."

I ended the call with Cade and explained the situation to everyone gathered around the table (since they'd already heard my side of the conversation and were all watching me with various degrees of curiosity). Then I turned to Luke and asked if he would go with me to the library.

He stood with a nod. "I'd be glad to."

Mother was not happy. "You have to leave right now?"

"A man has come from New York to see me," I repeated. "It would be rude to expect him to wait while I sit around here and visit."

If my mother was anything, she was polite. So she sighed in defeat. "Well, at least let me send some leftovers for you to eat later."

I never turn down food, especially my mother's. So I gave her a grateful smile and said, "If you insist."

Mother sent my father to get her a little cooler from the garage and then hurried into the kitchen.

Madison, ever one to look out for herself, asked, "Will you still be able to babysit for me?"

"I can't imagine that I'll have much to say to an art broker from New York, so I'm sure I'll be through soon. Just call me on my cell phone when you're ready for me to come to your house."

Luke and I said our good-byes and grabbed Luke's jacket from the closet as we made our way to the door. My mother met us there a few minutes later and pressed the cooler into Luke's hands. Then she kissed me on both cheeks and made me promise to call after my meeting so I could tell her everything the art broker said.

Finally we escaped from my family and stepped outside. As I filled my lungs with warm, fresh air, I felt a kinship with Robby Baxley, who would, on Wednesday, taste freedom again after a long incarceration.

On the way to Luke's rental car he said, "I wonder why an art broker from New York wants to see you about Mr. Dupree's paintings."

I shook my head as he stowed the cooler in the backseat. "I can't imagine why an art broker from *anywhere* would be interested in JD's paintings. But there's only one way to find out."

CHAPTER SIX

WHEN LUKE AND I PULLED up in front of the library, we saw Cade standing near the entrance, looking miserable. A man with very curly, very black hair was pacing up and down the sidewalk.

Cade rushed toward us with hope in his eyes.

"We shouldn't have come in such a hurry," Luke muttered.

I pressed a hand over my mouth to keep from laughing as Cade rapped the knuckles of one hand against my window. Luke rolled it down for me. I cut my eyes over at him and mouthed, "Thanks a lot."

He grinned and I returned my attention to Cade.

"I'm glad you're here," he said unnecessarily.

"I can tell," I replied as I climbed out of Luke's rental car.

The sarcasm was lost on Cade. "Come up here and let me introduce you to Mr. Thorne." He put his hand on my back and pushed me toward the sidewalk.

Luke followed behind us with an amused expression on his face.

"Mr. Thorne, this is Kennedy Killingsworth." I noticed he didn't try to claim me as his wife. "And, uh, Luke Scoggins," he added as an afterthought.

The pacing man stopped walking and shifted his leather briefcase to his left hand. Then he extended a very white, certainly manicured right hand first to me and then to Luke. At closer range I could see that Mr. Thorne was a little older than I had guessed from a distance. His hair was definitely dyed (to hide the fact that he was turning gray) and probably permed (to cover up the fact that he was going bald). His plaid pants, brown shirt, and orange tie might be stylish in New York, but the only person in Midway who would wear such an outfit was a circus clown.

"Nice to meet both of you . . . folks." Mr. Thorne spoke slowly and a little louder than necessary—the way you might address a young child. Apparently the short amount of time he'd spent in Cade's company had convinced him that all Southerners were idiots.

Cade walked to the library's front door. "Kennedy, why don't you open the library so Mr. Thorne can get in out of this heat?"

I did as he suggested, knowing he was just trying to dump Mr. Thorne off on me. And I was right. I unlocked the door and stepped inside. Luke and Mr. Thorne followed me. While I was turning on the lights in the lobby area, Cade leaned in through the open doorway and waved.

"Now that I've got the two of you together, I'll go on." Then, without waiting for a response, he hurried down the street—no doubt headed for a rendezvous with his favorite weekend anchorwoman.

Luke closed the library door and locked it to prevent anyone else from wandering in.

Mr. Thorne took a handkerchief out of his shirt pocked and dabbed his forehead. Then he carefully enunciated, "I would like to see the paintings, please."

"This way," I replied in the same deliberate way. Then I led him down the hall to my office. Once we were there, I pointed to the paintings stacked in the corner.

He looked through them quickly and then nodded. "Yes, these are all Jarrard Dupree originals."

I raised my eyebrows. "Was there ever any doubt?"

"Forgeries abound in the world of art," Mr. Thorne said importantly.

I wanted to ask what JD's paintings had to do with the world of art, but I restrained myself.

"I have an exclusive contract with JD," Mr. Thorne was continuing. "I buy all his paintings, and the ones I've purchased in the past sold briskly."

Luke and I exchanged a glance. Then Luke said, "Well, how about that?"

Mr. Thorne returned his handkerchief to his pocket. "So when I heard about the auction, I came straight down."

"The auction isn't until Wednesday night," I told him.

Mr. Thorne dismissed this with the wave of a hand. "I have a business to run and can't wait here for two days. So I'd like to buy the paintings from you as a group and eliminate the need for an auction altogether. I will give you a fair price for them."

"And then you'll turn around and try to sell them for a much better price," Luke guessed.

"I'll admit that," Mr. Thorne said. "It's called free enterprise. You might be able to sell them at auction for more than I'm willing to pay—but I doubt it. By selling to me you save yourself time and trouble and make a tidy sum for the library."

I tried to figure out exactly what it was about him that I didn't like. The insulting way he talked to us? That awful curly black hair? Or maybe it was that his hands were just too white? Whatever it was, I really didn't want to sell JD's paintings to him. But I had to ask, "How much are you offering?"

He flashed me a smile. "I'll give you a thousand dollars apiece."

I gasped. "You're going to give me $10,000 for those?" I pointed to the paintings stacked in the corner.

Mr. Thorne was still smiling. "Yes, I am."

I stared at the pile of old lumber daubed with paint and marveled that I could convert them into $10,000 to benefit the library.

"If he's willing to give you that much, you might be able to make double that at an auction," Luke cautioned.

"Or I might make half as much—or less," I pointed out.

Luke shrugged. "True."

I was really tempted, I'll admit. And it wasn't optimistic greed that made me say no. It was the fact that JD had given us the paintings with the specific instruction to auction them off. He was dead and I wanted to fulfill what ended up being his near-final wishes. And the fact that I didn't like Mr. Thorne was incidental.

So I said, "Thank you very much for your offer, Mr. Thorne, but I'm going to have to decline."

Luke's smile was almost worth losing a $10,000 bird in the hand for the library. Almost.

Mr. Thorne, however, was not amused. "I was hoping we could handle this like civilized people."

I was surprised to hear that he had such high expectations based on the way he'd been talking to us.

He opened his fancy briefcase and removed a single piece of paper with a flourish. "As I mentioned, I had a written agreement with

Mr. Dupree to purchase all his paintings. So you can't sell those," he waved the paper toward the paintings in the corner, "to anyone but me."

"You had an agreement with Mr. Dupree, not Kennedy or the Midway Library," Luke said and there was a little edge to his voice. "Kennedy received them as a gift and can sell the paintings to whoever she wants."

Mr. Thorne tapped his alleged contract. "If you don't make a deal with me now, I'll take you to court, and there is a good chance that Dupree's estate—not this little library—will end up with the proceeds of the sale."

I didn't want to let him intimidate me, but I hated to be responsible for costing the library so much money either. I was starting to waver. "We've already advertised the auction on TV and through word of mouth—which in the South is actually more effective. It would be impossible to let everyone know that the auction has been cancelled. We'd have people come and then find out there were no paintings, and it might create bad will in the community."

"So you are going to refuse an offer of $10,000 to save yourself a little bad PR?" Mr. Thorne demanded. "That's irresponsible. I'm sure when the county library board hears what you've done, they will have some questions about your ability to run this library."

This hurt because I knew I was underqualified for my position and figured that my lack of abilities was already discussed by the library board on a regular basis. But I stood firm. "No, sir. I can't sell them before the auction."

I'm not sure what I expected Mr. Thorne's response to be, but his next words took me completely by surprise.

"I'll give you $1,500 per painting, but that is my final offer."

I did the math—twice to be sure. "Fifteen thousand dollars?"

Luke looked more suspicious than surprised. "Those paintings just appreciated by fifty percent in less than five minutes, Kennedy. I say you hold on to them."

Mr. Thorne turned to glare at him. "And I say you stay out of this."

If I hadn't already made up my mind, that remark would have clinched it. I stood and said, "Sorry, Mr. Thorne, but these paintings are not for sale until the auction on Wednesday and then only to the highest bidder."

By now Mr. Thorne's face was almost purple with anger. "I don't have time for this hillbilly nonsense! My flight back to New York leaves in two hours. If you don't let me buy those paintings according to my prearrangement with Mr. Dupree . . ." He shook the paper in his hand to ensure that I remembered he had legal proof. "I will sue you!"

I guess he thought this was the final straw that would break my art-negotiating back. But actually this threat was the weakest part of his argument. I wanted the money for the library, and I was nervous about turning down so much. But the only thing of value that I own is my old truck, and since it was at the engine repair shop in Albany (and not expected to recover) the threat of a lawsuit didn't really worry me. But that hillbilly remark did sting a little.

"I've given you my final answer," I said. "And now I'd like you to leave."

Mr. Thorne seemed prepared to argue, but Luke stood and walked to my office door. He didn't make any threatening gestures, but his intentions were clear. Mr. Thorne would either leave of his own free will or he would be thrown out. And in this strange moment, I felt a deep tenderness for Luke.

Realizing that he had no choice in the matter, Mr. Thorne returned his alleged legal paper to his fancy briefcase and, while clutching it in his white hands, sailed past Luke as if he had demanded that he be allowed to leave instead of being required to do so. We followed him to the front door and locked it securely behind him. Then we stood by one of the plate glass windows and watched him drive away.

As the taillights of his flashy rental car disappeared down Main Street, I sighed. "I hope I did the right thing."

Luke put an arm around my shoulders. "You did. I don't exactly know what he was up to, but if Miss Eugenia had been here, she would have definitely thought he was fishy."

Laughing, I turned into his embrace. Being close to him felt so good, so natural. He kissed me once and it was wonderful. We were about to kiss again when my cell phone started ringing.

"It's probably my mother," I murmured against his lips. "I'll call her back later."

Luke laughed softly. "No way. I'm trying to get on your mother's *good* side."

He stepped back, and I pulled out my phone. "Hello," I said impatiently.

It was not my mother, it was Cade and he sounded even more aggravated than he had been when he left us in Mr. Thorne's clutches.

"You didn't sell those paintings, did you?" he asked.

I glanced out the window in the direction Mr. Thorne had taken when he left. "No. I thought it would be unethical to sell them now when we've been advertising an auction on Wednesday."

"Well it's a good thing," Cade informed me. "Because the sheriff just got a call from a judge in Albany. JD's lawyer filed a complaint."

I deal with complaints every day, but I was surprised to learn that JD had a lawyer. "What kind of complaint?"

"Apparently Mr. Meyer, the guy who runs the convenience store out there on Highway 46, convinced the judge that you and Miss Eugenia coerced JD into giving you the paintings."

I was furious with Mr. Meyer for calling my character into question. "We did not coerce him! How could we?"

"The judge wants to check into the accusations," Cade continued. "So he approved some kind of injunction or something. Anyway, you can't sell the paintings until the judge decides who owns them—you and the library or JD's estate. There's going to be a hearing on Wednesday morning so you'll know in time for the auction."

I sighed. Nothing can ever be easy. "Thanks for letting me know."

"You're welcome," Cade responded. "The sheriff will give you more information about the hearing. And he wants to be sure the paintings are kept in a safe place until the judge decides about them. Should I pick them up so we can store them in the vault at the sheriff's department?"

"It's up to you, but I think they'll be fine in my office."

"I guess I'll let the sheriff make the call," Cade replied. "I'll call you back if he wants to move them today."

I closed my phone and explained the situation to Luke.

He shook his head. "To be some of the ugliest paintings I've ever seen, they are causing a lot of commotion."

I laughed and moved back into his arms. "Now where were we?"

After a couple of nice kisses, Luke pulled away. "I hate to end the most pleasant visit I've ever had to a library . . ."

"But you're going to?" I guessed. "End it, I mean?"

"I have to," he said. "My father has been begging me to come see him, and I promised I'd come this afternoon."

I was surprised and not completely pleased. "It's not fair."

"What, that I can't stay here and kiss you?" he teased.

I rolled my eyes. "No, that your father neglected and ignored you for most of your life. But now that he's in jail he's trying to force a relationship that never existed when you were the one needing love and time and attention."

Luke pressed a warm, strong hand to my cheek. "But I'm not like my father. I won't ignore my responsibilities."

I turned my face so I could kiss the inside of his palm. "No, you're nothing like your father and I'm glad. Even if he doesn't deserve you."

He tilted my chin so I had to look into his eyes. "You've got to go babysit for Madison anyway."

I'd forgotten that. "True."

"So how about this. I'll bring a pizza to your apartment tonight. We can watch a movie and maybe I'll kiss you again."

I pushed his hand away and gave him a smirk. "If the pizza's really good, maybe I'll kiss *you*."

He laughed as we walked toward the door. "So it's a date?"

I unlocked the door and pushed it open. "Unless I get a better offer."

***

After Luke dropped me off at my apartment, I just had time to unload the cooler full of food my mother sent home with me before Madison called. She needed me to be at her house in twenty minutes, which I could do if I didn't confine myself to legal speed limits.

I hurried out to the Torino and drove as fast as I dared to Albany. While driving—and watching for speed traps—I called my mother. I gave her a full report on the meeting with the art broker.

And then she said, "Well, he sounds like a perfectly dreadful man. And the nerve of that Mr. Meyer taking you to court!"

It's not often that I agree completely with my mother, so I cherished this moment.

Then Mother started talking about Miss Winnie down the street who had surgery for her ingrown toes and how her third cousin's grandson had won a prize for best calf at the county fair. I stood it as long as I could and then told her I had to go.

As soon as I ended that call I dialed Miss Eugenia's number. When she answered I told her about my visit from the New York art broker and his offer to pay $1,500 for each one of Mr. Dupree's paintings.

"Well, I declare, who ever would have imagined those paintings were worth so much?"

"Not me," I assured her. "And I doubt we've seen the last of Mr. Thorne. He seemed to want those paintings pretty bad, so he'll probably be at the auction on Wednesday. And since we're not expecting the bidding to be brisk, he'll probably get them all for a fraction of what he offered me today."

"There's got to be a way to prevent that," Miss Eugenia said. "Maybe I'll tell Annabelle and Whit to come. They can drive up the prices, and if they end up having to buy one, it won't be a tragedy. They can both afford it!"

I laughed. "That's a great idea. Assuming the judge lets us sell them."

"What judge?" Miss Eugenia asked.

I told her about Mr. Meyer's accusations and the subsequent stay of sale issued by the judge.

"Well, I never!" Miss Eugenia fumed. "Accusing you of coercing that poor man. The very idea!"

I noticed that she didn't include herself as an accused "coercer."

When I got to Madison's house the two babies were asleep and the two boys were awake, so the two hours I spent there seemed like an eternity. But finally Madison and Jared returned to take responsibility for their own children. Relieved of duty, I rushed home.

I was tired and hot and hungry. I planned to take a shower, eat a piece of my mother's pecan pie, and sleep until Luke arrived for dinner and a movie. But all my plans changed suddenly when I pulled into the Midway Store and Save parking lot and saw a sleek, silver Mercedes parked in front of Mr. Sheffield's office.

At first I thought it might be Sloan, risking a daylight visit. But as I pulled up closer I was able to tell that the man behind the wheel was someone I'd never seen. Assuming it was a potential customer wanting to rent a storage unit, I climbed out of the Torino and walked toward the office. The driver of the car met me by the door.

He was in his late thirties with dark blond hair that needed a trim. He wasn't overweight but neither was he fit. He wasn't tall or short, good looking or ugly—just an average guy. Sticking out a hand, he introduced himself as Rayford Cottingham, Mr. Dupree's lawyer.

I narrowed my eyes at him. "So you're the one who just filed a complaint against me in court?"

"I'm sorry about that," he said. "Mr. Meyer insisted on it."

"Are you his lawyer too?"

Mr. Cottingham shrugged. "I guess I am now."

I glared at him to be sure he knew my feelings on this matter. Then I asked, "And what can I do for you?"

The lawyer gave me an engaging smile. "I was hoping we could talk."

I knew I was under no obligation to speak to Mr. Cottingham, and I was pretty sure that this was a case where exercising my right to remain silent would be wise. But refusing would be rude, which for some reason was a bigger etiquette infraction on Sundays than on other days of the week. So the years my mother spent teaching me good manners worked to Mr. Cottingham's advantage. I waved to a wicker bench that Mr. Sheffield had confiscated from an abandoned storage unit. "I'll give you a few minutes."

Once we were settled on the bench, Mr. Cottingham said, "I hope you won't take this legal action personally. I was just acting in the interest of a client, and Mr. Meyer can be very forceful."

The complaint itself and the accusation behind it did feel personal to me, and I told Mr. Cottingham so. "I don't know why he'd say I coerced Mr. Dupree into giving me those paintings. He was there and heard me try to talk JD out of the whole thing."

"I don't know either," the lawyer admitted. "Even if he thought you tricked Mr. Dupree, having the paintings returned to the estate doesn't benefit Mr. Meyer in the least. He's not a beneficiary. In fact there are no heirs so the entire estate will eventually go to charity."

I shook my head in bewilderment. "Then why does he care?"

"Mr. Meyer probably misunderstood the situation," Mr. Cottingham proposed. "And I think there's a very good chance you'll be able to talk the judge into letting you proceed with the auction," Mr. Cottingham continued. "Just bring the paperwork and your witness."

I stared back blankly. "Witness? You mean Miss Eugenia Atkins?"

"If she was there when Mr. Dupree gave you the paintings, then she's a witness."

"I guess I can ask her to come." I knew Miss Eugenia wouldn't mind making a court appearance. In fact she'd probably be delighted. However, she would definitely consider this visit from Mr. Cottingham "fishy."

"I don't understand why you're here, telling me how to get around the complaint you filed on Mr. Meyer's behalf. Isn't it a conflict of interest or something?"

He blushed. "I feel that my first obligation is to Mr. Dupree. I was his lawyer, and I want to make sure that his final wishes are carried out. And I believe he wanted you and Midway Library to benefit from the sale of those paintings."

I barely knew Mr. Dupree before his death, and his gift, while generous, had already caused me a good bit of trouble even though I'd yet to realize a dime from it. However, Mr. Cottingham's words made me sad and a little sentimental toward the lonely old man who'd painted horrible pictures that were apparently appreciated in New York. And I wanted to know more about him.

"How long have you known Mr. Dupree?"

Mr. Cottingham thought for a few seconds and then said, "A year or so, I guess. I was contacted by a national organization called Return to Dignity. It's a charity that takes people off the streets, gives them a place to live, and helps them find a job. They had chosen JD for their program. I found the trailer for him and got him a job at the tire plant in Albany. But his drinking cost him his job and his driver's license. He would have been back out on the street if his artwork hadn't become popular enough to support him."

"Apparently he made a very good living with his paintings," I said. "Which makes me wonder why he lived so . . ." I searched for a word that would be accurate without being insulting and finally settled on, "cheaply."

"JD was a character. He could have lived better—but he chose not to. I don't know why. Artsy people are known for being kind of eccentric."

"I guess it doesn't matter." But I couldn't shake the feeling of melancholy.

"Since the paintings are fairly valuable, it might be wise to keep them in a temperature- and humidity-controlled environment," Mr. Cottingham suggested.

I thought about the first time I saw the paintings, lined up against JD's rusty old trailer, exposed to wind, rain, and sun. "I think they'll be okay at the library until Wednesday. Hopefully the auction will be allowed to take place as planned."

"Ironically the paintings will probably be worth even more now that JD is dead," Mr. Cottingham remarked. "If the judge clears the way for the auction, I'd be glad to offer my legal services to the library. With my contacts I might be able to help you get a higher price."

"I presume that your services come at a fee?"

He handed me a business card. "I'm very reasonable—especially if the cause is good and the lady involved is as charming as you."

The way things were going, I might need a good lawyer so I nodded. "I'll keep this just in case."

He smiled. "I'm only a phone call away."

He was obviously flirting with me. Since my hair was still striped and my church clothes were wrinkled from hours of wrestling with Madison's children, I knew he couldn't possibly find me attractive. So I assumed his behavior was a ploy to drum up business. With JD gone, he had one less paying client.

He stood up and extended his hand toward me again. "Anyway, I just wanted to be sure there were no hard feelings."

Mr. Cottingham was engaging and genuine, and I couldn't make myself be mad at him, even if he did file a complaint against me in court. So I smiled and said, "I don't have any hard feelings against you. However, I can't say the same about Mr. Meyer."

The lawyer laughed. "As long as you don't consider me guilty by association. I'll see you on Wednesday."

"In court." I waved and then watched from the bench until Mr. Cottingham and his Mercedes had disappeared from view. When my unexpected company was gone, I climbed the stairs to my apartment and unlocked my door.

The living room was stifling hot, so I opened all the windows and turned on the old window unit. Then I took a shower and put on some shorts and a T-shirt. I was considering a run down to the drugstore for a box of Miss Clairol when Luke knocked on the door with a pizza in hand.

He gave me a quick kiss on his way into the kitchen. He deposited the pizza on my little table and ate a piece as he watched while I heated up the leftovers my mother had sent home with me after lunch. Finally we settled around the table to eat our veritable feast.

I didn't really want to know about his visit to the state mental institution where his father was incarcerated, but I asked him anyway.

"It was fine," he replied.

"I guess your father was glad to see you?"

"Yes."

"Are you planning to go back?" I tried.

"At some point."

Based on his short, uninformative answers I got the impression that he didn't want to talk about the time he spent with his father. So I told him about my visit from JD's lawyer. I summarized our conversations, emphasizing the humorous elements. When I finished, I expected Luke to be smiling, but he wasn't.

He put down his fork and gave me his full attention. "So he didn't want anything—just apologized for blocking the sale of the paintings?"

"He offered to help me sell the paintings at the auction, for a *reasonable* fee."

Luke's frown deepened. "That doesn't justify coming all the way out here on a Sunday afternoon."

I couldn't argue. "He said he wanted to make sure that JD's final wishes were carried out. He wants me to bring Miss Eugenia and the paper JD signed to the hearing on Wednesday morning."

"All of that could have been handled with a simple phone call tomorrow."

The way Luke put it made me feel a little uneasy. "Why do you think he really came?"

"I don't know, but if he comes again I wouldn't talk to him alone. He's not your friend, Kennedy. You don't even know him. You don't even know if he was good to that JD guy."

I felt stupid. "He seemed nice."

Luke smiled. "It's better to suspect everyone than to trust the wrong person."

"I'm pretty cynical, but I'm not even sure I agree with that!"

"Maybe suspecting everyone is a little much, but this whole thing with the lawyer seems peculiar to me."

After we stacked our dishes in the sink, I divided the last of the pecan pie into two generous pieces. Then we sat on the couch and watched TV until I dozed off while leaning on his shoulder. He awakened me gently.

When I opened my eyes he was standing over me. "I've got to go."

"So early?" I asked around a yawn.

He smiled. "It's not that early, and I've got to drive to Atlanta tomorrow so I need to get some sleep."

He started for the door and I trailed after him, yawning again. "You'll call me when you find out about your scholarship?"

"I'll call you," he promised. Then he pressed a quick kiss to my lips and stepped out onto the front porch. "Lock your doors."

Once the door was securely locked, I got Sloan's bedding from my room and put it on the end of the couch. Then I lay down beside it, intending to wait up, in hopes that Sloan would come to spend the night downstairs again. But I was exhausted and fell asleep almost immediately. I woke up the next morning with sunlight streaming through the windows. I was still on the couch, and the bedding was still stacked neatly beside me. Sloan had not come.

***

I worried about Sloan while I got ready for work. I kept telling myself that he was a grown man, a trained FBI agent, and capable of taking care of himself. But I couldn't shake the feeling that he needed help. No one else even knew he was in trouble. If I didn't help him, who would?

Finally I decided that the best thing to do would be to involve someone else. By sharing what I knew with someone trustworthy, I hoped to increase Sloan's chances of success and decrease my personal responsibility for his safety. And the only person I could trust with Sloan's life was Mark Iverson. I looked his number up in my phone book and dialed. While the phone was ringing I composed what I was going to say. When the answering machine picked up, I left my name and number and asked him to call me back.

Then I locked my front door and headed down the steps. I was surprised to see Mr. Sheffield's car parked in front of his office. He usually only comes on the tenth of every month to pick up the rents I've collected. And I was even more surprised to see a van with ALBANY SECURITY SERVICES emblazoned on the side parked beside Mr. Sheffield's car.

"What's going on?" I asked when I reached the ground.

"It's the most amazing thing," Mr. Sheffield told me. "This is one of the best security companies in Albany, and they are trying to expand their service area. So they offered to give me a top-of-the-line security system completely free. All I have to do is post their sign in my yard as advertisement."

"Well, that does sound like a good deal," I replied, wondering how Sloan had worked that out since he was cut off from his assets.

Mr. Sheffield dug an envelope out of his coat pocket. "Here are the instructions on how to operate it. You'll need to choose a code and enter it one minute after you open the door."

"We have an alarm system at the library, so I'm familiar with how they work."

"Well, this is a very nice system," Mr. Sheffield reminded me. "So be sure to read about it."

I promised him that I would.

"Their servicemen are installing one in my office now. Then they'll put one in your apartment."

I nodded. "Just keep an eye on them," I requested. "I wouldn't want any of my valuables to turn up missing."

Mr. Sheffield frowned. Apparently the possibility that the security men themselves might not be trustworthy hadn't occurred to him. Then with a wave he went into his office, no doubt to watch the installers to be sure they didn't steal anything of his.

I drove to the library, and even though I was five minutes early, Miss Ida Jean was already standing by the entrance when I arrived. She waved frantically as I drove past her—like there was some chance I hadn't seen her.

Already aggravated before I even had to hear her say her first annoying word of the day, I parked in the section of the side lot reserved for employees. Then I was tempted to go around to the back door and let Miss Ida Jean wait outside until the official opening time. But I knew she'd tell my mother. So I accepted my fate and walked to the front of the library.

"I've been waiting here for fifteen minutes," she said the minute she saw me.

"It's not nine o'clock yet," I told her. "I wasn't supposed to be here fifteen minutes ago."

She didn't commend me for my rare punctuality. "I can't believe that it's only two days until Robby's party!" She followed me inside and walked right behind me as I turned off the alarm, turned on the lights, and headed toward my office. "I hope we haven't forgotten anything important."

"Mother and the other church ladies are experts at giving parties," I reminded her. "I'm sure they've remembered everything." I pushed open my office door. The room was a shambles. The chairs had been overturned, my Monet print knocked off the wall, and the contents of my desk and the bookshelves spilled onto the floor. A soft breeze blew in from a large hole in the window. And JD's paintings that had been stacked in the corner were gone.

I stared at the vandalized room in grief-stricken silence. Miss Ida Jean threw her hands up into the air and screamed at the top of her lungs.

As soon as the jarring sound faded, I said, "Go up to the main desk and call Sheriff Bonham. Ask him to come here fast."

And for once, Miss Ida Jean did as she was told.

***

I stood in the doorway, staring at my office in shock and despair. This room had been specially designed for me by Drake Langston and Sloan. It had been a place of peace and tranquility. Now it would never be the same.

I knew Miss Ida Jean had fulfilled her assignment when I heard the front door open and then slam closed. A few seconds later Sheriff Bonham was standing beside me. Cade was right behind him, looking rumpled and tired.

"Are you okay?" Cade demanded.

I nodded. "It happened before I got here."

"They stole JD's paintings?" the sheriff guessed.

I nodded miserably. "Yes."

"But they didn't take any of your new computers?" he asked.

I shook my head.

"So they came here specifically for the paintings."

I looked around. "I guess. But why did they have to mess up my office too?"

"Maybe they were looking for something else," Cade suggested.

I rubbed my hands up my arms to ward off a sudden chill. "It feels personal. Like someone did it to scare me so I wouldn't look too hard for the paintings."

This annoyed Cade. "You wouldn't be looking anyway. That's our job."

"The thief probably knew that the dinky little security system you have installed here only covers the doors," the sheriff said. "By coming through the window, he didn't set off the alarm."

I looked at the broken window. The cheap little security system had seemed totally sufficient for Midway. Until now. "Several people told me I should move the paintings to a safer place," I admitted. "Now I wish I had listened."

The sheriff turned to me with a frown. "It was my call, and I decided to leave them here. So it's my fault, not yours."

I appreciated his attempt to accept responsibility, but I didn't feel any better.

"Did many people know you were keeping the paintings specifically in your office—not just at the library?"

"I told a few people. Why?" I asked.

"Because that might be another reason that the thief chose to come directly in through your office window," the sheriff explained. "If they knew the paintings were here they could save time and effort by coming straight here."

"Mr. Thorne!" I announced with enthusiasm.

Cade looked up from a text message he was typing into his phone. "The art broker?"

"He wanted those paintings real bad," I said. "He offered me $1,500 apiece for them. That's fifteen thousand dollars total!"

The sheriff whistled. "That's a lot of money. But you couldn't sell them because of that court order."

"I had decided not sell them before you even told Cade to call to tell me about the judge. I told Mr. Thorne he'd have to come to the auction and bid on them like everyone else."

"How did he take that?" Sheriff Bonham asked.

"Badly. He threatened to sue me. And he called me a hillbilly."

I could tell the sheriff was offended in my behalf. But all he said was, "Who else?"

"My family, Cade, and Miss Eugenia Atkins and Luke," I itemized.

"Scoggins?" the sheriff confirmed.

I nodded. "He was here when I met with Mr. Thorne."

The sheriff cut his eyes over at Cade. He didn't say so, but I felt sure Cade had been officially assigned to stay with me and had shirked that duty. The sheriff looked back at me. "Go on."

I concentrated to be sure I didn't forget anyone. "And Rayford Cottingham. He's JD's lawyer, and he came by my apartment yesterday afternoon to apologize for filing that complaint against me in court. He's one of the people who suggested I move the paintings to a safer place. And we can probably assume that Mr. Meyer knew where they were since Mr. Cottingham is now his attorney too."

Cade decided to give us a few seconds of his undivided attention. "And if you consider that each of these people could have told several other people . . ."

The sheriff nodded. "Yes, we'll have to figure that a lot of folks knew where the paintings were being stored."

The other two deputies who worked day shift walked in. One took digital pictures of the crime scene while the other wrote down my statement. Once the picture-taking was done the sheriff went into my office and looked around. Cade stayed in the hall with me but seemed distracted and spent most of his time texting or receiving texts.

Carmella arrived and walked over to join me in the hall, her eyes as wide as saucers. After one glance into my office, she burst into tears. I patted her back until she got herself under control.

Finally she said, "This is awful."

I agreed that it was.

"Maybe the sheriff will be able to recover the paintings in time for the auction?"

"Maybe." I tried to sound more hopeful than I felt.

The sheriff returned to the hallway in time to hear this. He said, "We'll do our best. I know it will be a big financial blow if we can't find the paintings."

"It isn't just the money." My voice shook with emotion, and I swallowed to regain my composure. Then I tried to explain. "We weren't counting on the money, so it's not like we'll have a budget shortfall. I just feel so bad for JD. He wanted to do something nice for the library, and the thief stole that along with those paintings."

"Kennedy?" I heard Miss Ida Jean's voice, more shrill than usual, call to me from down the hallway. "You've got people up here wanting to check out books!"

I looked at Carmella. "Do you think if I ignore her she'll go away?"

She shook her head and gave me a tremulous smile. "Probably not."

These words proved prophetic a few seconds later when Miss Ida Jean walked around the corner. She looked anxiously back into my office and then asked, "This won't keep you from having Robby's party on Wednesday, will it?"

I tried to overlook her selfishness in my time of trouble. "I don't see why it will be a problem. I'm about to call a glass place in Albany right now, but even if they can't get the repair made before Wednesday, we can go ahead with the party."

"But for the rest of today the library will be closed," the sheriff told Miss Ida Jean. "So I'm going to need you to go home." He turned to Carmella. "Can you notify the other patrons? And once everyone has left, lock the front door."

Carmella's head bobbed. "Yes, sir." Then she rushed off to do his bidding. Miss Ida Jean trailed behind her, a little less excited about following his orders.

"Hurry on now, Miss Ida Jean," the sheriff encouraged.

I was eternally grateful to the sheriff, although I knew that the minute Miss Ida Jean got home she'd tell my mother all about the robbery. I wanted to get to my mother first, but I didn't want to get caught up in a long conversation with her. So I was going to ask Cade to make the call, but his phone rang and he walked outside to take it. Left without options, I called her myself.

Mother was upset, as I knew she would be. She demanded to speak to the sheriff, who did his best to reassure her. Then the only way I could prevent her from coming up to the library was by promising that I would come to her house as soon as the sheriff was finished with me.

I didn't want Luke to hear the news from someone else either, so after ending my call to my mother, I dialed his number. He was halfway to Atlanta and sounded happy to hear from me at first. I was sorry that I had to spoil his good mood by telling him that the library had been robbed and JD's paintings were gone.

He offered to turn around and come back. "I can reschedule my meeting at Georgia Tech."

"No, that might hurt your scholarship chances," I said bravely. "The sheriff is here so I'm in good hands. Don't worry."

It took a little more doing, but finally I convinced him to keep driving toward Atlanta.

Then while Cade talked on his cell phone and the sheriff searched my office for evidence, I walked up to the circulation desk and found a phone book. I looked up the number for a glass company in Albany and arranged to have them come and replace my office window.

The sheriff walked up just as I ended that call. "Well, I think everything is secure here. We've got a piece of plywood over your broken window, and I'll have deputies drive past the library regularly." He glanced over his shoulder to make sure Cade wasn't listening. When he realized I'd noticed this strange behavior, he lowered his voice to a whisper and said, "His new connection to the local press makes me a little nervous."

I was surprised, both by the sheriff's wisdom and his willingness to share his concerns with me.

Then he surprised me further by adding, "So you think this Thorne guy from New York is our thief?"

"I think he's the best suspect, although I don't care for Mr. Meyer either, so I wouldn't mind if it was him."

"That's an interesting approach to finding suspects," the sheriff said. "Investigate all the people you don't like first."

I laughed. "There are a lot more people I don't like, but Mr. Thorne and Mr. Meyer are the only two who I think might be guilty. Luke thought it was strange that JD's lawyer took the time to come and visit me on a Sunday afternoon, so I guess we should consider him too, although I hope he's not the thief because I liked him."

"Well, I'm going to set up the hillbilly version of a think tank this afternoon, and I'd like you to be a part of it."

Now I moved way past surprised to at least astonished. "Me?"

He nodded as if this was the most logical thing. When I was trying to get Foster Scoggins's murder investigated, I couldn't get the sheriff to listen to a word I said. Now he wanted me to be a part of his think tank. Amazing.

"I'm going to invite Mark Iverson to come and represent the FBI," the sheriff continued. "And I've asked the county for an extra deputy who I can assign specifically to this case."

"Maybe we *will* find those paintings by Wednesday!" I started to feel hopeful.

"I also want to look into JD's death and make sure it was accidental," the sheriff said.

You could have knocked me over with a feather. "You think there was something . . . fishy . . . about Mr. Dupree's death?"

"I didn't," the sheriff replied, "until these paintings were stolen. But now I feel like we have to go back and rethink the whole thing. And if whoever stole the paintings did have something to do with JD's death, I'm going to make sure he regrets it."

I wasn't sure how I felt about this, but I knew Miss Eugenia was going to be thrilled.

"And I learned my lesson last time about not using all the resources I have available," the sheriff was continuing. "Since you were one of the last people to see JD alive and since you were in possession of the paintings when they were stolen, we need your input."

I'll admit I wanted to be a part of the investigation, but I had to be honest. "Miss Eugenia Atkins would be more helpful to you than me."

He didn't look thrilled with this suggestion. "I don't know about that. Chief Jones says Miss Eugenia is a pain."

"But she's experienced at solving crimes and has good instincts," I reminded him. "And she was with me when I visited with JD, so she's as qualified as me."

He nodded reluctantly. "Okay, Miss Eugenia can come too. We'll have our first meeting in my office at five thirty." He stepped a little closer and lowered his voice. "But I'm including you with the understanding that you can't discuss the case with Cade."

I wasn't completely comfortable with this disloyal not to mention inconvenient arrangement. "How can you run an operation here without Cade's knowledge?"

"I'll keep him busy elsewhere during the day, and his shift ends at five o'clock. That's why we're starting the meeting at five thirty."

The sheriff was in charge, so I nodded.

"For starters I've asked for Jarrard Dupree's body to be autopsied. I'm going to ask the FBI to do background checks on all our major suspects, and based on your suspicions about Mr. Thorne, I'll see if we can get a warrant to search his properties for the stolen paintings."

"Mr. Meyer is from New York and Mr. Thorne is from New York," I said. "Geographically speaking, that's a huge coincidence down here in Georgia."

The sheriff narrowed his eyes. "You think they might be working together?"

"I think it's a possibility." I couldn't believe I was speaking so confidently with the man who had always intimidated me.

"Doing what?" the sheriff asked.

"I don't know. But Mr. Thorne was in my office trying to buy paintings very quickly after JD's death. You might want to check on his whereabouts Saturday evening."

"I will do that," the sheriff promised. "Don't forget the meeting at five thirty."

"I'll be there and I'll bring Miss Eugenia."

He started for the door. "I'll see you then." He paused and looked back over his shoulder at me. "In the meantime, you be careful."

I nodded as my phone started ringing. I checked the screen. "My mother again," I told him.

He smiled. "You go reassure her. We'll keep an eye on things here."

I thanked him and while walking out to the Torino, I answered my mother's call.

The first thing she said was, "I thought you said you were coming over here!"

"I'm on my way," I promised.

"Well, hurry. I have a surprise for you. Not that you'll enjoy it since you've just been robbed."

Mother met me on the front porch. I let her hug me and stroke my hair for as long as I could stand it. Finally I pulled away and said, "I'm fine, Mother. Really."

She didn't look convinced. "Well come on in. I made you breakfast."

I didn't have the heart to point out that it was after ten o'clock—way beyond the normal time for eating breakfast. So I walked into my mother's kitchen where she fed me crispy bacon and scrambled eggs and biscuits slathered with butter and homemade jelly. And to be honest, this time I didn't mind the fussing too much.

While I ate I told her how nice Sheriff Bonham was being to me and how determined he was to bring the thief to justice. This seemed to relieve her greatly.

When my meal was over I helped her wash up the dishes and then she showed me her surprise. It was a box of hair color—and not the brands available in drugstores. She'd gone to Bonnie's Beauty Supply in Albany and picked up professional-quality hair dye.

I grabbed the box and clutched it to my chest. "You are the best mother in the whole entire world!"

Mother smiled and pointed me toward her bathroom. "Come on, my little tiger. Let's get rid of those stripes."

CHAPTER SEVEN

AN HOUR LATER MY HAIR was back to its normal light-brown color. I thanked my mother from the bottom of my heart and headed for Haggerty. While I was driving, I called Miss Eugenia and told her I was coming. She'd heard about the robbery and was anxious to get firsthand details.

While I had her on the phone I mentioned that I'd left a message for Mark Iverson and hadn't heard back from him.

"Mark's out of town on business," Miss Eugenia said, and I remembered that this had been announced at church on Sunday. "But I'm sure he's checking in with Kate so you can give her the message and ask her to pass it on. And I'm also sure she'll want to hear all about the big library heist. So just meet me over there."

When I turned onto Maple Street I could see Miss Eugenia standing on the Iversons' front porch. She waited for me to join her and then led the way inside. As we walked past the family room I waved to the Iverson children, Emily and Charles. They were building a tower with Legos, and I saw no evidence of a new foster baby yet.

Miss Eugenia and I walked into the kitchen to find Kate seated at the table conversing quietly with a tall black woman dressed in a dark business suit. Their conversation ceased abruptly when they saw us.

If Miss Eugenia noticed this, she didn't mention it.

"Kennedy, this is Special Agent Miracle Moore of the FBI," Miss Eugenia introduced us. "Miracle is Mark's supervisor and normally she works in Atlanta, but while Mark is away she'll be filling in for him."

"Nice to meet you, Agent Moore."

"Call me Miracle," she invited as I sat down in the chair beside Kate.

"Kennedy needs to get a message to Mark, and I told her you could pass it on," Miss Eugenia continued.

"I wouldn't bother you," I said. "But it's important and kind of sensitive."

"Will Mark be back soon?" Miss Eugenia asked.

"Mark may not be home for several days," Kate replied with a glance at Agent Moore.

"He's on special assignment," the agent added vaguely.

"But if you need help from the FBI, you can talk to Miracle," Miss Eugenia suggested.

"I would trust her with my life," Kate added. "In fact I have, several times."

I studied the other woman. She stared back, steady, calm, but not necessarily inviting. "I'll help you if I can."

I really wanted to talk to Mark Iverson, but since that wasn't a possibility, I took a deep breath and began. "It's about another FBI agent named Sloan." Belatedly I realized that I didn't know if that was his first or last name. "I don't know him well, but he saved my life once and I want to help him if I can."

"That handsome construction worker who came to Midway with Drake Langston?" Miss Eugenia asked.

I hated to give more details than absolutely necessary, so I kept my reply vague. "Yes, he's been undercover for a while."

"What kind of trouble is he in?" Kate asked.

I hesitated. Sloan's life could depend on the choice I made. I looked into all their eyes and saw varying degrees of concern and compassion. I felt like I had to trust someone. And these three women were all I had.

So I said, "He's in trouble with the IRS and the FBI. He said he stumbled onto some criminal activity while investigating another case. He collected evidence, including some pictures, and submitted a report to his supervisor. But nothing ever came of it."

"There's a limit to the number of cases the Bureau can handle," Miracle said. "Maybe his supervisor just didn't think it was a priority."

"His supervisor said he never got the report," I told them. "Then Sloan's laptop and personal files were stolen, which prevented him from duplicating the report. And then the IRS accused him of tax fraud and got a warrant issued for his arrest, even though he has paid his taxes every year."

"And you know for certain that this Agent Sloan paid his taxes and filed the report with his supervisor?" Miracle asked.

"I only have his word," I admitted. "But I trust him."

Miracle considered this. "You think someone within the Bureau framed him for the tax evasion—to keep him from pursuing the illegal activity he wrote about in the report that went missing?"

"Yes. Well that's what Sloan thinks, anyway. He wouldn't give me any details because he was afraid that might be dangerous for me."

Miracle nodded in apparent agreement. "And where is he now?"

"I don't know. He spent Friday and Saturday nights in the office below my apartment. But he didn't come last night, and I haven't heard from him. He said he was going to prove his innocence no matter what it took—even if it cost him his life. So I'm worried."

"Of course you are," Kate said kindly.

"Sloan suspects that his supervisor is the one who destroyed his report and gave false information to the IRS. And until he finds out for sure, he doesn't dare trust anyone in the FBI—except Mark."

"But you've decided to trust Miracle," Miss Eugenia pointed out.

"Yes." I glanced at the other agent. "I don't know what Sloan's plan is. I assume he's going to confront his supervisor and try to prove his innocence. But he's at a disadvantage since he doesn't have access to the FBI's resources."

"And he can't even go out in public without the risk of getting arrested," Miss Eugenia added, "making his situation even more hopeless."

"I was going to ask Mark to check into the supervisor and see if he could find anything . . ." I glanced at Miss Eugenia, "fishy."

Miracle nodded. "I can make some discreet inquiries."

I felt greatly relieved. "Thank you."

"Now, tell us about the library robbery," Miss Eugenia requested.

"There isn't much to tell. Someone broke into my office and stole the paintings."

"Miss Eugenia says they were quite valuable," Miracle commented.

"Apparently so, although I didn't have possession of them long enough to find out for sure," I acknowledged. "An art broker from New York offered me $15,000 for the group."

Miracle looked impressed. "That's a lot of money."

"Especially if you'd seen them," Miss Eugenia told her. "They were terrible."

Miracle asked, "And the artist died in an accident on Saturday night?"

"Just a few hours after he gave the paintings to Kennedy," Miss Eugenia confirmed. "The timing seems suspicious to me."

"Well, Sheriff Bonham agrees and is holding a meeting at five thirty this evening to discuss the case," I informed them. Then I turned to Miss Eugenia. "And he would like you to be present."

Miss Eugenia looked surprised. "Sheriff Bonham has invited me to be a part of his investigation?"

"Well, unofficially at least. He said he learned his lesson last time about ignoring people who can help him solve a case." I wanted her to feel welcome, so I didn't mention that I had suggested her involvement.

"Humph," Miss Eugenia said dismissively. "Learned his lesson indeed. Sheriff Bonham doesn't have a humble bone in his body. He's up to something. If he's inviting us to be a part of his investigation, it's probably because he's afraid we'll solve it before him again and make him look bad."

Kate laughed. "He has good reason to worry."

"We were some of the last people to see Mr. Dupree alive," I mentioned. "And I was the robbery victim. So hopefully we can be of help."

"I'm sure we can," Miss Eugenia agreed.

"You'll come to the meeting, then?"

"Of course," she said, "because whatever the sheriff's motives are for inviting us to the meeting, we want him to find out the circumstances around JD's death."

"I think it makes good sense to involve the two of you in the investigation," Miracle said.

I smiled. "Good, because you're probably going to be invited to the meeting yourself. Sheriff Bonham told me he was going to ask Mark to come, but since he's gone and you're filling in for him . . ."

Miracle nodded. "I'll be glad to help the sheriff with his investigation."

"He seems much more serious this time than he did when Foster Scoggins died," I told them. "He's already ordered an autopsy on Mr. Dupree."

"I'll call and offer my services to the sheriff," Miracle said. "And then I'll flag the autopsy so it will be rushed through."

I felt like I was helping the investigation already.

"Does the sheriff have any suspects?" Miracle asked.

"Well, a few persons of interest, anyway." I told them about the art broker, Mr. Meyer, and JD's lawyer, Mr. Cottingham. Then I described each man and the circumstances surrounding my interactions with them for Miracle's benefit.

"It could be someone who hasn't even been considered yet," Miracle said.

"That's true," I agreed. "To say this investigation is in its early stages would be an understatement."

Miss Eugenia asked Kate for a piece of paper and a pen. Once she had these items in front of her she said, "I'll be working on a list of everything we need to discuss this evening."

I could just imagine Sheriff Bonham's reaction when Miss Eugenia walked in with a list and tried to take over his meeting.

"We need to find out more about those paintings," Miss Eugenia continued. "How many did JD do and who bought them?"

"Why do you need to know that?" Kate asked.

"Partly just curiosity," Miss Eugenia admitted. "They are so . . ."

"Ugly?" I provided.

"I was going to say *odd*," Miss Eugenia revised. "But they sell so well that the art broker was very anxious to get this last batch. And I'm just wondering what kind of people buy them and hang them on the walls of their home."

"Do you think someone who already owns a painting stole the others or killed Mr. Dupree?" Kate asked.

"Maybe not, but they are at least providing a market for the paintings," Miss Eugenia said.

I had to agree. "And a motive for robbery."

"And possibly murder," Miracle added. "At this point, all information is potentially useful. We can trim away what we don't need later."

"So someone will get the assignment to find out who the ultimate consumers are for JD's paintings," Miss Eugenia scribbled on her list.

"We need to get detailed background checks on our persons of interest," Miracle said. "I have a researcher in my department in Atlanta who is a computer genius. I think I'll put her on that."

"You might mention that to Sheriff Bonham when you call him," I suggested.

"And try to make it sound like it was his idea so he won't think you're trying to take over his investigation," Kate added with a meaningful glance in Miss Eugenia's direction.

Miracle smiled. "Yes, it's better to let the sheriff think he's running things."

I stood. "Well, I've taken up enough of your time, so I'll head back to Midway. Would you like me to pick you up for the meeting tonight?" I asked Miss Eugenia.

"She can ride with me," Miracle said.

Miss Eugenia nodded. "That will work out nicely. Then she turned to me. "But if you're not in a hurry, while you're here why don't we go back out to George Ann's farm and see if anyone has stolen more wood?"

"Luke and I checked yesterday and everything looked the same," I told her.

"But you wouldn't want George Ann to feel neglected just because you have another case to work on," Miss Eugenia pressed.

I narrowed my eyes at her. "You are concerned about Miss George Ann's *feelings*?"

Miss Eugenia shrugged. "Of course I am. And while we're out that way we could go by JD's trailer and look around there too—just as tourists."

I understood that Miss Eugenia wanted to nose around JD's trailer and was using Miss George Ann's wood theft as an excuse. "I guess we could do that."

Miracle saw through the ploy as well and gave us a stern look. "Don't stay long and keep your cell phones in your hands at all times."

I nodded.

"And if you find anything that you think might be important, don't touch it," she cautioned. "Call the sheriff and let him handle it officially."

I nodded again.

Miss Eugenia pushed back from the kitchen table and stood up. "While we're gone, Kate can give her children some attention and Miracle can start acting like an FBI agent instead of a house guest."

Kate rolled her eyes.

Miracle said, "Yes, ma'am."

"It shouldn't take us long. Then maybe we can all meet at Haggerty Station for lunch. Today's special is chicken-fried steak and creamed potatoes."

"Just call us when you're on your way there," Kate suggested. "And if I feel like I've spent enough quality time with my kids by then, we'll join you."

Miss Eugenia ignored the sarcasm. "You'd better come. You know how much Little Charles loves creamed potatoes."

***

While we were riding out to Miss George Ann's farm, Miss Eugenia made me repeat every word Sheriff Bonham had said in relation to the investigation. When I was finished she shook her head.

"He's definitely up to something. He's never this cooperative."

"He was more than cooperative," I said. "He was downright *nice*."

"There has to be a reason for this uncharacteristic behavior. We need to be careful what we say and do when we're around him."

I was mildly alarmed by the comment. "You mean withhold information from the sheriff?"

"Not exactly," she hedged. "But it's possible that we're suspects and he's just pretending to include us in the investigation so he can collect incriminating information."

Now the fact that the sheriff hadn't originally invited Miss Eugenia to join his think tank seemed to loom large. She couldn't be a suspect, but maybe I *was*.

"But we didn't do anything wrong," I pointed out. "So there's nothing he can find that incriminates us."

"Don't be naive," she said. "Lots of innocent people go to jail."

This was a sobering thought.

Then she softened her tone and said, "I am sorry that the library lost all those paintings and the money they would have brought."

I sighed. "Me too. But maybe the sheriff will find them."

Then she surprised me by asking, "Who do you think took them?"

"I hope it was the art broker from New York since he called me a hillbilly. Or I wouldn't mind if it was Mr. Meyers either, since he basically accused me of stealing the paintings from JD in the first place. But it could have been the lawyer or anyone who saw the bit on the weekend news."

"True," Miss Eugenia agreed. "Under the circumstances I feel that I should return the painting I bought for Annabelle's birthday. That way you can proceed with the auction on Wednesday. With all the publicity surrounding JD's death and the robbery at the library—you'll probably get an inflated price for it."

I appreciated the offer very much and told Miss Eugenia so. But then I said, "With the paintings stolen, we had to cancel the auction. I asked Hannah-Leigh Coley-Smith to announce it on the news, and Mother is having the church ladies call around. If we're able to recover the paintings by Wednesday night we can always reschedule it. But that painting is yours. Just don't mention it to anyone until after we solve this case or you might get robbed too."

We drove past Meyer's Grocery and I noted the CLOSED sign on the door. "Apparently he's gone fishing again."

Miss Eugenia nodded. "I told you he's almost never open."

"Good thing we weren't desperate for a two-dollar Pepsi."

I turned at the old boiled peanut sign and followed the dirt roads from memory until we reached Miss George Ann's farm. Thanks to so many visitors lately, the grass between the house and the barn was pressed down into a nice little parking spot.

We walked around to the barn and determined that no new wood had been stolen.

Miss Eugenia frowned. "I guess JD's death was good for George Ann."

"Yes, without a customer, there's no point in stealing wood."

She started down toward the car. "We've seen enough here. Let's go over to JD's trailer."

Since I knew this was the actual purpose for our visit, I didn't argue, even though we'd only been at Miss George Ann's farm for about three minutes.

When we pulled up to Mr. Dupree's place, I gasped in unhappy surprise. The door to his trailer was not just open but had been torn off the hinges and thrown into the yard. The assortment of beer containers and paint cans in the yard had been joined by books and dishes and chairs. We got out and walked carefully through the debris. There was a full carton of milk and a stick of butter, indicating that the contents of the refrigerator had been emptied and discarded.

We reached the door and looked inside where there was further evidence of wanton destruction.

"Who would do something like this?" I whispered.

"Someone who was really mad at JD," Miss Eugenia replied.

"Because he gave away the paintings?"

She shrugged. "It's possible. But one thing is for sure. We've got to call Sheriff Bonham."

I placed the call to the sheriff, and he wasn't happy when he found out where we were and what conditions we had found. He told us to wait in the Torino with the doors locked until he could get there. I didn't argue.

He arrived in a cloud of road dust fifteen minutes later. He had a young, fresh-faced deputy with him whom he introduced as Mac Cross. "Deputy Cross is on loan to us from the Albany headquarters. He just got his degree in criminology and he's anxious to get some hands-on training."

Obviously in response to the sheriff's request for an extra deputy to help with the new investigation, the state had sent him an inexperienced kid.

I followed the sheriff's lead and addressed the newcomer with the respect that his title deserved—even if he hadn't earned it yet. "Nice to meet you, Deputy Cross. I'm Kennedy Killingsworth and this is Miss Eugenia Atkins."

The deputy shook hands with each of us and then, after surveying the damage quickly, said, "What happened here?"

I looked at the sheriff, and he closed his eyes in what might have been a short prayer for patience. Then he said, "It looks like the trailer has been vandalized and maybe robbed."

The deputy raised his eyebrows. "Really. What do you think they took?"

"It's going to be hard to figure that out since we don't know what was here to begin with," the sheriff said. "The best thing to do is to take pictures of the scene that we can refer to later. That's why I told you to bring the camera."

The deputy shrugged. "Okay." He pulled a digital camera from his pocket and started for the trailer—stepping on the carton of milk. He looked down at his milk-drenched shoe in horror. "Did I just ruin evidence?"

"Probably not," the sheriff comforted him, "But you did ruin your shoes, so watch where you're going from now on."

After the kid walked over to the trailer, the sheriff fixed me with a stern look.

"When I said I wanted you to be a member of my think tank, I meant that I needed your help with research and ideas—not actual police work. In the future if you think something needs to be investigated, I want you to tell me. Then I will send deputies to check it out.

I tried to look repentant. "Yes, sir. I'm sorry."

He seemed appeased. "I understand your desire to get the case solved, but you can't risk your safety."

"No, sir."

"Or contaminate evidence," he added.

This remark was punctuated by a squeal from Deputy Cross. We turned to see him wiping some unidentified substance from his hand onto his brand new uniform pants.

"Yes, your deputy seems well-trained in how to examine a crime scene without contaminating evidence," Miss Eugenia said.

The sheriff ground his teeth together. "That boy is going to be the death of me."

I laughed softly.

Miss Eugenia waved to encompass the trailer and the area immediately around it. "This could have just been a robbery. Some criminals watch the papers to see when someone died. Then they go out and steal what they want."

"That's possible," the sheriff replied. "But because of JD's death and the paintings being stolen, I think we'll consider this connected to the case."

"Maybe someone thought JD had more paintings out here."

The sheriff nodded. "Maybe he did."

Miss Eugenia stared at the devastation. "If he did, they're gone now."

***

We left the sheriff and Deputy Cross to process the crime scene and headed back to Haggerty. I dropped Miss Eugenia off at Haggerty Station but politely declined her insistent invitation to join her and Kate's family and Miracle for lunch.

"I need to get back to the library," I told her firmly, although I, too, love creamed potatoes and chicken-fried steak. "If the sheriff's department is through looking for evidence, I can clean up my office. It's very unsettling—having it all torn up like it is."

Miss Eugenia seemed to understand and finally accepted no for an answer. With a promise to see her at the sheriff's office that evening, I said good-bye and headed on to Midway.

By the time I arrived at the library, everyone was gone. The broken window was boarded up, and someone had kindly cleared away the broken glass and put the furniture back into place. The books were back on the shelves but not in the correct order. I wanted to fix them but felt uneasy about staying in the empty and recently robbed library by myself. So I went to the grocery store and then back to my apartment.

I was lugging boxes of Diet Pepsi up the stairs when Luke texted me. He said he was on his way home from Atlanta. I tried to get him to tell me if he'd gotten his scholarship transferred, but he said he wanted to tell me in person. I figured this probably meant he got it, but he might want to deliver bad news personally too. So I couldn't be sure.

I had time to put the Pepsi into the refrigerator before the next string of words appeared on my little cell phone screen. "Will you go out to dinner with me?"

This seemed like a celebration—more evidence that his trip to Atlanta had been successful. Regretfully I typed back that I had a meeting with the sheriff at five thirty and didn't know how long it would run. So if he was going to eat dinner with me it would have to be hot dogs from the Jiffy Mart.

My phone rang almost immediately. "Why are you meeting with the sheriff?"

"He says he wants me to be a part of a think tank he's creating to investigate the robbery at the library and JD's death."

"I thought those college kids ran over him while he was passed out drunk on the road."

"They did, but the sheriff has ordered an autopsy to be sure he wasn't already dead when they hit him."

"Wow, this is getting more complicated by the minute."

"I was honored to be included in the sheriff's think tank. But Miss Eugenia thinks that I'm a suspect in the case and the sheriff only invited me to join so he can question me without making it official and upsetting my parents."

There was a brief silence, and then Luke said, "In that case I'll go to that meeting with you tonight."

I didn't think the sheriff would object—not openly anyway—and I liked the idea of having a staunch supporter with me. So I said, "What about dinner? Are you going to buy me a hot dog or not?"

He laughed. "I'll pick you up at five. That should give us enough time to run by the Jiffy Mart, wolf down some hot dogs, and get to the meeting."

"I'll supply the Pepsi," I said. And then we ended the call.

I had almost two hours before Luke was coming to pick me up. So I ate a MoonPie, figuring this wouldn't ruin my dinner appetite and then sat on the couch to watch reruns of *Family Feud* back when the host kissed everyone (another object of my morbid fascination).

I planned to watch for about thirty minutes, giving my MoonPie time to digest. Then I was going to wash my newly dyed hair and style it as best I could before Luke got there to pick me up. But I fell asleep, and that put me behind schedule. Consequently when Luke knocked on my door, I had washed my hair but hadn't had time to dry and style it.

So I answered the door with a towel wrapped around my head.

He glanced at the towel and then his eyes moved down to mine. "New hair again?"

I smirked at him. "Very funny. Come in. I'll be ready in a minute."

"You'd better hurry or we won't have time for hot dogs."

I was hungry so I said, "I'll hurry."

I dried my hair, and as I tucked it behind my ears I blessed my mother. I looked so much better without the blonde stripes. I quickly touched up my makeup and rushed out to the living room.

Luke smiled when he saw me. "You do have new hair."

"It's just my old hair, back again." I moved close and grabbed two fistfuls of his shirt. "Now tell me. Did you get that scholarship?"

He grinned, and his chipped tooth looked exceptionally cute. "I got it."

I pressed my face against his chest and listened to his heart pounding in my ear. "That's good," I whispered.

He stroked my hair. "I'm glad you think so." Then he pulled away and took me by the hand. "Now let's get to the Jiffy Mart. I'm craving an overcooked hot dog served on a stale bun."

***

Luke parked at the Jiffy Mart and then ushered me inside. We ordered our hot dogs and ate them while sitting in the front seat of his rental car. Between bites he told me about his interview and the details of his scholarship. A lot of it I didn't really understand, but the fact that he was going to be living in Atlanta by the end of July caught my attention. It wouldn't require an immediate adjustment, and by the time he actually moved, I knew I'd be ready.

Then he asked about my day, and I told him about my visit to Kate Iverson's house—leaving out the part about Sloan—and the destruction we'd found at JD's trailer. We finished our hot dogs, disposed of our trash, and drove to the sheriff's office. We arrived at the same time as Miracle Moore, with Miss Eugenia in tow.

Greetings were exchanged on the sidewalk as we headed for the door. But just before we entered the sheriff's department, Miracle put a hand on my arm and said, "Can I speak to you privately for just a minute?"

Luke looked a little surprised by this request but didn't object. He said, "I'll wait for you inside," and went in with Miss Eugenia.

Once we were alone Miracle said, "I've checked on your friend Sloan. His full name is Alexander Sloan, and he has been with the Bureau for almost ten years. He's not a typical agent—which is common with undercover guys—but there was nothing negative on his record until the last six months. He got a new supervisor about then, a guy named Wade Norman. Apparently the two didn't get along. He wrote Sloan up constantly."

"For what?" I asked, although I wasn't sure I really wanted to know.

"Apparently Agent Norman comes from an administrative background and can't comprehend undercover guys," Miracle began. "So he had problems with Sloan's tendency to miss meetings and call-ins. He complained about late and sloppy reports. He accused him of insubordination three times."

"In just six months? That seems excessive!"

Miracle nodded. "But the biggest problem between the two was related to the Drake Langston investigation. Agent Norman felt like Sloan had evidence that would enable the FBI to prosecute but was withholding it because he likes Langston."

I was careful not to meet Miracle's eyes, because I was afraid this might be true and I wanted her to keep helping Sloan. "Did you see anything about the report Sloan said he filed recently about some kind of criminal activity?"

"No, none."

"So what does that mean?"

Miracle lifted her shoulder in a slight shrug. "It means either Sloan is lying or his supervisor destroyed the report and all reference to it."

"I trust Sloan," I told Miracle. "Were you able to question this Agent Norman?"

"No. Agent Norman didn't show up for work today." Something about her tone made my heart pound.

"Do you know why?"

"Human resources said he sent an e-mail this morning saying he was taking a couple of days off."

"But you think his absence has to do with Sloan?"

Miracle raised an eyebrow. "Don't you?"

I hung my head. "Sloan was desperate. He said he had a plan worked out. I guess his plan was to kidnap his supervisor."

"There's something else you should know," Miracle said softly. "But you can't tell anyone." She tipped her head toward the building. "Even your boyfriend."

I nodded, terrified.

"Mark Iverson is not on assignment from the FBI," Miracle informed me. "I'm his supervisor, and on Sunday I received an e-mail from him saying he would be taking a few days off."

I made the unhappy connection quickly. "Just like the supervisor. Sloan kidnapped Mark too?"

"Apparently. Mark never takes time off unexpectedly, so I called Kate. When I found out she thought he was on an FBI assignment, I decided to come and stay with his family and cover his work assignments until he's through with . . . whatever."

I felt a guilty responsibility for Sloan's actions. "Kate must be beside herself with worry."

"Kate's handling it okay."

I felt a little better. "And if Sloan did kidnap Mark, he won't hurt him."

"You said he was desperate," Miracle pointed out.

I remembered Sloan's words: "I will go to any length to clear my name—even if it costs me my life." Then I thought about Sloan flinging himself toward the exploding trailer that used to house the Midway Library—just to protect me. I squared my shoulders. "He's not a bad person."

Miracle nodded. "Then we'll assume that if he kidnapped Mark, he only wants his help. I'll keep trying to find out information and will keep you posted. However, we need to limit any communication by land line or cell phone. If we're going to be discussing specifics, we need to talk in person." She stepped back and moved toward the building. "Now let's get inside before your boyfriend thinks that I've kidnapped *you*."

We found Luke and Miss Eugenia already seated in Sheriff Bonham's office. The sheriff and his clumsy temporary deputy, Mac Cross, were there as well. Luke gave me a questioning look as I took the chair beside him. I smiled in a way that I hoped was both reassuring and casual at the same time.

Sheriff Bonham cleared his throat and said, "Well, now that we're all here, the meeting can begin. Has everyone met Miracle Moore from the FBI?"

We all said that we had.

"Well good." He referred to a piece of paper, and I noticed that his hand was shaking slightly.

I was concerned and glanced at Miss Eugenia to see if she'd noticed, but she couldn't see me. So I returned my attention to the sheriff.

"Then I'll move straight to the reason for our meeting. We are looking into today's robbery at the library and Saturday's suspicious death of a local artist, Jarrard Dupree." He still seemed nervous and oddly formal. I assumed this was because the FBI was present at the meeting.

He continued. "I received preliminary autopsy results on Mr. Dupree this afternoon thanks to Agent Moore, who convinced the county coroner that it was a top priority. The toxicology report showed that in addition to an extremely high blood-alcohol level, there were traces of a drug called Rohypnol in JD's system."

"In sufficient doses, Rohypnol causes paralysis," Miracle explained. "When mixed with alcohol it's often fatal. Since there was plenty of alcohol in Mr. Dupree's system, even if the students hadn't run over him, he probably would have died on Saturday night. In fact, he might have already been dead by the time they hit him. We'll have to wait for the full autopsy report to know for sure."

I could barely breathe. "So now this is a murder case?"

The sheriff shook his head. "First we have to prove that JD didn't take the drug himself—either on purpose or by mistake."

"How will you do that?" Miss Eugenia asked.

"If the drug was administered without the artist's knowledge, it was most likely mixed in with a drink—probably beer," Miracle said.

"So I sent a crew out to JD's trailer this afternoon to collect up all the beer cans and bottles," the sheriff added. "If we can find one with some of the drug in it—we can dust it for fingerprints."

"There were hundreds of beer cans and bottles at JD's trailer," I said.

The sheriff nodded. "We only collected the ones that looked fresh."

Miracle sighed. "Of course the fact that the trailer was ransacked at some point after his death is not to our advantage."

"The tainted cans might have been inadvertently destroyed," I guessed.

"Or purposely taken away by the murderer," Miss Eugenia said grimly.

The sheriff reclaimed our attention. "To be cautious, I'm not calling it a murder case, but what we've got is enough to open a full-scale investigation."

"It's a good thing you've already got a think tank in place," Miss Eugenia said, obviously proud to be involved.

The sheriff nodded slightly. "Yes. Now, Agent Moore has done detailed background checks on several persons of interest in this case. I'll let her report these findings."

"Thank you." Miracle accepted the floor but did not stand. "I'd like to clarify here that while we are investigating the robbery and Mr. Dupree's death together in order to conserve time and resources, they are two separate events and may not be connected."

"You mean someone might have killed JD and then someone else found out that his paintings were valuable and stole them?" Miss Eugenia clarified. I felt sure she understood exactly what Miracle meant and was just repeating this for everyone else's benefit.

"Exactly," Miracle agreed. "However, I will say that it is my opinion that Mr. Dupree was killed and that the same person, or persons, stole the paintings. Both crimes were well planned and even resemble each other."

Miss Eugenia's eyebrows shot up. "How?"

"Well," Miracle began her explanation, "the person who drugged Mr. Dupree was most likely a friend or someone he was familiar with—and someone who knew he had a drinking problem. Once he was in a drunken stupor, he was carefully laid on the road where the students, who travel back and forth several times a day, were sure to run over him. This also indicates a person who knew the area well."

"That's true," Miss Eugenia agreed.

"The paintings were stolen from the library by someone who knew exactly where they were being stored. One window was broken. The alarm was not tripped. And no actual damage was done to Kennedy's office. Some chairs were overturned, the painting was taken off the wall, and the books knocked off the shelf. But it had the same staged look."

"What about the vandalism at JD's trailer?" I asked.

"It did not look staged," Miracle replied. "It looked angry."

"Were you about to tell us who our suspects are?" Miss Eugenia prompted.

Miracle smiled. "Thank you, Miss Eugenia. You always keep me on track. We have checked out three individuals as possible suspects. They are Bryce Thorne, Randall Meyer, and Rayford Cottingham. Mr. Thorne is an art broker in New York City. He has a small gallery in Queens and carries art objects that would only appeal to people with very eclectic tastes. He's had some legal problems in the past relating to import and export irregularities."

"Smuggling?" Miss Eugenia asked.

Miracle nodded. "However, he was never convicted."

"Any ties to organized crime?" the sheriff asked.

Miracle shook her head. "None that have been proven. However, because the art broker has a police record and a business relationship with our deceased, we were able to get a warrant to search his home and business. The stolen paintings were not in either place."

"If he stole them, he could have put them somewhere else—like a storage building," I suggested hopefully. I really didn't want to lose Mr. Thorne as a suspect.

"We are looking into that, but as of now, we can't tie Mr. Thorne to the burglary. And he has an alibi for Saturday night when Mr. Dupree died."

Discouraged, I asked, "What's his alibi?"

"He was on a plane, flying down here from New York," Miracle told me.

This seemed a little odd. "Did he say why he was coming?"

"To pick up the paintings," Luke guessed.

Miracle nodded. "At least that's what he said. It's true that he had an exclusive arrangement with Mr. Dupree. The artist was contractually prohibited from selling his paintings to anyone else. We don't know what the judge will rule on Wednesday regarding the gift of the paintings to the Midway Library, but I suspect it will be allowed since Mr. Dupree had the forethought to get the transfer of ownership signed and witnessed."

"Even if one of the witnesses now says he thinks I was coercing JD?" I asked.

Miss Eugenia frowned. "I don't see why it matters anyway since the paintings have been stolen."

"But we're working hard to recover them," the sheriff said. During this exchange I thought back to my one and only meeting with Jarrard Dupree. Finally I said, "I think Mr. Meyer knew that Mr. Thorne was coming to get the paintings."

Miracle raised an eyebrow. "Why do you think that?"

"Because when JD asked him to write up a transfer of ownership and witness it, Mr. Meyer kept asking him if he was sure he wanted to do this. I think he knew the art broker was coming and that there would be consequences if the paintings were gone."

"I agree," Miss Eugenia said with a proud smile in my direction. "That was a good observation."

"It could mean that Thorne and Meyer were working together," the sheriff said. "Or it could just mean that Meyer was aware of the business relationship between JD and the art broker."

Miss Eugenia nodded. "It's too early to draw conclusions, but it's something to consider."

"Which brings us to our next suspect, Mr. Randall Meyer," Miracle said. "He was a very successful attorney in New York until a year ago. Unexpectedly he resigned from his law firm, cashed out his piece of the stock market, and bought several acres of unproductive land in rural Dougherty County. He converted an old gas station into a country store . . ."

"Which is never open," Miss Eugenia contributed.

"And he charges two bucks for a canned Pepsi!" I added.

"It's true that his store hours are irregular and his prices are inflated," Miracle confirmed with a smile. "He claims to be an avid fisherman, but that might just be an excuse for spending a lot of time wandering around the countryside."

"Doing what?" the sheriff asked.

Miracle pointed a finger at him. "That is what we need to find out."

"Maybe he was forcing JD to paint pictures so he could sell them at the gallery in New York!" the sheriff proposed.

Luke frowned. "Or maybe he really is fishing."

"That will be determined during our investigation," Miracle said.

"Any connection between Meyer and the mob?" the sheriff asked.

"The law firm he was with does sometimes represent Mafia clients—but then a lot of big law firms do," Miracle said. "I didn't find anything that specifically connects him to illegal activity."

Miss Eugenia said, "And we've already discussed the unlikely coincidence that Mr. Meyer and Mr. Thorne are both from New York and just happen to have ties to this small corner of the world and the obscure artist Jarrard Dupree."

"We will explore the possibility that Mr. Thorne and Mr. Meyer might have been working together," Miracle promised. "The last—and weakest—suspect that we have at this point is Rayford Cottingham, Mr. Dupree's lawyer. He's really on the list only because of his suspicious Sunday afternoon visit to Kennedy's apartment yesterday and his knowledge that the paintings were being stored at the library."

"Did he know they were in Kennedy's office?"

Everyone turned to look at me.

I tried to remember. "I don't think I specifically said they were in my office."

"So if the lawyer's the thief, it was just lucky that he broke into her office?" Luke asked.

"What if he just chose to break the office window since it faces the alley and it's small?" Miss Eugenia suggested. "Once he was inside the library, he knew he'd be able to find the paintings."

"That would seriously increase our suspect pool to include everyone with access to a television," Luke pointed out.

"Yeah, I don't like that," the sheriff said. "I want to check out everyone who knew where the paintings were before we start suspecting the whole state of Georgia."

"We can temporarily mark Mr. Cottingham off our list of suspects," Miracle agreed. "I've checked his finances and he does okay—makes a good salary and has some investments. He lives in an apartment in downtown Albany but also owns a nice house in the suburbs where his ex-wife and two kids live. He's been divorced for about a year. The official reason was irreconcilable differences, but unofficially he cheated on his wife—repeatedly."

I remembered how flirty he'd been with me and could see how his friendly nature could have gotten him in trouble—just like Cade.

Miracle was continuing to share information on Mr. Cottingham. "He was retained by a charitable organization called Return to Dignity to represent them in the Albany area. He assisted the group in helping several homeless people, including Jarrard Dupree, get off the streets. Once Mr. Dupree started painting, he separated himself from the group and since then paid Mr. Cottingham from his own income."

"What about his money?" I asked. "If JD made a lot for each painting, he should have been rich."

Miss Eugenia nodded. "He told us he was saving to build a log cabin on his land."

"But he lived like he was, well . . ." I searched for the right word, *destitute.*

"According to Mr. Cottingham, he lived in that trailer by choice and spent a lot of money on booze. He had about twenty thousand dollars in assets at the time he died."

"That's a lot of money for someone like JD," the sheriff said. "But a long way from what he would need to build a log cabin."

"Maybe the lawyer charged him more than he should have?" the sheriff suggested.

"We'll see," Miracle assured him. "I've requested Mr. Dupree's bank statements, which should give us some idea."

Suddenly I felt very sad. When investigating a murder it was easy to get caught up in the clues and evidence and plans and forget that someone who had been alive was now dead. A few days ago JD had been painting ugly pictures and planning to build a log cabin. Now he was gone.

"Did we ever find out the names of any of the people who bought JD's paintings?" Miss Eugenia asked.

"No," Miracle said. "I posted questions on several art blogs, but no one admitted to owning one of Mr. Dupree's paintings. In fact, so far no one admits to ever hearing of him."

"The owners are probably embarrassed for anyone to know they bought one," the sheriff said.

Miss Eugenia frowned. "But now that JD is dead it seems like the people who own his art would be putting out feelers to see if their paintings have appreciated or something."

"The complete lack of discussion is odd," Miracle agreed.

"The thing that bothers me about all this," Luke said, "is that the broker and the lawyer were making money off the artist. Mr. Meyer, too, since JD bought all his groceries there. So why would any of them want to kill him and lose that easy source of income?"

Miracle raised an eyebrow. "That's a valid point."

Luke's question got me thinking. "Another strange thing is that the paintings were stolen after JD died. But before his death they were left outside his trailer where anyone could have taken them. And supposedly they were valuable all along."

"That is another inconsistency," Miracle acknowledged.

"And what about the college students running that experimental farm?" Luke asked. "Are they going to be investigated?"

"My staff researcher did background checks on them and their professor. They are all from the southeast region of the country but come from different social and economic backgrounds. None of them are from New York or have police records or any other ties to Dupree or the other suspects. Why?"

"Well, they did run over Mr. Dupree," Luke pointed out. "And they could have drugged him and laid him out in the road first."

I didn't want to believe it, although it was certainly possible. "Tripp seemed so upset after it happened."

This didn't sway Luke. "If he murdered Mr. Dupree, he planned it well—including a convincing reaction. But even if they didn't kill the artist, I think there's something strange about that whole farm thing. They seem uncommonly dedicated, driving out to the farm at all times of the day and night."

I felt that I should confirm this statement. "It's true that I've seen some of the students every time I've been out there except for this morning."

"Maybe they just want a good grade," Sheriff Bonham said.

"Maybe," Luke allowed, "but for the last few months I've been closely associated with college students, and I think it would be difficult to get this level of dedication from a bunch of kids if the only reward is a good grade."

"You think they're growing something else?" the sheriff guessed. "Something a little more profitable and a lot less legal?"

Luke nodded. "I think it's a very real possibility. And if the artist found out . . ."

"They might have felt like they had to kill him to protect their income," the sheriff said softly.

"And then they came and stole the paintings?" I asked.

"Remember, we may be dealing with two separate crimes and could have two separate criminals," Miracle cautioned.

I wasn't about to let my favorite suspects off the hook. "If the students killed JD—either by mistake or on purpose—that leaves Mr. Thorne or Mr. Meyer to steal the paintings from the library. Or both of them working together."

Miracle nodded. "It's a reasonable theory. We'll dig a little deeper on those college students. And we'll keep checking on Mr. Thorne and Mr. Meyer."

"And I'll send someone out to snoop around the farm and see if they've got any cash crops mixed in with the official ones," the sheriff said.

"I guess that's it for tonight." Miracle stood. "We appreciate everyone's input. You've done a good job at this meeting."

"Yes, thank you," the sheriff added. "Okay, folks, Agent Moore said that was it for tonight."

"Call me Miracle."

The sheriff looked pleased and a little embarrassed.

He accepted her invitation by repeating, "Miracle."

Suddenly I realized the reason for his awkward nervousness throughout the meeting. It wasn't just that she was an FBI agent. The sheriff found Miracle attractive. And since his wife had been dead since I was in elementary school, I thought it was about time he made friends with a nice lady.

If the FBI agent realized the effect she was having on the sheriff, she didn't let on. "Sheriff, would it be possible for me to have some office space here?" she asked. "That will make it easier for us to confer on these cases and save me a lot of time driving back and forth from the FBI field office in Albany."

Sheriff Bonham was more than happy to accommodate her. "Of course. We have an empty office you're welcome to use."

I knew Cade had been eyeing that office, trying to work up the nerve to ask the sheriff if he could have it. As senior deputy he thought he deserved it. So when he found out that an FBI agent was ensconced there, especially one the sheriff was sweet on, he would be disappointed.

"Deputy Cross!" the sheriff boomed.

I think he woke the boy up.

"Sir!" the deputy yelped as he jumped to attention.

"Get your stuff out of that front office. Agent Moore is going to use it while she's here."

Deputy Cross scurried out of the room to do the sheriff's bidding.

Then Sheriff Bonham lowered his voice and said, "To make sure we keep this investigation out of the news, we'll need to give Deputy Burrell an excuse for your being here."

"Tell him I'm investigating a case of mail fraud in Midway," Miracle suggested.

The sheriff looked surprised. "Is there a case of mail fraud here?"

Miracle grinned. "There will be by tomorrow."

***

While Luke was driving me home from the meeting at the sheriff's office, I was filled with conflicting emotions. Had Sloan seriously kidnapped two other FBI agents? Even if he was trying to prove his innocence, this was dangerously reckless and borderline insane. Had someone killed Mr. Dupree? Were the students from the experimental farm growing marijuana for extra credit? Did the sheriff really have a crush on Miracle Moore?

It was almost too much to comprehend at one time. Luke was quiet during the drive, allowing me time to go over the things that had been said, theories that had been presented, and disclosures that had been made. But after parking his rental car under the Midway Store and Save sign, he turned to face me with a grim expression.

"At the risk of being like Cade . . ." he began hesitantly.

I shook my head. "There is no resemblance at all between you and Cade."

Some of the tension left his shoulders, and he gave me a little smile. "I'm glad you feel that way. But with a robbery at the library and a possible murder out by the farm you've been checking on, I'm worried about your safety. Especially here at night by yourself."

I could only imagine how he'd feel if he knew Sloan had slipped into my apartment twice during the night. But what he didn't know couldn't worry him. "I'll be fine. Mr. Sheffield had a new alarm system installed today. I have my cell phone and my father's .45. And I know how to use it."

"If you're sure," he said, but it was obvious he didn't like it.

And I felt that I'd learned something important about Luke. Even though he and Cade were alike in their concern for me, Luke had enough respect to allow me to make my own decisions—even if he thought they were the wrong ones.

To reward him for this, I leaned across the car and granted him a gratitude kiss. Then I asked him what his plans were for the next day.

"I've got to go with Nick to buy some supplies for the salvage yard in the morning." This was his nice way of saying that he didn't trust his brother with actual money. "I'm free after that. Do you want to meet at the Flying J for lunch?"

"I've been craving creamed potatoes, and they're good at Haggerty Station."

"Then I'll meet you there," Luke promised. "What time?"

"Let's say noon, but call if your supply-buying trip runs late, and we can push back the time." I climbed out of his car and then leaned down and said, "Thanks Luke. You're a good friend."

He gave me a lovely smile. "I'm glad you think so. I've been trying since the third grade."

"I'll see you tomorrow." Then with a wave I climbed the stairs and unlocked the door to my apartment and entered the security code. I noticed that Luke waited until I was inside and had all the lights on before he drove away.

CHAPTER EIGHT

IN A BREAK FROM MY normal routine, I woke up early on Tuesday morning and had plenty of time to shower and dress before it was time to leave for work. With Sloan most likely a kidnapper, the expensive paintings stolen, and a possible murderer on the loose, I had no reason to be optimistic. But inexplicably I felt very hopeful.

I drove to the library and arrived ten minutes early. Of course Miss Ida Jean was waiting for me, but I was determined not to let her spoil my day.

"Good morning, Miss Ida Jean," I greeted as I unlocked the library doors. I looked around for a broken window or other signs of burglary, but everything was as it should be. "Did you need to check out a book or something?" I asked, although I knew her request wouldn't be that simple. And I was right.

"I want to talk about decorations for Robby's party tomorrow," Miss Ida Jean said.

I frowned. "Mother said she'd collected ribbon and had volunteers tying bows up along Main Street."

"Oh, she did," Miss Ida Jean confirmed. "I'm talking about here, in the library."

I looked around. It hadn't occurred to me that I would need to decorate inside. Fearfully I inquired, "What do you have in mind?"

"I thought we could just continue the yellow ribbon theme," Miss Ida Jean said. "We can do yellow streamers and put bows everywhere."

"It sounds very . . . yellow," I replied. "But I'm afraid I don't have time."

"I'll help her," Carmella said kindly. "It won't take too long."

"Why, how nice, Carmella," Miss Ida Jean said. "I don't care what anybody says, I've always thought you were a good person."

Proving this, Carmella just accepted Miss Ida Jean's backhanded compliment with a nod. "Thank you, Miss Ida Jean."

Having already had my fill of Miss Ida Jean, I left them to their decorating plans and walked back to my office. Shortly thereafter the glass people came to install the new window. It didn't take long and when they left I sat and stared at the beautiful, uncracked glass. I was glad to have the last visible evidence of the break-in a part of the past.

The sheriff called at ten o'clock and asked if I could come to his office. So I left the library and Miss Ida Jean in Carmella's capable hands and walked across the street. The sheriff, Deputy Cross, and Miss Eugenia were all gathered in Miracle's temporary office. There was no sign of Cade.

"So did you find out anything?" I asked, a little breathless from my walk.

"A couple of things," the sheriff confirmed. "First some news about your good friend Mr. Thorne."

I rolled my eyes.

Miracle picked up the dialogue. "The search of his home and office are done, and they didn't find the stolen paintings. But the officers didn't find any of JD's older paintings either. So it's possible they are being stored somewhere else."

"He did say that they sold briskly," Miss Eugenia reminded them. "Maybe they've already been purchased."

"Not only did he not have a single painting in his gallery inventory," Miracle restated. "But there was no record that he'd ever processed any of Jarrard Dupree's paintings."

Now that was shocking. "None of them?" I confirmed. "Ever?"

"Nothing."

I was confused. "Why would the broker continue to buy paintings if he's not selling them?"

"Maybe this Dupree guy isn't the real artist," Deputy Cross suggested. "If they stole the paintings from someone else and just pretended like they were his—maybe that's why the art broker didn't sell them in his gallery."

This earned him a scowl from the sheriff. "Of course they weren't stolen. Who would they be stolen from? We know JD painted them. He always had paint splatters on his arms and clothes."

"And under his fingernails," I provided.

"I don't think the paintings were stolen either," Miracle concurred more gently. "But feel free to give us your opinions, Deputy."

Deputy Cross blushed. "Yes, ma'am."

The sheriff sighed in frustration. "Anyway, the broker has to be selling JD's paintings. It makes no sense for him to buy them otherwise. But if he's not selling them through his gallery, how is he selling them?"

"Black market?" Miss Eugenia suggested.

The sheriff shook his head. "That's what I thought at first. But then I remembered you talking about how Mr. Thorne had some trouble with import and export laws. Which made me wonder if he might be a smuggler on a large scale. In which case he could use the paintings to help him transport drugs or whatever he's moving illegally."

I was confused. "How could he use JD's paintings to smuggle drugs."

"This is just a guess," the sheriff prefaced.

I nodded. "I understand."

"If they pack up big crates that are supposed to be full of expensive paintings, they'd have to pack them carefully to provide stabilization during transport. Like some sandbags or special pads or something."

I considered this. "That sounds reasonable."

"But what if instead of sand the bags are full of drugs?" the sheriff said. "And the genius of it is that if anyone checks one of the crates, they are concentrating on the paintings—not the packing."

"And those paintings do catch your eyes," I affirmed. "Under those circumstances their ugliness would be a helpful distraction."

Miracle laughed. "I can just imagine the customs people standing around talking about who in the world would buy these paintings instead of looking more closely at the packing materials."

"Is there a big market for exporting drugs?" I asked. "I thought the problem was other countries bringing them in."

"He might ship the paintings out to an associate in another country," the sheriff said. "They could then repack them, with the special supplies, and send them back."

It just didn't feel right to me. "But if that's the case, why did they need a continuous supply of new, awful paintings? They could have just used the same ones over and over."

Miss Eugenia nodded. "And the broker wouldn't have been so anxious to get the last paintings from Kennedy."

I frowned. "Yes, anxious enough to break into my office."

"I like the smuggling angle," Miss Eugenia continued, "but I think that there is value associated with each painting—rather than them just being something distracting to mail along with drugs hidden in the packing supplies."

The sheriff looked annoyed. "But what value could they have? We've seen them. They're terrible."

Deputy Cross decided to give another try. "Maybe they write the numbers of offshore accounts with invisible ink on the back. Or hollow out the wood and fill the paintings with drugs."

The sheriff shook his head, and I thought he was angry with the young deputy again. But I realized it was just frustration when he said, "It may be impossible for us to figure this out since the paintings were stolen."

Miss Eugenia looked at me and I nodded.

"I have one," she said.

Everyone else turned to stare at her.

Finally the sheriff said, "You have one of JD's paintings?"

"Yes, I bought it from the Midway Library in an exclusive, pre-auction sale."

"I sold it to her out of the trunk of my car right after JD gave them to me," I clarified. "That was before we knew they were valuable and before the judge issued his stay of sale order."

"And why haven't you mentioned this before?" The sheriff's tone was beyond impatient.

He didn't scare Miss Eugenia at all. "Because I didn't think it was important."

The last thing I wanted was a fight between Miss Eugenia and the sheriff. It would be so humiliating for him to lose a battle of words with an old woman in front of his new girlfriend. So I stepped in. "I told Miss Eugenia not to tell anyone that she had one of the paintings so she wouldn't get robbed."

The sheriff still looked mad. "And Miss Eugenia takes orders from you?"

"It wasn't an order," I said calmly. "It was advice."

After rubbing his hair vigorously in a show of extreme aggravation, Sheriff Bonham said, "So can we see it now?"

"Of course," Miss Eugenia agreed graciously. "I'll call Winston Jones and see if he can pick it up and bring it here for us. That way it will be in police custody, so to speak."

"Chief Jones has a key to your house?" the sheriff asked.

Miss Eugenia continued digging in her purse in search of her cell phone. "He won't need a key. The doors aren't locked."

Sheriff Bonham rubbed his hair again. "You left the only unstolen painting in an unlocked house?"

"It's well hidden," she assured us.

The sheriff seemed a little relieved, and I was proud of Miss Eugenia for taking precautions. "We discussed the fact that there was a burglary risk."

Miss Eugenia waved this aside. "I wasn't worried about a burglar. I was afraid my sister Annabelle would find it before her birthday. She is the nosiest person in the world."

Coming from Miss Eugenia, that was saying something.

While Miss Eugenia made her call to Chief Jones, the sheriff paced.

"Well, at least now we know why JD's trailer was ransacked yesterday morning," he said. "They were looking for the last painting."

I remembered Miracle saying the destruction there looked "angry" and felt a little uneasy. "We need to make sure that no one knows Miss Eugenia had that painting they were looking for. We wouldn't want those angry searchers to go to her house."

"We don't know for sure that's why the trailer was searched so . . . thoroughly," Miracle amended with a glance in my direction. "But it is a possibility."

Miss Eugenia snapped her phone shut and announced, "Winston is headed to my house to get the painting and will be here as quickly as he can. Now, back to the smuggling idea. How would the broker ship the boxes of paintings? The post office? UPS?"

The sheriff shrugged. "If he's shipping large, heavy boxes internationally, he might send them by water."

"And in a busy shipyard they might not have time to search every crate," I pointed out.

Miracle nodded. "And if they were familiar with Mr. Thorne's company and the paintings, when they opened the box and saw the contents, they probably wouldn't examine it any closer."

The sheriff still looked frustrated, and I thought Miss Eugenia was the source until he said, "I feel like we're missing something."

Miracle smiled. "We're missing a lot of things—but it's early in the investigation. We'll know more once we examine the painting. And in the meantime I think I'll call my researcher and have her look through Mr. Thorne's shipping records very carefully. If he's been making regular shipments of large crates . . ."

The sheriff's mood improved suddenly. "We should be able to find out who he's sending them to and how often and maybe we'll be real lucky and catch one that's waiting at the docks to be sent and search it."

This gave me an idea. "I wonder if Mr. Thorne has a warehouse or rents some kind of space at the docks to store items awaiting shipment or things that have just arrived."

"If he does, that would be a wonderful place to keep stolen paintings!" Miss Eugenia said.

Miracle pulled out her phone. "I'll get my researcher working on that right away."

As Miracle stepped out into the hallway, I asked, "What about Mr. Meyer?"

"We haven't found a connection between him and Thorne yet, but we'll keep trying," the sheriff said. "I'm not ready to turn loose any suspects yet."

I was pleased to hear that. "Good. Because I've got a feeling about Mr. Meyer. He's up to no good."

"You're just mad that he filed a complaint against you," Miss Eugenia teased.

"I have been known to hold a grudge," I admitted.

"Ladies, we're trying to solve a case here," the sheriff scolded mildly. "We searched the area around that old bottling plant and the experimental farm but didn't find any signs of marijuana growing. However, the background checks Miracle did on the students and their teacher turned up some unusual things."

"What kind of things?"

"Well, according to a secretary at Heatherly College, the teacher, Mr. Shepherd, is a corporate loaner," Miracle said.

I reached for another doughnut. "A what?"

"A corporate loaner is someone who isn't an actual employee of the college," Miss Eugenia explained.

"Shepherd works for a company called Solutions, Inc. They've loaned him to the college to teach this agriculture class," Miracle informed us.

"What about the students?"

"All six of them have had some improvement in their financial status over the past six months."

"How much of an improvement?" Luke asked.

"It varies," Miracle replied. "One has a new car, one just got back from an Alaskan cruise, two others just paid off substantial student loans, and none of them seems to be hurting for money."

"So they all have access to large amounts of cash," I mused. "Is there any other explanation—like a rich aunt who died and left them an inheritance?"

"For all six students?" the sheriff said. "I don't think it's likely that they all got a windfall."

"So if they aren't growing marijuana," I asked, "how are they making all that money?"

"I figure they are growing it," the sheriff replied. "I'm thinking because they've got this absentee, corporate teacher they saw an opportunity to make a little money on the side with no one the wiser."

"How will we prove that?" Miss Eugenia wanted to know.

"I've requested a warrant to search that old bottling plant that they're using to store their supplies and equipment. I hope I might find traces of something there. If not, we'll do an aerial search. I'll hire a couple of crop dusters who can get in real low. Sometimes they plant their crops in small fields that are nearly hidden by trees— almost impossible to find."

Miracle returned in time to hear this comment and said, "Not for you. If they're growing anything illegal, you'll find it."

The sheriff smiled in bashful pride. "I will certainly try."

"And we still have the mystery of the stolen wood taken from Miss George Ann's barn," Miss Eugenia mentioned.

"Yes," the sheriff agreed. "We need to figure out how that plays in."

Since the wood theft had not even been taken seriously up to this point, I was surprised when Miss Eugenia introduced the topic and even more surprised that the sheriff didn't dismiss it. So I asked, "Why is that important?"

"Because the stolen wood eventually became expensive paintings that might have been used, somehow, as smuggling vehicles," Miracle explained.

The sheriff frowned. "And they tie everything together—the students and JD and the paintings."

"Miss Eugenia felt pretty sure that the students were taking the wood and selling it to Mr. Dupree," I said. Then feeling disrespectful to the dead, I added, "And they almost certainly sold him more than the one truckload he admitted to."

Then Deputy Cross proved that he had been paying attention when he said, "Would they kill the artist just to keep him from telling the police where he got the wood?"

The sheriff shrugged. "People kill for crazy reasons all the time."

"We've got plenty of ideas," Miss Eugenia said. "What we need is some evidence."

"Why don't we follow the money in reverse," I suggested. "If we start with JD and find out exactly where all his money came from and then where it went."

"The bank is dragging their feet about providing me with the bank statements I've requested," Miracle said. "I could have my researcher hack into their system, but I prefer to do things the legal way when possible. Especially if I think I'm going to present them in a court of law."

Sheriff Bonham smiled. "If we were able to get a warrant for the guy in New York with these autopsy results, we can probably get one for JD's financial records. I'll work on that."

"And you should check into that charity organization that set JD up here in the first place—Return to Dignity," Miss Eugenia advised.

Miracle nodded. "They might have records that would tell us something about his past. So far my researcher hasn't been able to find much information about Jarrard Dupree before he came to Midway. I'm beginning to think that's not his real name, so I had the coroner send DNA samples and fingerprints to Atlanta. We'll run them through the government computers and see what we come up with."

Chief Jones arrived at that point, carrying the painting concealed with a black garbage bag under his arm. He placed it on the desk, and I stood back while the sheriff and Miracle did a thorough examination.

"What are you looking for?" Chief Jones asked as Miracle pried two of the wood planks apart.

"We're not exactly sure," Miracle admitted. "Maybe something that would aid in the smuggling of drugs. Numbers, letters, hollowed-out areas."

Deputy Cross leaned in close so he could watch closely. "It seems like if they were wanting to hollow out the wood, they would have used something thicker."

"And JD told us he painted on scrap wood and sheet metal sometimes," I remembered. "Which would be very difficult to use as a smuggling device."

"Maybe that's why they switched to this wood," Miracle said. "It's thin enough not to attract too much attention, but it does have a little space so that something could be put in there."

Chief Jones raised both eyebrows. "No kidding? You really think these paintings are used by smugglers?"

"It's one of several theories we're considering."

I could tell by Miracle's tone that she didn't want Chief Jones to know how totally clueless we were. A few minutes later JD's painting was in pieces, but we still had no idea why it was valuable. A pall of discouragement hung over Miracle's borrowed office.

I stared at the dissected painting and said, "I guess you need to start looking for something else to give your sister for her birthday."

Miss Eugenia shrugged. "No need for that. Once I glue it back together, it won't look any worse than it did to start with."

That was true. "Well, I guess I'd better head back over to the library." Actually I just wanted to make sure I wasn't late for my lunch date with Luke.

"And I need to get back to Haggerty," Winston Jones said.

"Thank you for bringing . . ." the sheriff looked at the pile of old wood on the desk, "this."

Chief Jones settled his hat onto his head. "You're welcome." Then he turned to Miss Eugenia. "You want a ride home since I'm here?"

She nodded. "I'll take you up on that."

"Call me if you get any more exciting information," I requested.

"We will," Miracle promised. Then she stood and said, "I'll walk you to the door."

Once we were away from the others I whispered, "Any news on Sloan or Mark?"

"Not really . . ."

"I've been thinking, and I wonder if the illegal activity Sloan stumbled onto was the same thing that got JD killed."

I could tell by the look in Miracle's eyes that this had occurred to her too. "It's possible."

"So I feel guilty for not telling the sheriff about Sloan and his problems with the FBI and the possibility that the evidence he found and reported weeks ago could be related to JD's death."

"Do you think the sheriff is telling you everything he knows about the case?"

I considered this. "Probably not."

"Then you're even."

I still felt uneasy. "But he's the sheriff."

"He's using you—your mind and intuition and ideas—to help him solve his crime. You don't need to forget that."

"Okay."

"And you don't need to feel guilty about withholding information about Sloan and Mark," Miracle said. "That's my call, and I'll decide when and if to mention it."

I felt greatly relieved. "Thanks." Then I waved good-bye and walked back across the street. Inside the library all was normal, except that Miss Ida Jean had hung up yellow bows everywhere. Carmella didn't complain when I told her I was taking a lunch break (because she really is a good person, no matter what Miss Ida Jean has heard people say).

So I walked out to Luke's Torino and drove to Haggerty. I arrived at Haggerty Station five minutes early, but Luke was already there. I decided to take this as a sign that he was anxious to see me. He was waiting by the front door and smiled when he saw me. He leaned down to kiss my cheek and pushed the door open. Then he told the restaurant's owner, a crabby woman named Nettie, that we were ready to be seated.

Nettie gave us menus, and a teenage waitress came to take our order. I chose a salad and a double serving of creamed potatoes. Luke got the Tuesday lunch special—fried catfish with hushpuppies and coleslaw. During our meal I filled him in on the meeting at the sheriff's office. I finished my detailed summary as the waitress arrived with our desserts—banana puddings.

"So what do you think?" I asked him in between bites.

"I think that you may be in the wrong profession," he replied. "You really seem to enjoy solving crimes. As badly as I hate to say it, maybe Cade was right and you should get a degree in something besides library science so you can pursue a career in law enforcement."

I knew Cade wasn't serious when he challenged me to get qualified for police work. So I hadn't given his remark a second's consideration. But after Luke's comments I did think about it. I'll admit I like the challenge associated with crime-solving, but I couldn't see myself making a career of it.

"No, I think the library is where I belong," I told Luke. "And my mother might have to be institutionalized if I decided to be a policewoman, so make sure you don't let her hear you encouraging me in that direction. Not if you want to stay on her good side."

"So you're just going to solve crimes as a sideline?" he asked. "Kind of like a ghoulish hobby?"

I gave him a smirk for "ghoulish." "I guess. That shouldn't be a big deal—how much crime can possibly take place in Midway?"

He shrugged. "Midway has had two suspicious deaths in about that many months."

"But it's some kind of anomaly. In the previous hundred years nothing exciting happened!"

He finished off his banana pudding and pushed back from the table. "I guess that's true. There's no sense in getting qualified to solve crimes that won't ever happen."

After lunch Luke followed me back to the library. When we walked in, no one expressed any surprise at seeing us together. Luke didn't know the significance of this, but I knew it meant the town had already classified us as a couple.

Luke surveyed the room. Finally his eyes came to a stop on Miss Ida Jean, who was tying a bow on our large unabridged dictionary.

"Do you see any bare spots?" Miss Ida Jean inquired.

Luke shook his head. "I think you've covered every square inch."

She beamed with pride. "Oh good!"

I waved for Luke to follow me and led him back into my office. "Hurry! We have to make our escape while she's distracted," I whispered.

He grinned as he stepped into my office and closed the door behind him. "Are we hiding from Miss Ida Jean?"

I nodded. "Not that there's any place on God's green earth where I can really do that. She's like an annoying bloodhound and can find me wherever I go."

Luke's eyes moved to my new window and his smile faded a little. He walked over to examine the workmanship. "I see the repairs are done."

"Yes, that glass company from Albany was quick."

"I just hope you won't need their services again."

"Me too," I assured him.

He turned and said, "So how long do you intend to stay in here?"

I pointed to the bookshelves. "Until I get those books in the correct order or Miss Ida Jean leaves the library, whichever comes first."

"You want some help?"

I smiled. "If you're volunteering, I'd love some."

We sat on the floor and removed all the books from the shelves then placed them back in the proper order. I told Luke the history behind some of them and showed him the first book I ever purchased specifically for the library—a tattered copy of *Gone with the Wind*.

He studied it with appropriate reverence. "So this was the beginning of the Midway Library."

I nodded. "I got it at a thrift store in Albany for thirty-five cents. Then I took it home and placed it on one of the shelves I'd built in my grandfather's barn."

He looked around my office. "You've come a long way."

"And I owe a lot of it to Drake Langston." I glanced at Luke for a reaction to Drake's name, but he kept his face carefully expression free. "I know you don't like him," I continued. "But the truth is he did change things for the better in Midway. And he didn't kill your uncle—he only created a situation that encouraged a greedy person to act out something that had always been inside them."

"I don't blame him for Foster's death," Luke reassured me. "But you're right, I don't like him. Maybe it's just because you do."

I couldn't deny this. "I barely know him."

"I'm glad he's gone." Luke lined up a copy of *Rebecca* with the book right beside it. "It's hard to compete with somebody rich and handsome and powerful. Besides, I think Midway needs to progress at its own natural pace."

"You realize that means *no* progress?" I clarified. "Right?"

He smiled. "It means slow progress. Remember you'd made it from your grandfather's barn to a double trailer by the city pool before Drake Langston arrived in Midway."

"I guess that's true." I handed him *To Kill a Mockingbird*. "There is no telling how much Drake spent on this library, and all he asked was that it be named the Willard G. Langston Memorial Library after his grandfather. The town council agreed to that originally, but after your uncle died and the housing developments didn't, well, develop, a lot of them blamed Drake. So now they don't want to honor their agreement—even though Drake kept every promise he made."

"That doesn't seem right," Luke said.

"He even bought this building and deeded it to the town of Midway."

Luke looked impressed. "That was certainly generous."

I didn't add that it was part of his plan to ensure that I got the job as library director. "So it seems only fair that they should call it by the name Drake asked for—especially since they promised." I sighed. "So I've written a proposal to present at the next town council meeting asking them to reconsider."

"Do you think they'll listen?"

"No, the town council will not listen to me, and the library will be named after somebody else's grandfather. But it makes us look bad. Drake did what he said he would. We should honor our part of the bargain."

Luke handed me an Agatha Christie novel. "If you think it would help, I'll write a letter to the town council telling them that my family has no ill will against Drake Langston and asking that they name the library after his grandfather as originally agreed."

I was touched. "Honestly I don't know if it will help or not, but I'd be grateful. And you never know—it might make a difference."

We finished reordering the books and Luke stood. "Well, I hate to leave, but I need to get back to the salvage yard and make sure Nick isn't playing video games instead of working on cars."

I waved at the neatly ordered books. "We're done here. Thanks for your help."

He grinned. "Anytime."

We walked together out of my office, and then I led him to the back door. "I'm afraid if you try to go out through the main entrance, Miss Ida Jean might try to tie a yellow ribbon on you."

"She is very serious about her decorating," he agreed. "I guess if my son had been gone for so long, I'd want to welcome him home in style too."

I felt a little bad for making fun of Miss Ida Jean. But just a little. "My mother cooks every night, and she'd be more than delighted to have our company. Should I call and tell her we'll come?"

Luke shook his head. "Your mother is a great cook, but I don't want to wear out my welcome."

I nodded. "You're right. Eating with my mother more than once a week is a mistake. The food is good—but it's not worth the mental anguish."

"I love your mother," he said.

"I know."

"Are we still meeting at the sheriff's office tonight?" he asked.

"As far as I know."

He leaned against the door. "Do you want to ride with me?"

"I've been gone from the library a lot today, so I think I'll just stay here until time for the meeting. Meet me here and we'll walk over together."

He gave me a quick kiss and walked outside.

With Luke gone, the rest of the afternoon seemed to stretch endlessly before me. I didn't want to go up front and subject myself to Miss Ida Jean and her yellow-ribbon decorating. So I returned to my office and tried to think of a way I could further the investigation into JD's death. Since we had narrowed our suspect list down to Mr. Thorne or Mr. Meyer, I felt comfortable calling the lawyer, Rayford Cottingham. And I was sure that an investigation of JD's finances would give us some much-needed information.

So I sat down at my desk and pulled out Mr. Cottingham's card. My call was answered by a secretary and relayed to voice mail. I left a message and was trying to think of something else to do when my phone rang. It was Mr. Cottingham.

"So," the lawyer said. "I was surprised when I heard your message."

"Mr. Dupree's life was such a mystery," I said. "I'm just trying to find out more about him."

That sounded weak even to my own ears, so I wasn't surprised when the lawyer laughed. "Seriously, do you really want to talk about JD or are you flirting with me?"

I assured him I was not flirting.

"Well, in that case I'll tell you what I can about JD. Although I'm sure you realize that I'll be limited by client privilege."

He might seem casual and a little silly, but Mr. Cottingham was, after all, a lawyer. "I was just wondering how he got money for his paintings. Did Mr. Thorne always come to pick them up personally?"

"I'm not sure about that," he replied. "I wasn't involved in that end of things."

I was disappointed but not surprised. "And how did Mr. Thorne pay him?"

"Automatic deposits into his checking account," Mr. Cottingham supplied.

"And is that how JD's bills were paid—automatically?"

"He didn't have much in the way of bills," the lawyer told me. "He owned the trailer outright so there was no rent or anything. I think Meyer's Grocery sent in a monthly bill and the bank cut them a check."

"How about your legal fees?" I asked. "Who determined how much JD had to pay you and how was the money paid? Did JD approve the charges or did you just send them through?"

There was a brief silence, and when Mr. Cottingham responded he wasn't quite so friendly. "I charged JD a standard retainer that he approved annually. There were occasionally other legal expenses, and I submitted these via invoice to the bank. I don't know whether they approved them specifically with JD or if they just paid them. But I do know I never overcharged him, if that's what you're really asking."

"I'm really just trying to understand how his finances worked," I assured him. "What if JD wanted to buy something from somewhere besides Meyer's Grocery. How would he access his funds?"

"I'm not sure he could," the lawyer said. "I think a safeguard was set up when JD was still under the protection of Return to Dignity, and I doubt that he ever changed it."

"So he couldn't get money out—like cash?"

"No, but that was just to protect him from being taken advantage of," Mr. Cottingham defended. "Someone who gets drunk a lot is an easy target. He could submit a bill to the bank or request that a check be sent to someone—but all expenditures had to be approved. He couldn't just walk into the bank and withdraw cash from his account."

I thought that was interesting—to have money you couldn't spend. It didn't even seem constitutional. "What do you know about Return to Dignity—the charity that helped JD get off the street?"

"Not much," he responded. "I haven't heard from them in more than a year. I figured like everyone else they are hurting for cash. So I guess Albany will get to keep the rest of their street people."

"Can you give me the names of any of the other people you helped Return to Dignity get settled in a better life?"

Mr. Cottingham laughed. "That would definitely be an invasion of their privacy and completely irresponsible on my part."

I made a mental note to ask Miracle to include the lawyer's files relating to Return to Dignity on her to-do list.

Then I tried, "What can you tell me about the group and when their charity was set up?"

I really expected Mr. Cottingham to say that he couldn't tell me anything, so I was surprised when he launched into a detailed answer.

"They had a representative who went around asking questions in the homeless community trying to figure out which ones were eligible for disability or social security or Medicare—whatever. Then the rep would choose one or two to work with at a time. With my help he got them a place to live. Then, once they had a legal address, my office helped file for government assistance. The group paid their monthly living expenses until a regular income was established."

"I appreciate that explanation and I understand that you can't give me specifics," I told him. "So you assisted the group in helping several people in the Albany area?"

"Yeah, this group was small scale but very well organized and successful. They picked their candidates carefully—which increased their chances of success. Then they stayed with them for longer than most charitable groups do."

"Because they were so small scale."

"Right."

"And was JD one of their success stories?"

"Yeah, he was. I know that he was still an alcoholic and didn't live what anyone would call well. But his life was much better in that trailer than living in a cardboard box on the streets of Albany."

An idea started forming. "Did this group, Return to Dignity, originate in the East—near New York?"

There was a brief pause, and then Mr. Cottingham said, "Now that you mention it, I think so."

"And do you know if they got JD started in painting?"

"I'm not sure how that came about," the lawyer said thoughtfully. "But it's possible. I told you they were thorough, and if they found out he had an interest in painting and some aptitude for it, it makes sense that they would have encouraged him to use it as a way to support himself."

"It makes sense to me too," I agreed.

Then Mr. Cottingham got cautious. "I probably shouldn't say anything else about them."

"Would it be too much trouble for you to look up the group's contact information?" I asked. "I don't know what else I can learn about their setup, but it seems wise to give them a call directly."

"Hold on."

There was a sharp click in my ear, followed almost immediately by soothing classical music. I waited for a good two minutes before a female voice came back on the line.

"Mr. Cottingham asked me to give you the number for a charitable group called Return to Dignity."

I could barely control my excitement. "Yes."

She recited the numbers and I jotted them down. Then I thanked her and after disconnecting our call, I dialed the number she had given me. This call was picked up by an answering service.

Using my most authoritative voice, I said, "I need to speak to someone from Return to Dignity."

"I'm sorry but that account is listed as inactive," the operator replied.

"What does 'inactive' mean?"

"That we no longer take messages for them," was her answer.

"But this is an emergency," I told her. "It's a matter of life and death that I contact them."

"Well," I could hear the uncertainty in the operator's voice. "I'm new here and I'm not really sure what to do in this situation."

I don't catch a lot of lucky breaks—so I'm particularly happy when I do. And there's nothing much luckier than dealing with an inexperienced person when you're digging for information.

"I understand that you can't take a message for them, since they no longer have an active account with your company," I told her. "But there must be a number listed for the group so that they can be reached in emergency situations like this."

There was a pause, and I was afraid the operator had wisely passed me on to a supervisor or other more experienced person. But finally she said, "There is a number, but it's not listed as an emergency contact. It's just typed into the notes."

"It's worth a try," I said quickly so she wouldn't stop and think things through. "Just give it to me."

She read off the number. I repeated it to be sure I had it right and then disconnected the call. I sat at my desk and stared at the number for a few seconds. It had a Georgia area code—the same one shared by all the other residents of Midway. The owner of Return to Dignity, the group that had taken JD off the streets and possibly set him up to create awful paintings, was a local. I was excited and terrified all at once.

With trembling fingers I finally dialed the number. It rang twice and then an answering machine picked up. "You've reached Meyer's Grocery. We're not open right now. Leave a message at the tone . . ."

I closed my phone, barely able to breathe.

I was still sitting at my desk, trying to decide what to do with my newfound information, when my phone rang. I answered it absently. It was Miss George Ann Simmons.

"I understand that you discovered a robbery out at Mr. Jarrard Dupree's trailer yesterday. The two crimes could be related, and I'm surprised that I had to hear about it from a third party since I've contracted with you to look for the person who stole my wood."

I noticed that she didn't say *hired*. "I'm sorry, Miss George Ann," I lied. "There was also a robbery at the library that the sheriff has asked me to help him solve (I couldn't help myself). I agreed to host a welcome-home party for Robby Baxley tomorrow and, well, it's been crazy."

Miss George Ann offered no sympathy for me or the many demands on my time. "Well, we need to find out if my wood is still on Mr. Dupree's property. If so, we can petition the court to have it returned to me. If not, we can add the wood to the list of stolen items."

Miss George and her wood would not have been a priority for me even if I hadn't had so much else going on in my life. But under the circumstances I couldn't have cared less if she ever got her wood back. And I was tired of the way she expected me to do all her footwork without a dime of compensation. So I said, "I can't remember if the wood was still there or not. If you want to find out, you can call the sheriff or the courthouse or the president of the United States. But I can't help you."

"I don't know what in the world the president of the United States could do about my stolen wood," Miss George Ann replied. "That is just a silly suggestion."

I rolled my eyes up to stare at the ceiling. "Don't call the president, Miss George Ann. And don't call me either. I am hereby officially resigning as your investigator. Check with the sheriff and see what steps you need to take to claim your wood."

There was a brief silence, and then Miss George Ann said, "Well, I never," and hung up the phone.

I listened to the dial tone in my ear for a few seconds, enjoying the sound of it more than Miss George Ann's voice. Then I called the sheriff's office and asked to speak to Miracle.

"I was just about to call you," she said when I was transferred to the line in her temporary office. "I convinced the New York Police Department to bring in Mr. Thorne and put a little pressure on him. As a result, he gave us the name of the one buyer who purchased every one one of Jarrard Dupree's horrible paintings."

"Mr. Meyer," I guessed.

"How did you know?"

"Because his number is associated with the charitable organization Return to Dignity, which took JD off the streets and, I believe, suggested that he take up painting in the first place."

"Meyers set Dupree up as a conspirator in his smuggling operation?" Miracle said.

"It certainly looks that way."

"Now we just have to figure out why," Miracle said grimly. "Can you come over here now?"

I hadn't given the library much time that day anyway, so I said I could.

"I think we'd better get together with the sheriff and others a little early," Miracle said. "I'll notify the sheriff and Miss Eugenia if you'll call your boyfriend."

"So Luke is an official part of the team now?" I asked.

"I don't know if there's anything official about this motley crew," Miracle replied. "But Luke did have some good comments. And since you're prone to doing foolish things, I like the idea of your having a devoted bodyguard."

I didn't know about Luke taking the role of my bodyguard, but I liked the devoted part.

"So try and get him to come on," Miracle finished.

I called Luke and explained the new information briefly but didn't mention that Miracle considered him my bodyguard, devoted or otherwise. Then I asked him to meet me at the sheriff's office, and he promised to come right away. When I got there, the sheriff, Deputy Cross, and Miracle were gathered in the front office.

"So Mr. Meyer killed JD?" I asked breathlessly as I rushed in.

Miracle smiled. "We aren't quite to the point of drawing that conclusion yet. But I do think we had it backward. We thought the art broker was the brains behind the operation and that he arranged for

Dupree to make the paintings and possibly sent Meyer down here to watch him as part of a smuggling operation. But now, according to what Thorne told the NYPD, it was Meyer who started the whole thing."

"He established Return to Dignity just to locate a man he could force to make paintings for his scheme?" I asked.

The sheriff nodded. "It looks like JD was the only person Meyer was interested in. The other people the organization helped were just to cover up JD's involvement in, whatever."

Miracle paced and thought out loud. "Meyer set Dupree up in that trailer out in the middle of nowhere and had him start painting on old wood. Then he contracted with the art broker to handle the purchase and sale of all the paintings."

"But if he was going to buy all the paintings himself anyway, why did he need the broker?" I asked.

"To separate himself from the illegal activity," the sheriff said. "It's a common thing that criminals do."

"And this would be nice and tidy if we hadn't run into a snag on our smuggling theory," Miracle said with a frown.

"What kind of a snag?" Miss Eugenia asked as she walked in. Luke was right behind her, and it surprised me how glad I was to see him.

Luke sat on one side of me and Miss Eugenia on the other. Miracle brought them up to date on the case developments succinctly. Then she answered the "snag" question.

"We can't find any evidence of smuggling. Mr. Thorne runs a small business, selling mostly to locals. He's only made three overseas shipments in the past five years—all to Europe. And he hasn't received a single shipment from outside the U.S.—ever, that we can find."

"No big crates full of terrible paintings packed with illegal drugs?" I asked.

"Not a one." The sheriff's disappointment was obvious. "Mr. Meyer either. Miracle even checked the Return to Dignity foundation."

"No shipments?" I guessed.

Sheriff Bonham shook his head. "Not now or when they were actually functioning."

"There's always the possibility that Meyer set up another company or organization and handled the smuggled drugs that way," Miracle said. "But my researcher is thorough, and she doesn't see anything."

"Can you get a search warrant and look at Mr. Meyer's place for JD's stolen paintings?" I asked. "If we find them, we can make him answer some of these questions."

"We could get a warrant and we could look for the paintings," the sheriff confirmed. "We might even find them—but we couldn't make Mr. Meyer tell us anything."

"He'd lawyer up so fast," Deputy Cross agreed.

"And the robbery is only part of the investigation," the sheriff continued. "The most important question is who gave JD that drug and laid him in the road. If Meyer is guilty of murder, we want to get him for that—not just stealing some paintings."

"Which brings us back to the question—if the artist was central to whatever scheme Meyer is running, why would he kill him?" Luke asked.

"Unless JD wanted out," Miss Eugenia proposed. "Or was going to expose Meyer and the whole operation for some reason."

"But if JD was trying to get away from Mr. Meyer by giving away the paintings, why did he call him over and get him to fix up that transfer of ownership?" I asked. "It seems like he would have wanted to keep his intentions secret."

"Maybe he did want to," Miss Eugenia said, a finger pressed to her chin in what I presumed was a gesture of deep thought. "But when Mr. Meyer walked up, he knew he couldn't keep it a secret anymore. So he used Mr. Meyer help him by doing the legal paperwork—in front of witnesses. *Us!*"

"Mr. Meyer really didn't want to do it," I remembered. "He kept asking JD if he was sure and reminding him how much time it was going to take to replace the paintings."

"Which was ridiculous," Miss Eugenia said. "It wouldn't have taken him fifteen minutes to redo that sloppy artwork."

"Maybe more than fifteen minutes," the sheriff said. "He had to glue the boards together and all."

Miss Eugenia brushed this aside. "Well, you know what I meant. The paintings involved no special techniques or even deep thought. He opened a can of paint and sloshed some on the wood. They were not time consuming." Then she turned to me. "We need to try and remember everything JD said that day because any of it could have been very important."

I tried to think. "He's the one who suggested the auction for the library, and we thought he had visions of grandeur since the paintings seemed worthless to us."

The others listened attentively as Miss Eugenia continued. "He wanted press coverage but declined when you offered to have someone pick him up so he could actually attend the auction."

I nodded. "We thought he was trying to save himself embarrassment, but he knew that the paintings would attract buyers. So there was another reason he didn't want to be there."

"Maybe he planned to leave," the sheriff suggested.

"Or maybe he knew that because of his actions it was possible that he'd be killed," Miracle said.

"And hoped that the press coverage would guarantee an investigation," Miss Eugenia proposed.

Luke shrugged. "Which it has."

I liked this. I hoped that we were following JD's wishes. "I don't know if this is important and it's definitely not a fact . . ." I began.

The sheriff waved for me to continue.

"But during the short time I was with JD and Mr. Meyer together, they seemed friendly," I concluded.

The sheriff glowered at me. "What do you mean, friendly?"

I didn't take his tone personal. "Like they were comfortable with each other and probably spent a lot of time together. I guess what I mean is that I don't think JD was scared of Mr. Meyer."

"Well," Miracle said, "maybe he should have been."

"Maybe," I acknowledged. Then I said, "I had a little talk with JD's attorney, Mr. Rayford Cottingham, this afternoon. He's the one who gave me the phone number for Return to Dignity, which eventually led to my discovery that Mr. Meyer was involved with that organization. And according to him, JD couldn't get his own money out of his bank account."

"How is that possible?" Luke asked.

"He said that a 'safeguard' had been set up when the charity first took JD off the streets and gave him a job. His monthly bills were paid automatically and extra things, like legal fees for Mr. Cottingham, were submitted to the bank. If the bank approved them, they paid them. Mr. Meyer kept a tab for JD at his grocery store and submitted it to the bank monthly."

Miracle frowned. "So if Dupree did want to leave, it would have been difficult since he didn't have any access to his money."

"They were holding him hostage!" Miss Eugenia said.

I felt awful. "Poor JD. There we were on Saturday morning, talking to him. He was in all that trouble, and we didn't even know it. I wonder why he didn't just tell us that he needed a ride to the police station or something."

"We still don't know exactly what his situation was," Miracle interjected. "We have a lot of information and some good ideas, but we've got to get some proof, or our investigation can't move forward."

Miss Eugenia was frowning, and finally she held up a hand. "I think we've been missing the point."

"How?" the sheriff wanted to know.

"We all agree that JD's paintings weren't very good," she began.

"We do all agree about that," the sheriff concurred.

"So let's think it through," Miss Eugenia directed us. "Mr. Meyer starts up a charitable organization—very small scale—and sends a representative out to find homeless people who could be receiving an income either from the government or something similar. He picks out reasonable candidates and sets them up in some type of living quarters. According to Mr. Cottingham, he picked about six people in the Albany area. And we assume that all of this happened under Mr. Meyer's direction."

I nodded. "Especially since Mr. Meyer himself had moved here—leaving behind a successful law career in New York."

"So we don't know what happened to the other five homeless people, although that would be something to check on." Miss Eugenia looked at Sheriff Bonham.

"I'll look into it," he promised.

Miss Eugenia continued. "Mr. Meyer put JD in that trailer, which just happened to be right by the land he'd recently purchased."

"He said he tried to buy Miss George Ann's farm," I remembered suddenly. "But she wanted an outrageous price for it."

"So he chose to buy land in a very remote area," Luke said. "And he wanted to buy a lot of it—I guess to reduce the risks associated with close neighbors."

"I wouldn't be surprised if he didn't try to buy that old bottling plant too," Miracle said.

The sheriff nodded. "He should have tried harder to buy it. I'm convinced that those kids, driving up and down the dirt road constantly, were a big part of what ruined his whole scheme in the end."

Miracle turned to Miss Eugenia. "Now go on with your theory."

The old lady squinted her eyes, obviously thinking hard. "So Mr. Meyer sets JD up out in the middle of nowhere and gets him started painting. Then he contracts with Mr. Thorne, whom he knew from New York, to buy the paintings at inflated price and then sell them back to him."

"Talk about a snag," the sheriff said. "That's where the whole thing stops making sense."

"We've already agreed that each painting had value," Miracle reminded him. "Otherwise they could have had Dupree paint a few and then reused them."

"And there was some reason why JD had to do it," the sheriff said. "If he wasn't important to the process, they could have slapped paint on some wood themselves."

Miss Eugenia nodded. "I've been chasing this idea around in my mind ever since Miracle said that she thought we didn't have JD's real name. And I finally caught it just now. I believe that Mr. Meyer set up his charitable organization with the intention of finding JD—someone with no family or connections, no future, no hope. He set him up in that trailer and then created, out of an old drunk, an eccentric artist named Jarrard Dupree."

She paused to make sure we were all following.

"Go on," the sheriff encouraged.

"We discussed before that art is in the eye of the beholder and what is beautiful and valuable to one person might not be to another," Miss Eugenia said.

"That's true," I agreed. "I've seen paintings and sculptures that were completely unfathomable to me."

"So the ugliness of the paintings could easily be explained away," Miss Eugenia said. "If the IRS or an auditor checked Mr. Meyer's records—as long as all the paintings purchased did exist and Jarrard Dupree was a real person—the value on paper could not be questioned."

Miracle gasped. "You think it's some kind of money-laundering scheme?"

Miss Eugenia nodded. "Or some way of hiding assets or cash from the government. If Mr. Meyer had money coming in from some illegal source and needed a way to explain it—or was investing money in something that wasn't on the up and up—he could use the paintings to make up for holes in his financial statement."

"So he paid Mr. Thorne a broker's fee but really paid JD very little," Miracle said. "That's why there's such a small amount in his bank account!"

"And that's why they've got it set up so he didn't even have the ability to access his own funds," Luke said. "Because it wasn't really his money. It was Mr. Meyer's."

"And if anyone ever wants to see Meyer's assets, he has stacks of paintings that he can show an auditor and list whatever value he needs them to have?" Miracle guessed.

Miss Eugenia nodded. "At tax time the values might have been relatively low and at other times . . ."

"That's why he has to own them all," I realized. "Otherwise someone could take them to an appraiser and have an official value established. Then he wouldn't be able to change the values so easily."

Luke shook his head. "But again, if Dupree was central to Meyer's adjustable asset scheme, killing him would be a really bad thing."

The sheriff shrugged. "If JD was going to blow the whistle, he may not have had any choice."

"And JD's death might not have meant the end of his scheme," Miracle said. "Meyer could continue using the paintings—selling them back and forth between companies he owns as necessary. In fact, if he needed to use larger amounts, Dupree's death would be a good excuse for even more inflated prices since often an artist's work appreciates after they die."

Deputy Cross looked confused. "So Mr. Meyers is our murder and robbery suspect?"

"Yes," the sheriff confirmed. "I feel certain that we'd find those stolen paintings if we searched his place."

"So what do we do now?" I asked.

The sheriff frowned. "I think it's time to question Mr. Meyer."

Luke seemed surprised. "You aren't going to arrest him?"

"Not yet," the sheriff replied. "I don't want to tip him off. So I think I'll question everyone involved—Mr. Meyer, the students and their elusive professor, the lawyer, even Miss George Ann Simmons. That way nobody will feel singled out."

I thought this was a completely brilliant idea.

"When you bring George Ann in for questioning can you keep her locked up overnight?" Miss Eugenia asked. "That would be like the best thing that ever happened to me."

Sheriff Bonham chuckled. "I can't do that, because I value my life—not to mention my pension."

Miss Eugenia sighed. "I love the thought of George Ann sitting in a cold metal chair in a dark room with a single lightbulb hanging from the ceiling while you question her into the wee hours of the night."

Even Deputy Cross, who didn't know Miss George Ann, smiled at that.

Miracle said, "Rather than have the suspects come here for questioning, it might be better for the sheriff to go to them."

"That would be a little less official," Miss Eugenia agreed.

"And when you visit Mr. Meyer's place, you might get lucky and see some of JD's paintings lying around," I added.

Luke cleared his throat. "I think it's important to remember that while Miss Eugenia's idea is a really good one, it's still an unproven theory and you should keep your mind open to other possibilities."

I held my breath, waiting for Miss Eugenia's reaction. But Luke's remark didn't bother her at all.

"You're exactly right, young man. Narrow-mindedness is the surest way to miss the obvious." She glanced at the sheriff, and he did look a little offended.

"I'm not narrow-minded," he claimed.

Miss Eugenia stood. "Well, if you have a change of heart and decide to bring George Ann in, give me a call. I'd gladly drive back to Midway to see it."

"I won't change my mind," he said.

Miss Eugenia waved this aside. "If she's not going to be in handcuffs or anything, I'll just wait until tomorrow to hear what she has to say."

"I want to hear what everyone has to say," I admitted.

"We're all anxious to hear," Miracle agreed.

The sheriff smiled. "Let's meet here in the morning and I'll fill everyone in. Will eight o'clock work for everyone? I'll provide the doughnuts and plenty of bad coffee."

***

After leaving the sheriff's office, Luke took me by Hardees. We both ordered a hamburger, fries, and a milkshake. Then while we ate, we discussed the events of the next day, which promised to keep us busy.

I held a french fry up to help me itemize. "First we have the meeting at the sheriff's office where we'll try to prove that Mr. Meyer murdered poor old JD."

Luke nodded. "And the sheriff is providing breakfast."

"I hope he goes by the Piggy Wiggly in Haggerty and gets Krispy Kremes," I wished aloud. "If he picks up those they make themselves at the Exxon, I'll have to pass."

Luke smiled. "So you'll eat hot dogs cooked at a convenience store but not doughnuts made at a gas station?"

"A girl has to have some standards." I waved my French fry again. "Then after our meeting with the sheriff, I'll go to court in Albany and try to prove that I didn't coerce an old man into giving me a bunch of terrible paintings."

"Only one of which remains in your possession," Luke added.

"Actually it's in the sheriff's vault, and it really belongs to Miss Eugenia. She gave me a hundred dollars for it before we learned that it was actually worth at least fifteen times that much."

"Or maybe it's worth nothing if Miss Eugenia's money laundering theory proves true."

"It will still have some sentimental value." I popped the French fry in my mouth. "Then I'm hosting the welcome-home-from-jail party for Miss Ida Jean's son, Robby. And even if he's only a fraction as annoying as his mother, he'll be a new misery in my life."

"Maybe with her son home, Miss Ida Jean won't have as much time to spend at the library."

I was cheered for a moment by this thought. Then I shook my head. "No, things never work out like that for me."

Luke wadded up his hamburger wrapper. "Would you like me to pick you up for the meeting at the sheriff's office?"

"Then you'd be stuck with me all day, and only a true glutton for punishment would want to be on my schedule."

"Then I'm a glutton," he said. "I'm planning to hang out with you through thick and thin."

I was touched. "Through court appearances and welcome-home parties too?"

He nodded. "Your torture is my torture."

I leaned forward and kissed him right there in front of all the five or six customers in Hardees. That may not seem like a big deal to some people, but for me kissing in public took our relationship to a whole new level.

When Luke dropped me off at my apartment, he asked again if I wouldn't feel more comfortable spending the night at my parents' house.

"I'll be fine here," I assured him. It wasn't exactly that I minded staying with my parents. But my mother makes such a fuss, and I don't like giving up my independence—even for a few hours. Besides, there was always the chance that Sloan might come by during the night, and if he did, I wanted to be sure I was there.

Luke didn't argue. He just made me promise to set the new alarm and keep my doors locked. And to call if I needed him. We leaned toward each other and shared one last breathtaking kiss. Then I got out of the car and climbed the steps to my apartment.

I opened the door and turned on the living room lights before entering the code in my new alarm. I left the door open while I made a full rotation of the limited space—taking the time to check under my bed, in the closet, and behind the shower curtain. Finally certain that I had no unwanted guests, I walked back to the front door and waved down to Luke. He waved back and then started his rental. I locked the door, set the alarm, and headed for the shower. It had been another long day.

CHAPTER NINE

THE NEXT MORNING WHEN LUKE knocked on the door to my apartment, I opened it and found him smiling broadly.

"What?" I asked.

"It looks like you're not going to be needing my Torino anymore."

I frowned in confusion, and then my heart started to pound. Was it really possible? I stepped out onto the front porch and saw my old truck parked in its normal spot below.

I took the steep stairs as quickly as I dared, and when I reached the hood, I touched it just to be sure I wasn't dreaming.

Luke pointed at the driver's window. "The keys are in the ignition."

I climbed in and reverently turned the key. The engine sprang to life, and I was afraid I might cry.

"Your dad?" Luke guessed.

I nodded. "I don't know how he did it, but I'm about to find out."

I dialed the number at my parents' house, and I knew Daddy had to be sitting right be the phone because he answered, and he never beats my mother to a phone call. "Hello!"

"You have some explaining to do, young man."

He laughed. "Are you talking about that old junky truck I had Maxwell's drop off at your place this morning?"

I turned on the air conditioner, and it spewed cold air toward me. "The air even works!" I cried. Then I realized that this miracle couldn't have come cheap. "How did you do it, Daddy?"

"Well, the head mechanic over at Maxwell's has a '57 Chevy that he's been wanting to restore, and I told him I'd help him with it in exchange for having your engine rebuilt and fixing your air conditioning."

"Oh, Daddy, how can I ever thank you?"

"You just did," he said. Then he lowered his voice and added, "We don't have to mention any of this to your mother."

And I understood the full extent of his gift to me. My mother saw my truck problems as a way to get rid of the noisy and unladylike vehicle she hated so much. By negotiating a way for me to get the repairs my truck needed, he had deliberately defied her wishes. And that was something my father never did.

As if he could read my mind, he said, "I love your mother, but that's not *her* truck."

"I won't say a word," I promised. And then, before I became a sobbing heap of sentimentality, I told my father good-bye and hung up.

Luke had been standing silently beside me throughout my conversation. Even though he didn't know my father well and couldn't hear everything that was said, I was pretty sure he'd gotten the gist of it.

He reached in and rubbed his hand along the old steering wheel. "When I have kids, I want to be just like your dad."

Tears threatened again as I said, "You could do worse."

"So you want to drive me to the sheriff's office?"

I reached up and adjusted my mirror. "I'd love to."

***

When we arrived at the sheriff's department a few minutes after eight o'clock, the others were already assembled in the front office. There were several boxes of Krispy Kreme doughnuts on Miracle's temporary desk along with a carafe of steaming coffee and a stack of Styrofoam cups. I took a doughnut as we passed by the desk.

We sat in the only two available chairs, and as the sheriff launched into his report on the interviews he'd held the night before I bit into the warm, soft, sweet pastry.

Reading from a yellow legal pad covered with scribbled notes, Sheriff Bonham said, "Well, let's see. I talked to the college boys, and they admitted to stealing wood from George Ann's barn for JD."

"I knew it!" Miss Eugenia was pleased.

"That one kid, Tripp, seemed like the leader," the sheriff said. "According to him, JD found the barn during one of his walking expeditions and cut down a few boards himself. Then he asked them to get more for him. He did pay them fifty dollars for each truckload."

"So that much of his story was true, at least," Miss Eugenia muttered.

"Why didn't he just say that when we asked him?" I demanded.

The sheriff shrugged. "He said he was afraid we'd tell him he couldn't come back to the experimental farm. If that happened he wouldn't pass his agriculture class, which would mean he wouldn't graduate and his parents would kill him."

"And I'm sure he never expected that his petty theft to be investigated so thoroughly," Miss Eugenia predicted. "Next time I ask him a question, he'll think twice before he lies."

"I talked to two other students who work on the project, and there are two more who are supposed to call me," the sheriff added. "I called the number at the company where that adjunct college teacher was supposed to work, but the phones have been disconnected. Apparently they have gone bankrupt, so we may never be able to talk to the guy."

"If the teacher has quit and doesn't turn in grades for the students, they won't get credit for the class," Miracle pointed out.

"Unless the college makes some kind of arrangements, it sounds like those boys may not be graduating this semester, after all," Luke said.

I didn't feel sorry for them. "It would serve them right."

The sheriff spoke again. "Next I went to see Miss George Ann Simmons. She welcomed me into her home, made me sit in her living room, and then proceeded to tell me the approximate value of all the possessions she keeps there. I barely got a word in edgewise, but I'm pretty sure she doesn't know anything about the case."

Miss Eugenia shook her head. "George Ann is so self-absorbed she probably wouldn't have noticed anything illegal if it was happening right in front of her face."

"Are you going to tell Miss George Ann that Tripp took her wood?" I asked, dreading the answer.

"Only if I have to," the sheriff replied. Then he referred to his notes. "I didn't talk personally to the art broker since he's already been interviewed by the NYPD. I spoke with Mr. Cottingham, who was very cordial, although he claimed there was not much he could say because of client privilege. He said that if we ever get around to filing charges against someone, he'd be glad to relinquish his records— under court order."

"Lawyers tend to be picky about doing things by the book," Miracle said.

The sheriff continued. "Then I went to visit Mr. Meyer, but he wouldn't even open the door. He said if I didn't have a warrant, I was trespassing on his property."

"Well!" Miss Eugenia was offended in the sheriff's behalf. "It would serve him right if you did exactly that—came back with a warrant and forced him to answer your questions."

The sheriff sighed. "I could probably convince a judge to give me one, but Meyer is a cagey character and a lawyer. He'd refuse to talk, and we'd be no better off than we are now."

Miracle said, "We need a way to flush the guilty party out into the open."

"A catalyst," Miss Eugenia agreed.

Miracle nodded. "If we could come up with a reason to get everyone together, I believe that something would happen."

"I would be hard to get everyone in the same place at the same time since Mr. Thorne is in New York," the sheriff pointed out.

"Maybe we could gather the students at least," I suggested. "And Mr. Cottingham would probably come if I asked him."

"But Mr. Meyer is the main one we need, and I can't imagine what we could possibly do that would make him come to us without a warrant," Miracle said.

Miss Eugenia gasped. "There's only one thing that will draw Mr. Meyer out of the safety of his private property. My painting!"

The sheriff's eyebrows shot up. "The one that we broke into a bunch of pieces last night?"

"Of course I mean that painting," Miss Eugenia replied crossly. "There's nothing wrong with it that a little glue can't fix. We'll have the auction tonight just like we'd originally planned—right after Robby Baxley's welcome-home party."

"But we cancelled the auction after the other paintings were stolen," I said. "Hannah-Leigh made an announcement on television. Then my mother and the other church ladies spent hours on the phone calling to let people know."

This did not concern Miss Eugenia in the least. "Your mother and the church ladies can call everyone again to let them know that the auction is back on. And ask Hannah-Leigh to announce it on the midday news."

I was overwhelmed by the scale of this assignment. "There's no way we can be sure that we reach everyone."

"We don't need to notify everyone," Miracle said. "The only people who absolutely must be invited are the suspects in our investigation."

Miss Eugenia smiled. "Exactly."

"How will we get Mr. Meyer to come?" Deputy Cross asked.

"All we have to do is make sure he knows that the one remaining painting is going to be up for bids tonight," Miss Eugenia said. "He will have to come if he wants to buy it, which we know he does."

"Unless he decides to steal it before the auction," the deputy said.

The sheriff scowled. "I'd like to see him try."

"I'll call Mr. Cottingham and ask him to come—hinting that the library might need his legal services," I offered. "But how will we get Tripp and his friends and his professor here?"

"I'll get my researcher to see if she can find out anything about that company the teacher works for," Miracle said. "Maybe we can contact him through another former employee."

"And I think the sheriff should call Heatherly College and ask them to send the students as a delegation of goodwill since this auction will be basically a memorial service for JD," Miss Eugenia suggested. "And as insurance I'll call Tripp privately and tell him that if they aren't all at the auction, we'll tell George Ann that he stole her wood."

I had to smile. "That should do it."

***

When Luke and I got to the library, I led him past all the yellow ribbons to my office. From there I called Hannah-Leigh Coley-Smith.

I asked her to reannounce the auction at the library. She didn't sound happy, but she did agree, which was all I cared about.

Next I called my mother and asked her to have the church ladies call around about the auction.

"For heaven sakes, Kennedy," Mother said. "I'm trying to get the refreshments ready for Robby's party. If it's only one painting, can't we wait and have the auction next week?"

"No, Mother, we can't have the auction next week. It has to be tonight when we have a big crowd gathered."

"Well then you'll have to hope that someone who comes to the party will have an interest in the painting, because I really don't have time to make calls advertising the auction today."

"I know you're busy," I commiserated. "But could you just ask some of the ladies from church who aren't helping with refreshments to make a few calls? There are only a couple of people I need you to speak with personally."

"And why can't you call them?"

"Because I'm the director of the library, and it will look like I'm begging if I call and ask people to come."

My mother certainly didn't want anyone to think I was begging. "All right," she agreed. "Tell me who to call."

I gave her Mr. Meyer's name along with a few others. "If you don't get to speak to them personally, be sure to leave a message on their voice mail."

"I know how to make calls, Kennedy," Mother said impatiently.

"Thank you so much! And I'll see you this afternoon."

***

Ten minutes before Luke and I planned to leave for the courthouse in Albany, I got a phone call from the sheriff. He said that Mr. Meyer had withdrawn his complaint against me.

"That's nice of him," I said. "Now that he's stolen most of the paintings I was going to sell."

"But it clears the way for you to sell the last one at the auction tonight," Sheriff Bonham pointed out.

"Do you think that's why he withdrew the complaint?"

"I think he's heard that you have the painting, and he knows that stealing it from my vault will be impossible," the sheriff said. "So buying it is his only option. And that can only happen if there's no court order preventing it."

After hanging up with the sheriff, I turned to Luke and explained. "So our morning just got a little less complicated."

"Kennedy!" Miss Ida Jean's shrill voice called to me from down the hall. Seconds later she was knocking on my office door.

Luke grinned. "You spoke too soon."

With a grimace I pulled the door open. "What do you need, Miss Ida Jean?"

"The men from the Baptist church are here with the tables. Can you come out and tell them where to set them up?"

"When is Mother coming?"

Miss Ida Jean shook her head. "Not until later. She's still working on refreshments and then has to go get the flower arrangement that Cecille at Floral Occasions is donating."

I didn't know where Mother wanted the tables set up. So for the next hour Luke and I moved tables around and set up folding chairs. Then mother arrived, and of course we had done it all wrong. So we spent another thirty minutes moving everything to what she considered the proper locations. But at 10:55, I told my mother we had police business to attend to. Then I pulled Luke out the front door and headed down to Midway's only restaurant, in the truest sense of the word, the Back Porch.

Luke frowned when he saw our destination. "You lied to your mother."

"I did not," I denied as we sat in a booth with a good view of the television. "I need to see the eleven o'clock news to be sure Hannah-Leigh announces the auction." I waved to a waitress. "But as long as we're here, we might as well eat."

I ordered a plate of mozzarella fries with an ice-cold Pepsi. Luke got hot wings and a Pepsi of his own. Then we shared the food while watching the news. Right after the weather, Hannah-Leigh's lovely face filled the television screen. She gave a heart-wrenching description of JD's lonely life spent painting and drinking. She mentioned the log cabin he was saving for but would never build.

Hannah-Leigh told her viewers about his generous donation of paintings to the library that were later stolen in what she called, "Midway's most recent crime spree." Then she announced that the one remaining painting would be sold at auction at seven o'clock that night and invited all of her listening audience to attend. Then with a cute wink she encouraged everyone to bring plenty of cash.

When her segment was over I shook my head. "That Hannah-Leigh is something else."

"She did a good job," Luke replied. "She passed on the information and did it in an entertaining way so that people would actually pay attention. If you end up solving this crime, you may have to thank her."

"I'll have to thank her anyway for taking Cade off my hands," I muttered and Luke laughed.

We were trying to decide whether we wanted to share a banana split or a piece of apple pie à la mode when my cell phone rang. I answered it absently, still concentrating on the dessert menu.

"Miss Killingsworth, this is Randall Meyer."

I sat up straight and mouthed "Meyer" to Luke. Into the phone I said, "Hello, Mr. Meyer. I guess I should thank you for saving me a trip to Albany this morning."

"You're welcome," he replied.

"But I don't think that's why you're calling."

"No," he confirmed. "I've heard that you have one remaining painting that you plan to auction off tonight."

"That is correct."

"Well, I'd like to save you the trouble," Mr. Meyer said. "I'm offering you $10,000 for it."

I widened my eyes at Luke. "That's an interesting amount."

"Most people would say it's *extremely generous*," he countered.

"I'd say it's the exact amount Mr. Thorne offered me for ten of JD's paintings—the ones that were stolen from the library. That makes me wonder if you have a guilty conscience."

"You don't know me at all, Miss Killingsworth. Therefore you are in no position to judge my conscience. I can come by in thirty minutes if you'll have the painting ready."

"I'm sorry, Mr. Meyer," I lied. Actually I was enjoying every second of our conversation. "But I can't let you buy the painting before the auction begins. Since it's the only one, it wouldn't be fair to the rest of the art-buying public."

"I'm tired of playing your little games, Miss Killingsworth. I just offered you $10,000 for one painting. You're in no financial position to refuse."

I was tired of playing games too. "You don't know me well enough to judge my financial position," I said. "And it's a shame I don't have the other ten paintings for you to bid on since you seem to be such a fan of the late Jarrard Dupree's masterpieces. But I'll see you tonight at the auction, and if you're the highest bidder, I'll be glad to accept your check."

"Miss Killingsworth, be reasonable . . ."

"I've given you all the time I can spare," I told him, and that was no lie. Then I closed the phone, hanging up on Mr. Meyer. To Luke I said, "The nerve of that man! It's like he can't take no for an answer."

"I guess he thought he was making you an offer you couldn't refuse."

I scowled at the phone, remembering the conversation. "Well, he was wrong."

"He does seem to want that last painting pretty bad," Luke mused. "I just wish we could figure out why."

Mr. Meyer had ruined my appetite, so we decided to forgo dessert. We went back to the library, and as we walked into my office a terrible thought occurred to me.

"The sheriff didn't want Mr. Meyer to know we're suspicious of him. What if I said too much during our phone conversation? If I've scared Mr. Meyer off and he runs away instead of coming to the auction . . . well, I'll never be able to forgive myself."

Luke laughed. "Well instead of hating yourself, you should call the sheriff and tell him Meyer might be thinking of running. Then the sheriff can be watching him and catch him if he does."

"You're brilliant!" I told Luke. Then I called the sheriff, who informed me he already had someone watching Mr. Meyer.

"And as a matter of fact," the sheriff said, "he did leave his house just a moment ago. But according to the man who is following him, he doesn't seem to be running. In fact, it looks like he's coming straight to you."

"He's going to try and make me take that check!" I fumed. "He offered me $10,000 for the one painting I have left."

The sheriff whistled into the phone. "He is serious about getting that painting. Do you want me to come over?"

"No, Luke's here," I said. "And Mr. Meyer is going to find out that I can be just as stubborn as he is."

After making me promise to call and report on my conversation with Mr. Meyer as soon as it was over, the sheriff ended our call. A couple of minutes later Carmella called to tell me I had a visitor.

"Send him on back," I said grimly.

***

I was sitting behind my desk and Luke was standing in the corner of my office, leaning against the newly repaired window, when Mr. Meyer walked in. He glanced in Luke's direction, but if he thought his location significant, he gave no indication. Instead he walked over and sat down in one of the chairs facing my desk.

I expected him to start with an insult or to try and bully me, but his initial remarks took me completely by surprise. "I am a private man, Miss Killingsworth. It is painful and difficult for me to discuss personal things. But I've decided that I need to explain everything to you and then ask for your understanding."

I nodded for him to continue. And I'll admit that I was intrigued.

"JD was my half brother. My mother found herself an unwed teenager expecting a child during a time where such situations were not socially acceptable. She gave him up for adoption and then spent the rest of her life wondering and worrying about what had become of him. She died a couple of years ago and on her death bed told me that I had a brother and begged me to find him."

It was a tragic story. Whether it was a true story, I didn't know. I wasn't ready to trust Mr. Meyer yet, but I did want to hear the rest of what he had to say.

"Finding him was not an easy task. I used the services of a private detective in New York. He can provide you with his records, showing the hours he spent searching and the results he was finally able to achieve."

"He discovered that JD was a drunk living on the streets of Albany?" I guessed.

"I'll spare you the unpleasant details of his years spent with his adoptive family, his military service, and the loss of his wife when he was still in his twenties. It's enough for you to know where he ended up."

I nodded and Mr. Meyer continued his sad tale.

"I consulted with a partner in my law firm who is also a friend, trying to decide how best to help JD. And together we came up with an idea."

"You established Return to Dignity."

"Yes," Mr. Meyer confirmed. "Originally that was a way to protect myself and my assets against JD if he were to turn greedy. According to my friend, that happens quite often."

"Very wise," I murmured. "By creating the nonprofit organization you were able to help your brother without his finding out anything about you personally."

"It may sound stingy to you, Miss Killingsworth. But I didn't know JD at the time, and while I wanted to help him, I didn't want to sacrifice everything I'd worked for in the process. So with my partner's help, we created the charity and I hired Mr. Cottingham to represent the organization in this area. JD was one of six Albany homeless people who were helped here."

He sounded proud of this fact.

"I presume that his name was not really Jarrard Dupree."

"No," Mr. Meyer admitted. "That was a pen name of sorts. His legal name is Jonas Donahue. He'd always used his initials, JD, as a nickname."

"So you set JD up in that nice trailer in the middle of nowhere. Then what?"

"I wanted to see him," Mr. Meyer said. "And possibly become a part of his life."

"But only if you could be sure that your brother wasn't going to try and take some of your money." I was starting to actually enjoy this interview.

Mr. Meyer looked annoyed, but he went on. "I came down and met him, but I didn't explain our relationship. This was based on advice I received from my friend." He paused to clear his throat. "I've never had any family except my parents, and my father died when I was a child. I was very close to my mother, and she hadn't been gone for very long so I was still missing her a great deal."

"I understand," I claimed, although I'd never been separated from my mother long enough to actually miss her.

After a short pause he continued. "I liked JD and enjoyed his company, and I loved fishing. Soon after that I lost interest in practicing law. I wanted to be near my brother—get to know him—and help him if that was possible."

"And to fish at any time of the day or night," I added.

"Yes."

I leaned my elbows up onto my desk. "So you retired and moved to Georgia?"

"I set up the store and established a relationship with JD, mostly through hiking and fishing. By living here I was able to make sure he had food and medical care if necessary. Unfortunately I wasn't able to keep him from drinking."

"And why did you have him start painting?"

"He needed an income so that he could feel independent and stop receiving the monthly stipend from Return to Dignity."

"And it needed to be something that you could ensure would be successful."

Mr. Meyer gave me a quick nod. "I suggested that he try painting. Once he did a few pieces I told him I thought they had potential. I asked if I could send them to an old friend in New York who owned a gallery."

"Then you arranged with Mr. Thorne to buy the paintings and sell them back to you."

"Yes. I wanted to give JD some pride and hope and confidence. I felt that this would help him to get over his addiction to alcohol. But even with assistance from the judge, who revoked his driver's license and forced him to take some counseling, the lifetime of chemical abuse proved too difficult for JD to leave behind."

"But you were still friends," I clarified.

Mr. Meyer smiled for the first time since I'd met him. "Yes. JD and I became very good friends."

"Until he gave me those paintings," I said. "You couldn't let them be auctioned off because JD thought they were valuable works of art, selling for more than a thousand dollars a piece. And at the auction they would be recognized for the worthless pieces of junk they actually were."

He flinched but nodded. "Yes, I couldn't risk that. JD's belief in himself was very delicate and closely tied to his paintings and their success."

"So you had Mr. Thorne try to bully me into a quick sale."

He sighed. "Yes."

"And when that didn't work out you got the court order."

"Yes and I'm sorry." He leaned forward in appeal. "But it was all to protect JD."

"And what are you trying to protect now?" I asked. "Your reputation? Your family name? All your money?"

He shook his head. "Just JD's memory."

For the first time since he'd entered my office I felt a little sorry for him. "You stole the paintings from my office?"

"Actually Mr. Thorne was the thief, but he was acting on my behalf," Mr. Meyer acknowledged. "I told him to get them at any cost and, well, I didn't realize how literally he would take my words."

I'm not the world's best judge of character (I'll use my first husband, Cade, as Exhibit A), but I believed Mr. Meyer and I had to steel myself against feeling sorry for him.

"I'll have to get the sheriff to check out your story," I warned.

He nodded. "I will cooperate fully with Sheriff Bonham." He took a check from his pocket and pushed it across my desk. "I want to pay for the paintings that were taken and the one that you still have in your possession."

"It's not here," I was quick to inform him. "The sheriff has it in his vault."

"I am not a thief." Mr. Meyer had the nerve to look offended. "And I also want to pay for the glass repairs." He waved a finger vaguely toward Luke and the room's only window.

I glanced at the amount of the check—$11,500 made out to the Midway Library. "That's too much."

He smiled sadly. "It was JD's final wish to make a donation of this magnitude to the library. I would like to, as his brother, fulfill that wish. Please don't deny me, Miss Killingsworth."

What could I say? "Well, if you put it that way, Mr. Meyer, I accept on behalf of the Midway Library. However, I do have one condition."

Mr. Meyer looked surprised.

There was no way the sheriff would let Mr. Meyer have that painting until the investigation was over. But rather than insult Mr. Meyer (again), I said, "Even though you'll own the last painting, I'd like to keep it at the library for a while. I'll hang it here in my office so you won't have to worry about it being scrutinized. But I'd like to have it as a reminder of your brother and his generosity."

Mr. Meyer nodded. "I think JD would be very pleased to have one of his paintings hanging in the library." His business concluded, he shifted in his seat, obviously ready to leave.

I hated to ask, but felt that I had to. "Do you know who killed your brother, Mr. Meyer?"

He shook his head. "I have no idea."

I stood. "Mr. Meyer, I'm going to have to ask you to go over to the sheriff's office and repeat the things you've told me."

He stood as well. "I'm headed there now." He held out a hand to me. "I hope we meet again in the future, Miss Killingsworth. Under better circumstances."

I shook his hand and after giving Luke a brief nod, Mr. Meyer walked to my office door and let himself out.

"Well," I said after he left, "that was unexpected."

"And unsubstantiated," Luke added. "He could have made it all up."

"He could have, but I don't think he did. There was no point in him coming and telling me lies that couldn't be proven. He had to know the sheriff would check it all out."

"He probably did know that," Luke agreed.

"If he wasn't going to tell the truth, he could have just stayed at his house and hidden behind legal procedures for years."

Luke nodded. "True."

I narrowed my eyes at him. "And I've noticed that you have a tendency to be a little cynical."

"And you have a tendency to be a little gullible, so we're a perfect blend."

I felt kind of warm all over. I wasn't sure if it was because Luke thought I was something less than hard as nails or if it was because he thought we blended well.

"So now we are back to square one," Luke pointed out. "We have a dead man and no suspect."

"Not square one exactly," I amended. "We do know who took the paintings."

"But if that crime isn't tied to Dupree's death, we're even further from solving that crime."

He looked so cute and serious standing by my recently repaired window. I walked over and gave him a hug followed by a couple of kisses. We were interrupted a few minutes later by my cell phone. It was the sheriff. He told me that he'd talked to Mr. Meyer. And like Luke, he wasn't willing to accept the story without verification.

"Miracle is checking out the key points," he told me. "And I think we should continue with the auction tonight just as we had planned. By gathering everyone together we still might get lucky and have a catalyst reaction or whatever it is Miss Eugenia is hoping for."

"What will we do when it's time to actually auction off the picture that is no longer for sale?"

"Hmmm," the sheriff murmured. "We'll think of something by then."

And actually, we didn't think of anything, but Miss Eugenia did. I called to report to her all that had happened with Mr. Meyer. She was a little disappointed that her money-laundering theory was in jeopardy. But like any good investigator, she took it in stride.

Then when I explained that we were going to go through with the auction, although we had nothing to sell, she suggested that we sell pieces of the scrap wood JD would have painted on eventually—if he'd still been alive.

"But that wood belongs to Miss George Ann," I reminded her.

"We'll have to make some kind of a deal with her," Miss Eugenia acknowledged. "She's money hungry, so maybe you could offer to split the proceeds with her. At the auction half of the money will go for the library to buy books and the other half will be used to repair her useless barn."

"I was pretty rude to her the last time we talked," I admitted. "I'm not sure she'll want to deal with me."

Miss Eugenia laughed. "People are rude to George Ann all the time. Who can help it? But she wants her barn fixed, and she's always looking for opportunities to get things for free. So don't worry, I'm sure she'll agree to a deal. I'll call her and work it out even if I have to agree to join that bell choir again."

"You'd make such a sacrifice in the name of justice?"

"It would be a sacrifice, I promise you," she said. "Now we need to get some of that wood stacked in the lean-to beside JD's trailer. Will you take that assignment?"

I checked my watch. "I can do that."

"But don't go alone," Miss Eugenia cautioned.

I smiled at Luke. "I've got an escort."

"Call me on your way back to town, and I'll tell you how we're going to make that old wood appealing to potential buyers."

I laughed. "I can't wait to hear that."

"Well," Luke said as I hung up the phone. "What now?"

"Now we're going to collect a little wood for the auction tonight."

"Old wood that used to be on a teetering barn?"

I nodded. "Remember, you said my torture was your torture."

CHAPTER TEN

LUKE AND I DROVE OUT to JD's trailer and filled the back of my truck with pieces of old barn wood. Then because it was a beautiful day and we were in no hurry to get back to the library, we climbed the hill behind the trailer and looked around. We could see Miss George Ann's dilapidated farm, the lake where Mr. Meyer and JD liked to fish, and the old bottling plant, surrounded by fields full of experimental plants.

There was a big U-Haul truck pulled up to a door of the bottling plant. Squinting, I could identify Tripp and his fellow students, loading the truck with equipment. "I guess the semester is ending, and their project is over."

Luke nodded. "Either that or Miss George Ann found out that the students stole her wood, and they are trying to make a getaway before she has them arrested."

I hoped that wasn't the case. It seemed a shame for Tripp not to graduate just because of a few old boards. "It's funny," I told him. "I hadn't ever been out here before last Saturday, and now I probably won't ever come again."

"It's not much to look at," Luke pointed out. "I doubt you'll miss it."

"You'd be surprised how attached I can get to unremarkable things," I told him. "I'll remember JD fondly. Mr. Meyer, too. It's sweet that he kept his promise to his mother and looked so hard to find and help his brother."

Luke took my hand and pulled me close. "I think you're pretty sweet for caring about all these people you barely know."

"It's not that often that anyone accuses me of being sweet," I told him. "In fact, I usually wouldn't like it—but when you say it, I sort of do."

He pressed a kiss against the corner of my mouth. I turned my face slightly so that the next kiss could land more accurately.

A few minutes later he murmured, "We'd better get that wood back to the library. It's not fair of us to leave your mother with all the last-minute party preparations."

I sighed. "I guess you're right. Not that we'll be much help, but we probably should go and at least provide moral support."

We turned to start our descent. As we rounded the hill we saw two men heading up. Their close proximity, in the middle of nowhere, was startling enough. But the fact that they were dressed all in black and holding guns was beyond alarming. I couldn't control a little scream as the two men charged toward us.

I've always heard that your life flashes before your eyes in moments like this, but for me that was not the case. Maybe it's because my life has been so boring that it didn't deserve even a flash. Instead my thoughts went to the future that I was never going to have. I'd never know if Luke and I were destined to marry and build a life together. I'd never have the children my mother was always nagging me about. Even the thought of missing Robby Baxley's welcome-home-from-jail party suddenly seemed tragic.

Luke yanked me from my grief-stricken reverie, literally. Still holding my hand, he pulled me back around the hill, and soon we were careening down the other side, headed toward the old bottling plant. I presumed the men-in-black were following us but didn't dare take my eyes off the uneven terrain long enough to find out. We were just a few feet away from the trees that would provide us with some cover when the shooting began.

I expected them to shoot at us, so I was terrified but not surprised. As the gunfire intensified, Luke tackled me to the ground and shielded me with his body. I appreciated his concern even though my cheek was pressed against what was almost surely poison ivy. But as the seconds passed without either of us being injured, I started to hope.

I lifted my head slightly and saw that the black-clad men on the hill were not shooting at us but at Tripp and his fellow students at the bottling plant. Luke and I were just pinned down by the crossfire. Although our situation was still dangerous, it was better than I had initially thought, and I moved from hopeful to optimistic.

"Is this a robbery?" I asked.

"I don't know," Luke whispered, "but we've got to make it to those trees before we get hit by a stray bullet. Stay as low as you can. I'm right behind you."

I pushed up and started crawling toward the tree line, which now seemed impossibly far away. Sweat dripped into my eyes, and sharp rocks scraped my hands and knees. After several minutes of slow but determined progress, we reached the relative safety of the trees without getting shot. And my feelings changed from optimistic to confident. The bell had not tolled for me. I would live to see another day.

We stood and moved deeper into the trees at a trot. Now we were less exposed to flying bullets, but the underbrush made running difficult, and low-hanging branches further impeded us. I didn't think anyone was following us, but I couldn't hear much of anything besides our ragged breathing and my pounding heart.

Finally we made it to the other side of the little forest. A few yards away, the bottling plant with its thick cinder-block walls, beckoned. During a brief lull in the gunfire, I pointed at it and whispered, "We should be safe there." I took a step in that direction before Luke stopped me.

"We don't need a place to hide," he whispered back. "We need a way out of here." He tipped his head toward the U-Haul truck that the students had been loading before the hostilities began. "Hopefully the keys are in the ignition. If not, I can probably hotwire it."

As he caught my hand in his, I gave the bottling plant one last longing look. Then we stepped out into the clearing. In my peripheral vision I saw a dark blur. I turned to see one of the men dressed in black coming toward us. Luke's attention was focused on the truck, so I screamed a warning. But I was too late. The man grabbed me with such force that I couldn't maintain my grip on Luke's hand as the man dragged me back into the trees. Without hesitation or a thought for self-preservation, Luke plunged into the woods after me.

My captor anticipated Luke's reaction. After pushing me to the ground behind a large oak tree, he turned toward Luke and crouched, ready for combat.

The men collided with a sickening thud. Then they grappled silently for a few horrifying seconds, ricocheting from tree to tree as they fought for the advantage. They seemed evenly matched, and I was looking for a way to tip the scales in Luke's favor when I saw that a few strands of long, silky black hair had escaped from under the ski mask that covered the head of Luke's attacker. And at this point I realized I had an emotional connection to both opponents.

"Sloan!"

He turned to me, and Luke caught him in the jaw with a nasty right hook. Sloan's blue eyes blinked once, and then he dropped to his knees, stunned. Luke stepped behind him and wrapped an arm around Sloan's neck.

"Don't hurt him!" I yelled. "He's a . . . friend."

Luke didn't loosen his hold.

"And an FBI agent!" I added.

This got Luke's attention. "FBI?" Reluctantly Luke released him.

Sloan pointed toward the U-Haul. "That truck is full of the evidence I need to prove myself innocent," he rasped as he rubbed his throat. "There are all kinds of flammable chemicals in the milk plant, and sooner or later a bullet is going to hit something and blow the place up. I need to get the truck out of here before that happens. Otherwise I'll end up in prison for tax evasion."

Luke looked confused. "Tax evasion?"

"I'll explain later," I told Luke. Then I said to Sloan, "We'll help you get to the truck." I stood and took a step toward the edge of the trees.

"No!" Sloan hissed as he stood up. "It's too dangerous for you to go out in the open. Just wait here while I move the truck. Once the students are under arrest, it will be safe. But stay in the woods until then."

I waved toward the hill above us. "Those guys are FBI agents?"

Sloan nodded.

"If they are having a shootout with Tripp and his fellow students, there must be more to it than stolen wood," Luke said.

"I'll have to explain that later too." Sloan moved toward the truck. "Stay here with Kennedy. The last thing we need is one of those students using her as a hostage."

I pressed closer to Luke, and together we watched as Sloan ran across the open space to the U-Haul truck. He made it to the driver's door and climbed inside undetected. But when he started the engine, he drew attention and gunfire from inside the old milk plant.

Sloan threw the truck into gear as a bullet shattered the passenger window. I clutched my throat, barely able to breathe, willing him to hurry. The truck shot forward, skidding on the loose dirt of the unpaved road. I heard Sloan shift into second gear as another bullet hit the back of the truck. Two more bullets were fired, but they landed harmlessly in the dirt. Sloan was out of range. I sighed with relief and slumped against Luke.

"Now can you tell me what's going on?" Luke asked.

But before I could even attempt to explain what little I knew, we were surrounded by men in black. One walked close to us, and as he whispered I recognized Mark Iverson's voice. "We're going to storm the plant. You two stay right here."

Luke and I nodded in unison.

"Are you armed?" he asked Luke.

Luke shook his head.

Mark pulled a revolver from his shoulder holster and pressed it into Luke's hand. "Use this only if it's necessary to protect yourselves."

Luke nodded and Mark moved to the edge of the clearing where the other agents were lined up, waiting for the signal to overtake the students in the milk plant by force. As Mark lifted his arm, a voice called out from inside the plant.

"Hold your fire!" Following this plea, several guns were thrown out the open doorway in an apparent show of good faith. "We're surrendering!" the voice claimed.

"Come out where we can see you and keep your hands up!" Mark called back.

Slowly four young men, including Tripp, came filing out of the building. Their hands were raised, their heads hung down in defeat. As I watched them trudge toward us, I felt a deep sadness. I didn't know exactly what they'd been involved in, but it was obvious that lives once full of hope and potential had now been ruined by bad choices.

While the boys walked forward under Mark's watchful eye, the men along the tree line removed their ski masks. When I saw Cade, Sheriff Bonham, and Chief Jones from Haggerty, I realized that it had been more than an FBI operation. It had been a collaborative effort between several law enforcement agencies.

Cade and Sheriff Bonham walked over to where we were standing. I felt Luke stiffen and was thankful he had promised to control his temper around Cade. We'd had more than enough drama for one day.

"You told me you didn't trust Cade to work on the investigation into JD's death," I said to the sheriff. "You said you were afraid anything we told him would end up on the news because of his . . ." I searched for the right word, "association with Hannah-Leigh Coley-Smith. You said you'd sent him to Albany to keep him out of the way. But you always trusted him. In fact you trust him so much you loaned him to the FBI!"

The sheriff did have the decency to look ashamed. "If I didn't trust Cade, I would fire him, not give him busywork in Albany. I'm sorry that I had to mislead you, but it was necessary."

The necessity of his lies was arguable. But I'd been less than forthcoming with all I knew about Sloan and his presence in Midway so I let that drop. However, there was another question I had to ask even though I was pretty sure I wouldn't like the answer. "You said you wanted me to be a part of your investigation because you valued my opinion. Was that true?"

"I do value your opinion," the sheriff claimed stubbornly. "But I'll admit that I had other reasons as well. I wanted to keep you out of trouble. After the whole thing with Foster's murder, I knew you wouldn't leave it alone and let the professionals investigate. So I decided it would be better to involve you."

"So you could keep an eye on me. Like a child." My feelings were really hurt, and I was suddenly glad for all the black smoke that was impairing our vision. Being hurt was one thing. Having everyone know it was worse.

Mark walked over at this point and said, "Sheriff, I'm going to ask you to take custody of our prisoners."

"I'll be glad to," the sheriff said. "I've got a deputy waiting by the main road. I'll tell him to come on in."

While the sheriff pulled out his cell phone, I looked at the prisoners. The students were all wearing handcuffs. Tripp wouldn't meet my eyes.

When the sheriff ended his phone call, Mark continued. "We'll discuss the charges later, but for now let's just keep them locked up in your jail."

Sheriff Bonham nodded, and a couple of minutes later Deputy Cross came driving up the dirt road in a sheriff's department van. We watched Cade and Sheriff Bonham load up the students.

As they drove away we heard several pops from inside the milk plant followed by a low hissing sound. "What is that?" I began.

Then the ground shook as the old cinder-block building exploded into flames. And, for the second time in less than an hour, Luke tackled me.

Under other circumstances I would have enjoyed the feeling of his arms around me. But with his weight pressing me into the layers of decaying leaves, I couldn't fill my lungs properly. I was afraid that I had survived gunshots and a bottle plant explosion only to be smothered by love. The irony was not lost on me.

Once he was sure that it was safe, Luke rolled over and helped me up. I gulped in air and dusted off my clothes, again. Then I gave him a stern look. "The next time you think I'm in danger, will you please just tell me instead of knocking me down?"

"I'm sorry," Luke said. "It's instinct."

"I appreciate your concern," I assured him. "But enough is enough."

"I won't knock you down again," Luke promised. "Unless I think you're about to be shot or blown up," he added with a smile.

I decided to accept these terms. "Thank you."

I stared at the burning milk plant in dismay. Even though we were a good distance away, the heat was intense and the smoke thick. Sloan came running up beside us, gasping for breath. He leaned forward and rested his hands on his knees and asked, "The kids blew the plant up?"

Mark nodded. "They probably started a fire before they surrendered." He frowned at Sloan. "Where's the U-Haul? Without the plant, all the evidence we have is in that truck."

Sloan pointed to the hill behind us. "When I heard the explosion, I asked a couple of Haggerty police officers to watch it while I came down here to check on things."

Chief Jones, upon hearing that his employees were in charge of crucial evidence, took off toward the hill at a trot. "I'll go and supervise."

"I'd appreciate that," Mark said. Then he scowled at Sloan. "You need that truck to prove your innocence and keep your job with the Bureau. You should have stayed with it."

Sloan looked embarrassed. "Sorry. It was a lapse of good judgment."

It was strange to see Sloan so humble and asking for forgiveness. Maybe several days on the wrong side of the law had changed him. Or maybe he just didn't want to alienate his major ally.

One of the men in black walked over and spoke to Mark. "So it looks like things are wrapped up here."

Mark nodded. "Yes, we managed to get the evidence without any loss of life, so I guess we'll consider the operation a success." Mark turned to me. "Kennedy, let me introduce a fellow agent, Wade Norman. Agent Norman, this is Kennedy Killingsworth and her friend Luke Scoggins."

Agent Norman nodded to each of us in turn. "Nice to meet you folks."

I turned to Sloan. "Are you going to explain all this?" I waved my hand to encompass the entire smoldering, police-ridden area.

"I'll be glad to try," Sloan said.

"Kennedy's truck is parked up the hill," Mark said. "Why don't we walk in that direction while we talk?"

I needed to get back to Midway as soon as possible, and the smoke was choking me, so I said, "I think that is a great idea."

Once we were walking, Sloan began his story. "I told you I stumbled on to something that looked like criminal activity a while back."

I nodded. "You did."

Agent Norman interrupted and said, in a very official tone, "Miss Killingsworth, remember that what you're about to hear is related to an ongoing FBI investigation and cannot be repeated without risk of prosecution."

I raised my eyebrows. "Duly noted."

Sloan tipped his head at the other agent. "Please excuse him. Agent Norman is pretty intense."

Mollified, I said, "I understand that I can't repeat what Sloan tells me."

Agent Norman seemed to relax, just a little.

"Now that we've got that settled, let's see where to begin," Sloan glanced up at the smoke-filled sky for a second. Then he asked, "Did I say that when I was working in Midway with Drake that pushy old lady, George Ann Simmons, insisted that we consider her pitiful little farm over there as a spot to build a subdivision?"

"No, you didn't," I said. "But Miss George Ann told me she'd tried to sell her farm to a developer without success."

"Drake told me to take a look at it just to get her off his back," Sloan continued. "He never really considered building anything out here."

"Of course he didn't," I agreed. "Drake can see potential that others don't. But here, well, there was nothing to see."

He gave me a smile. "Exactly. But anyway, while I was here, pretending that her property had potential, I saw the fields planted by the students. I was taking pictures of the farm for Drake, and I thought the fields were kind of cool, the way they had planted all different kinds of things in neat little squares. So I took pictures of the fields and the bottling plant too. I even talked to that kid . . . Tip?"

"Tripp," I provided.

Sloan nodded. "Yeah, Tripp. He told me about the project and the website and all. I went back to Midway and got busy with the renovations there and forgot all about this place. Then a couple of weeks later Drake said that Simmons woman was driving him crazy. He asked for my feasibility report on her property, so he could officially tell her he wasn't interested and why. I made prints of the pictures I took here and wrote up my report. And of course I recommended that Drake pass on the Simmons farm."

"Of course."

Sloan winked at me. I assumed this was my reward for being a good sport. "But when I was going through the pictures I saw those fields and was intrigued all over again. So before we left I came out here to look at them one last time. And to my surprise, in just two weeks the crops had more than doubled in size."

I looked over to the patchwork fields where Cade and his crew were working. I'd noticed their lushness but never realized they were growing at an amazing rate. "They have grown really fast."

Sloan continued. "None of the students was around that evening, so I decided to look for them over in the bottling plant. I didn't find any students, but I did find a fertilizer factory."

My eyes strayed back to the burning building. "They were making fertilizer there? Not growing marijuana?"

"Just fertilizer," Sloan confirmed. "But the whole setup was odd. The equipment was very new and obviously expensive, which didn't make sense. Why would anyone set up a state-of-the-art fertilizer lab in an old, boarded-up factory? Then I found some mailing labels for addresses in South America. At that point I was pretty certain whatever was happening there was at least suspicious and possibly illegal. So I took a few more pictures and collected some fertilizer samples. Then when I got back to the hotel room that night, even though I was tired after a long day of making the library in Midway a nice place for you to work . . ."

I rolled my eyes. "Keep talking."

"I did some more research," Sloan said. "I looked up the website that kid had given me and after reading the information there I was even more interested. So I called the college, trying to contact the professor in charge of the project, but I kept getting an answering machine. Finally I talked to the dean and found out the professor was a corporate loaner."

I waved my hand impatiently. "We already know all that. Solutions, Inc. was his employer and they are now bankrupt."

"I'm impressed," Sloan said.

"So what did you do next?" Luke asked his first question of the conversation.

"I fixed up my report and submitted it to my supervisor, Agent Norman."

I turned to the other agent with wide eyes. "*You're* Sloan's supervisor?"

Agent Norman nodded.

I frowned at Sloan. "But you said your supervisor had framed you!"

"I thought he had," Sloan confirmed. "Because the report disappeared."

"But I never got it," Agent Norman explained. "In fact for the past few months, I haven't gotten any of Sloan's phone calls or e-mails."

"Someone at the Bureau was interfering with our communications," Sloan said, and now he wasn't smiling.

"All because of your interest in the fertilizer?" I asked.

Sloan nodded.

"It was that important?" Luke asked. "Some fertilizer?"

"It's not just any fertilizer," Sloan assured him. "It's like a super-fertilizer that will enable the people who grow marijuana to produce twice as much in half the time. Which means they can quadruple their crop."

"And that qualifies as a crisis for the agencies responsible for the control of drug trafficking," Mark added.

"And a few college seniors were doing all of this?" I asked.

Sloan shook his head. "Not without help. We believe the drug suppliers in South America are financing the project. They found this deserted plant out in the middle of nowhere and bought it for next to nothing. They turned an FBI agent, who created Solutions, Inc., and then loaned himself to the college With the help of some students who needed money, our rogue agent was able to test the fertilizer and begin production without attracting scrutiny. After all, it was just some college kids doing a senior project."

"They needed privacy, so this place was perfect," Mark said.

"Until Mr. Meyers bought up the land that adjoins this property," Luke contributed. "Then he gave part of it to JD, along with that trailer he was living in."

"He set up that dumpy little store on the highway," I continued. "And to make matters worse, he took up fishing as a hobby. That meant he and JD were always walking around all over the place looking for new fishing spots."

"Which had to make the fertilizer makers nervous," Luke added.

Which brought me to a sad conclusion. "And finally JD saw something?"

Sloan nodded. "Something that got him killed."

"And in the meantime our rogue agent had intercepted Sloan's report about the fertilizer," Mark said.

"He tried to discredit me and get me into trouble with my supervisor." Sloan hooked a thumb toward Agent Norman.

"Not to mention the IRS," I added.

"Please don't mention them!" Sloan pleaded.

"Sloan was desperate," Mark said.

"So since I thought Agent Norman was my enemy inside the FBI," Sloan took up the dialogue, "I kidnapped him."

I groaned. "Sloan!"

He held up his hands in surrender. "I know it was a dumb, desperate thing to do, but I had to prove I wasn't a tax evader."

I rubbed my temples. "But first you kidnapped Mark, isn't that right?"

"Sort of," Sloan said.

"He didn't have to kidnap me," Mark said. "Once he explained everything, I agreed to help figure things out. And although Agent Norman took a little more convincing than I did, eventually he agreed to help too. So there was no real kidnapping involved."

"Good," I said with a stern look in Sloan's direction. "He's in enough trouble already."

"So these students that we've seen coming out to the farm have developed a super-fertilizer and were testing it on the legal plants in the little patchwork fields. But their ultimate intention was to sell it to people who grow drugs in South America?" Luke recapped.

"Yes," Sloan confirmed.

"And they killed Jarrard Dupree?" Luke asked.

"We're not really sure about that," Sloan admitted.

"They swear they didn't kill him," Mark said.

"Not that we think they are trustworthy," Sloan mentioned.

"True," Mark conceded. "But they say their teacher killed Dupree."

"The rogue agent?" I clarified.

Mark nodded. "These might not be model students, but I don't think they are cold-blooded killers either. I think the students were willing to ignore the law to make some money, but I don't think they murdered Dupree."

"What will happen to Tripp and the other students?" I knew I shouldn't feel sorry for them, but I did.

"If they didn't kill the old man, I don't think any of them will do jail time," Agent Norman said. "If they did, well, that's another matter."

"Even if they get off easy, JD's death will haunt them forever," I predicted.

Sloan nodded. "Yeah, they should have just stuck to making good grades and earning a living legally."

I asked Sloan, "So once you convinced Mark and Agent Norman to help you—what then?"

"We came out here so I could show them the setup, and we saw that they were taking it all apart. I guess they had gotten wind that we were on to them."

"So I contacted Sheriff Bonham and we worked out a plan to arrest them and seize their equipment," Mark said.

"Lucky for us they had put a lot of the evidence in that U-Haul truck before they blew the place up," Sloan said. "Otherwise we wouldn't have a case."

"That was lucky," I agreed as we reached my truck.

"Well, that's it—the whole story," Sloan said, rubbing his hands together in a hurry-up gesture. "Now it's time for you folks to go so we can finish up here."

"You won't have to ask me twice," I assured him.

"I need to collect your bulletproof vests so I can return them to the Albany PD," Agent Norman reminded them.

Sloan pulled off his black T-shirt and dropped it on the ground. Then he unfastened his vest and extended it toward his supervisor. Not the least bit self-conscious about his bare chest, he said, "Ahh, it feels so good to be rid of that thing."

Mark Iverson glanced at me, and I realized that he was going to wait until I was gone before removing his shirt.

So I excused myself by saying, "We do have some old barn wood that we need to get to Miss Eugenia before Robby Baxley's party starts." I looked at Sloan. "But I would like to talk to you again before you leave town."

He gave me a fearless grin. "I'll be looking forward to that."

I narrowed my eyes at him and climbed into my truck. When we reached the road, I stopped and stared at the charred remains of the burning building.

"Well, I think we can safely say that no one will be making anything in that bottling plant again," Luke murmured. "Agent Sloan did exactly what he set out to do."

"Yes," I whispered as I turned away from the bottling plant. "I'm ready to get out of here."

There were seven missed calls from Miss Eugenia on my cell phone. So I called her back while negotiating the dusty dirt road. Since I'd been warned by Agent Norman not to discuss an ongoing FBI investigation, I wasn't planning to mention the events of the past hour. But as it turned out, Miss Eugenia didn't give me a chance to say a word anyway.

"I don't know why you haven't been answering my calls, but you need to get that wood to your father's workshop immediately!" she nearly yelled. "He's going to cut it into little plaques and your mother has gotten some golden labels printed for us to stick on—if you ever get here with the wood, that is!"

"I'll be there in a few minutes," I promised. Then I closed the phone and stepped on the accelerator. Since all the law enforcement people were burning down the bottling plant, I didn't have to worry about speed traps. So I made it to Midway in record time.

Fortunately my mother was at the library, which meant that once we got to my parents' house, we were able to unload the wood and leave quickly instead of having to answer a hundred questions.

As we were leaving my parents' house, Luke asked, "Do you want to change before the party?"

I glanced at my cell phone and saw that I only had thirty minutes before Robby Baxley's bus was scheduled to arrive. But my hands were cut from crawling over sharp rocks, my shoes were filthy, and I smelled like smoke. If I showed up at the welcome-home party in my present condition, my mother would die of a heart attack on the spot.

"We don't have much time, but cleaning up is absolutely necessary."

"Then we'll make time."

When we arrived at my apartment, Luke moved to his rental car and waited there while I ran inside. After a quick shower, I opened my closet and pulled out the first thing I saw, which just happened to be the lavender suit I'd purchased a couple of months before.

I put it on, dried my hair, and applied a little makeup. Then I stood in front of the mirror and surveyed myself. The suit fit well and made me feel a little like the ever-stylish Hannah-Leigh Coley-Smith. My hair looked so much better without stripes, and the extra time I'd spent out in the sun during the past few days had given me a healthy glow. My palms and knees were scraped, but as long as I was careful to hide them, I'd look okay.

I rushed back down my porch stairs feeling confident and attractive. Luke reached over and pushed open the passenger door for me. The warm smile he gave me indicated that he approved, which made me feel even better.

As we drove to the library I leaned back against the headrest and thought about all that had been resolved during that one day. Sloan was safe and no longer in trouble with the FBI, Mark Iverson was not kidnapped, Mr. Meyer had paid for the stolen paintings, we'd mostly solved the mystery of JD's death and ended an illegal fertilizer operation. All in all I had to say that was a pretty good day's work—even if none of my favorite suspects turned out to be guilty.

Main Street was a pretty sight with all the yellow bows tied along the way. I was suddenly very proud of our town for giving Robby this welcome. I was a little disappointed, however, when Luke pulled to a stop in front of the library's front entrance with the obvious intention of dropping me off.

"I need to get cleaned up too," he explained. "And Robby Baxley certainly won't be upset if I'm not there to greet him the moment he arrives."

I had to smile. "Okay, but hurry back as quickly as you can. Robby Baxley might not care if you're there, but I do."

I climbed out of Luke's car and walked into the library. There an amazing sight met my eyes. The innumerable yellow ribbons bordered on overpowering, but my mother and the other church ladies had outdone themselves. The borrowed tables were covered with snowy white cloths and laden with an amazing assortment of delicious refreshments.

"You went way beyond the cake and punch I requested," I scolded my mother as I ate a juicy slice of pineapple.

"We wanted it to be nice for Robby," Mother replied demurely.

"Well, it is definitely nice." I looked around. "And yellow."

"He's coming!" Miss Ida Jean screeched, and everyone headed for the door.

Most of the crowd followed Miss Ida Jean across to the bus station where the town council was waiting to greet the guest of honor. The high school band lined the street, their instruments ready. I decided to stay in front of the library and watch the proceedings from a distance. I didn't realize my mother had stayed with me until she put an arm around my waist.

"You look lovely," she said.

I hugged her back, careful to keep my palms from view. "Thanks, Mother."

We saw the bus coming down the street at a painfully slow pace.

"Isn't this exciting?" Mother whispered.

I nodded and it was, although I couldn't help wondering how ecstatic Midway would be if we were welcoming home a real hero like a soldier, instead of someone from prison.

The bus pulled to a stop in front of the bus station and several people climbed out. Robby Baxley was the last one to step down. I recognized him because he looked just like Miss Ida Jean except forty years younger and nearly bald.

When he stepped off the bus the band began to play and the town council rushed forward to shake hands with him. Then they led him toward the library with the band marching enthusiastically behind them. When they reached the library I moved back to let the dignitaries pass inside. But as they reached the entrance, Miss Ida Jean stopped the whole procession.

"Where's Kennedy?" she demanded, her beady little eyes searching the crowd for me.

Left with little choice, I stepped forward into the limelight.

She beamed at me. "Here she is, Robby," she said, pulling on her son's arm. "Tell Kennedy how much you appreciate her wanting to have this nice welcome-home party for you."

Robby blushed. "Thank you," he said. "Mother told me this was all your idea."

I wanted to kill Miss Ida Jean (more than I usually do). "Actually the whole town is welcoming you," I told him firmly. "I just provided the library."

Robby gave me a warm smile as his mother led him inside.

My mother chuckled. "It looks like you have an admirer."

I was not amused. "That's what I get for helping Miss Ida Jean."

I followed Mother inside, and as I looked around the room I had to admit the party was a big success. The Baptist preacher, Brother Jackson, was there. The town council was well represented, along with most of Midway's merchants. The sheriff and Miracle Moore were standing by the relish trays, looking almost like they were on a date. Rayford Cottingham was talking to Mr. Sheffield, no doubt trying to drum up business.

Of course Tripp and his fellow agricultural students weren't there since they were in jail.

But before I could dwell too much on their fate, Madison arrived with all her children, plus Heaven. The result was instant chaos. The baby was crying and needed to eat so Madison invited herself to use my office. I picked up Maggie, mostly to keep her from getting trampled, while my mother helped Major and Miles get some refreshments.

Apparently she thought Heaven could handle herself. A few minutes later I saw her stick a finger in the punch and then lick it. Then she looked up at me with challenge in her eyes. I just turned away since germs in the punch were the least of my worries.

I was sitting in a corner feeding Maggie tiny bites of finger sandwiches when Madison found me.

"We got a house!" she announced.

Knowing Madison, I figured it was probably bigger and more expensive than the one they'd just sold.

But she surprised me by saying, "It's small but there's enough room for everyone, and we cut our monthly mortgage nearly in half. Maybe someday we can build our dream home again—but for now it's best that Jared is able to spend more time with us by less working."

"I wholeheartedly agree."

Madison leaned closer and whispered. "Jared has been much more romantic lately. I don't know if it's because I'm not pregnant for the first time in years or if it's because I'm not being so expensive—but whatever the reason, it's nice."

I held up a hand. "I told you not to tell me about your romance with Jared. It might scar me."

Madison laughed, apparently thinking that I'd been joking.

Then I saw Luke walk in so I handed Maggie to Madison.

"How do you expect me to hold two babies?" she asked.

I wanted to say she should have thought of that before she came to the library with two babies, but instead I smiled. "I'm sure Mother or one of the church ladies will help you, but I've got hostess duties to attend to." After making this grand statement, I walked straight past all the refreshments and greeted Luke with a warm hug.

He looked wonderful, even with the beginnings of a black eye—a result of his fight with Sloan.

"I'm so glad you're here," I whispered.

"And I'm glad you're glad," he replied. Then he pointed to the refreshment tables. "I'm starving. When are you going to cut the cake?"

"Right now." I got him a corner piece from the huge sheet cake and a little cup of punch. Then we settled at a table in a relatively quiet corner of the children's section. But it didn't stay quiet long. Mark and Sloan arrived, along with the supervisor, Wade Norman. They were all wearing black T-shirts with FBI emblazoned on the front and looked a little out of place at the party. I knew I should be grateful that at least they had taken off the bulletproof vests.

They spotted us in the corner and walked over.

Mark cleared his throat. "We wanted to thank you for your help with this combination of cases. The sheriff said you were a big help to him even if he did involve you under false pretenses."

"I'm still mad at him," I replied. "He said that he wanted me to be part of his think tank because he valued my opinion."

Sloan laughed as he sat down beside me. "I can't believe you fell for that."

I gave him a scowl. "I'm still a little mad at you too, so you'd better watch it."

Sloan appeared unconcerned.

"Have you seen Cade Burrell?" Mark asked. "We're supposed to meet him here."

I pointed toward the fruit table where Cade was filling his plate. "If he's supposed to meet you, he'll make his way here eventually."

Agent Norman checked his watch. "We've got a truck full of fertilizer equipment outside that needs to be taken to Atlanta. So we can't stay long."

I looked at Sloan. "Are you going back with Agent Norman?"

Both men nodded in unison.

"Since you never figured out who it was inside the FBI that framed you, how are you going to keep from getting arrested by the IRS?"

"I'm not worried," Sloan claimed. "Mark and Agent Norman will vouch for me until I can access my personal records and prove that I paid my taxes."

I shrugged. "If you're not worried, I guess I won't be either."

"After our successful operation today, I'm sure the FBI will give me the benefit of the doubt." Sloan's tone was flippant. "Even though the thugs we arrested were pretty low-level guys, I figure a couple less criminals on the street is a good thing."

"We can't change the world," Agent Norman said.

Mark nodded. "We have to be realistic."

Cade, Miracle, and Sheriff Bonham joined us at this point. I nodded vaguely in greeting but couldn't force myself to be friendly. After all, the sheriff had tricked me.

"And your distractions were a big help to us," Mark told me. "Since the students had to worry about you and your questions, they couldn't pay close attention to us."

"I'm glad we didn't get in your way," I murmured.

Mark waved this aside. "Miracle wouldn't have let that happen."

I looked at Miracle. "You knew?"

She nodded.

"And you betrayed me too?"

She gave me a sheepish smile. "Sorry. I had to put the good of the operation over personal feelings."

I tried to be understanding, but it was hard.

"Don't blame Miracle. It was my decision," Mark said. "We weren't sure that the fertilizer factory was connected to Mr. Dupree's death, so we ran them as completely separate operations. I contacted Sheriff Bonham and told him we were setting up a sting and asked for his permission to operate within his jurisdiction."

My eyes turned to the sheriff briefly.

"No hard feelings?" he asked.

I shrugged. "Just don't come running to me the next time you need help solving a case."

Everyone laughed, and I joined in to be polite. But I noticed that Luke wasn't even slightly amused. Apparently Sheriff Bonham was on his bad side.

Miss Ida Jean rushed up at that moment and said that she wanted to take my picture with Robby. It was the last thing I wanted to do, but I knew how relentless Miss Ida Jean could be. So the best way to get rid of her was to do what she asked. I told Luke I'd be right back. Then I gritted my teeth and followed Miss Ida Jean to the library's front entrance. I posed awkwardly with Robby while she took an absurd number of pictures. When she was finally through I was flashbulb blind.

Blinking in a vain attempt to improve my vision, I headed back to the table where Luke was waiting patiently for me. But Miss George Ann Simmons intercepted me in front of the cheese balls.

"Have you seen the little plaques your father made?" she asked.

"No, I haven't had a chance," I told her. I took another step toward the table and saw that the sheriff and Miracle were leaving. If I got stuck with Miss George Ann much longer, the table would probably be empty.

"I think they are very nice," she said as if I'd expressed an interest. "It's a very fitting way to immortalize my family's farm and the contributions we've made to this community."

I frowned. This had never been my intention, but anything that would end my conversation with Miss George Ann was a good thing. So I gave her a fake smile, took another step toward Luke, and murmured, "Oh, hmmm."

Miss George Ann followed me and began talking about all her father's fine qualities. I didn't care about her father, but neither did I want to lead her back to the table and include the others, especially Luke, in my torture. So I stood still and let Miss George Ann brag.

Fortunately she didn't require any comments from me since she thoroughly enjoyed the sound of her own voice. This left me free to study the men at the table in the corner. Agent Norman was standing a few feet away, talking on his cell phone. So it was only Cade, Sloan, and Luke who fell prey to my scrutiny.

Cade was about to marry Hannah-Leigh and I was surprised by the lack of emotion I felt about this now. I didn't love Cade or want to be his wife. I didn't even care if he was married to someone else. I smiled, realizing I'd come a long way since that horrible night at the drive-in.

Miss George Ann had moved from her father's saintly attributes to how much she was helping the library by allowing us to sell some of her old barn wood. I tuned her out again and looked at Sloan. I realized that I love him the way I love Superman. He's beautiful and brave and a little dangerous and completely not the kind of guy to settle down with a family. I would never be able to trust my heart to him, but I would always love him a little.

Finally my eyes moved to Luke. When we'd first become reacquainted a couple of months earlier I found him intriguing and attractive. But when I remember him as a little boy, ragged, dirty, and friendless, I still felt sorry for him and a little repulsed. Now when I remembered little Luke I felt sorry for the rest of us. We'd wasted the chance to know him and it was our loss. Of the three men at that table he was the only one I couldn't bear to think of living without. Just knowing that he was flying back to Indiana the next day was enough to make me want to cry.

"As much as I'd like to stand here and talk to you all evening, Kennedy," Miss George Ann was saying, "there are others here who will feel slighted if they don't get some of my time. So you'll have to excuse me." With that she walked away and I was blessedly free of her.

By the time I got back to the table, Cade had left. No one said he'd gone to meet Hannah-Leigh, but neither would anyone meet my eyes when I asked about him, so I drew my own conclusions.

Agent Norman ended his phone call and approached Sloan. "We've got to head to Atlanta," he said. "It will already be late by the time we can get there."

"Be careful while you drive," Mark cautioned. "All that fertilizer in the wrong hands could have been, well, disastrous."

"We'll be careful," Sloan promised.

Mark stood. "Well, I guess I'll go ahead and say good-bye then. I want to try and find a flower shop that's still open so I can make up with my wife for my disappearance."

"You're going to leave before the auction?" I asked.

"Miracle will be here for that," Mark said. "I've been away from my family for too long."

I thought that was really sweet.

"You'll call ahead and straighten things out for me with the FBI, right?" Sloan asked him. "Otherwise they might shoot me on sight."

"I'll take care of it," Mark promised.

After Mark was gone I turned to Sloan. "Don't you need to go by my apartment and get your picture disc before you head back to Atlanta?"

He flashed me a smile. "I already got it and gave it to Agent Norman along with the rest of the case evidence. He's promised to give it back when the FBI is finished with it, but I'm not holding my breath."

Agent Norman gave Sloan a rare smile. "They aren't that expensive. Buy yourself another one."

I was not smiling. "You sneaked into my apartment again and got it off my lampshade without even letting me know?"

"I've been telling you to get deadbolts on your doors," he teased. "So I guess you don't really want to keep me out."

"I do have a nice new security system now, but I'm betting you know the code."

Sloan just grinned.

"And how would deadbolts do me any good since you usually come in through my bedroom window?"

"Sloan comes into your apartment often?" Luke asked. "And through the *bedroom window?*"

I realized too late that it sounded much worse than it actually was. "Only a couple of times when there were warrants for his arrest. I mean, I knew he wasn't guilty and he needed a place to sleep and, I mean, he stayed downstairs!"

I could see the hurt and confusion in Luke's eyes.

"It doesn't matter. It's nothing to worry about," I promised him. But I remembered how I'd felt when I found out that the sheriff and Miracle had been less than honest with me.

"Well, it's time for me to say good-bye!" Sloan said.

I was torn, I'll admit. I knew that Luke was where my future lay and that he deserved an apology and needed reassurance. But once

Sloan walked out the door, I didn't know when I'd see him again, if ever. And I wanted to at least say good-bye. Before I could make a choice, Luke stood.

"If you'll excuse me for a minute, I have a niece who needs my attention." Then he walked over toward the cake table where Heaven was encouraging Major to smear blue icing all over his face. Certainly Heaven needed to be stopped, but I knew Luke had used the child as an excuse to give me some private time with Sloan. His sensitivity made me feel happy and sad at the same time.

Sloan regained my attention by taking my hand in his. Then while walking toward the door he asked, "Will you miss me?"

I looked into his hypnotic eyes and nodded. "Where are you headed after you make your truck delivery in Atlanta?"

"I'm not sure. I've asked for a leave of absence so I can get things straightened out with the IRS."

"That seems wise."

"Then I need to do something about Drake. I've either got to make a permanent break with him or the FBI. I can't keep working for them both."

I respected him for this. "You'll make the right decision."

We stopped by the front door and he leaned in close. Then he whispered, "I might drop in and spend the night with you again sometime."

"The office below my apartment is always available to you."

He smiled and tilted his head toward the cake table where Luke was standing. "Have you already given your heart away or do I still have a chance?"

I glanced over and saw that Luke was trying futilely to help Major wipe the sticky icing off with paper napkins. My lip trembled a little and I said, "My heart is taken, but I've always been told it's impossible to have too many friends."

"Do you want me to kiss you just to make him jealous?"

I shook my head. "No, thanks. You've done quite enough in that department already."

Sloan laughed. "He needs to appreciate how lucky he is to have a girl like you so he'll never take you for granted."

I shook my head. "Luke won't take me for granted. And I'm the one who is lucky. Good-bye, Sloan. Good luck and, like Mark said, be careful."

"I will," he promised.

"Let's go, Sloan," Agent Norman said a little impatiently from the door.

So I brought his hand up to my lips and kissed it quickly. Then I let it drop and waved.

With his amazing smile still firmly in place, he walked to the door and followed his supervisor out.

I went over to the cake table, intending to explain about Sloan to Luke and offer my assistance with the blue icing smears, which seemed to be getting worse instead of better. But my mother rescued Major before I could get there. I said, "Luke . . ." and he looked up at me. Then Robby Baxley stepped between us.

"Thank you again for throwing this nice party for me," he said. "And I wanted you to know that I was convicted of a white-collar crime." He blushed again. "I doctored the books a little, but I didn't want you to think I robbed a convenience store or anything like that."

I could think of absolutely nothing to say.

Robby, on the other hand, seemed unable to stop talking, a trait he shared with his mother. "I don't know that many people around here anymore, and my mother thought you might like to go out to the movies with me this weekend so we can get acquainted."

Robby had several strikes against him. He's at least fifteen years older than me, he's unattractive, and he's a thief. But even if I'd been the slightest bit interested in him, the fact that he's Ida Jean's son would have been enough to prevent me from accepting his invitation.

And I wasn't mad at Robby for asking me. But I was furious with Miss Ida Jean for creating this awkward situation. I was trying to think of a way to gently tell Robby that I would not to go the movies with him if he were the last man on earth, when Luke stepped forward.

"I know you're the guest of honor, but Kennedy is already involved in a relationship, so she not available for any movie dates." Luke draped his arm across my shoulders to punctuate his remarks.

And even though his arm was comforting, I couldn't help but notice he was careful not to say who I was in a relationship with. Robby didn't notice this fine point. He was visibly disappointed but wouldn't risk a confrontation with Luke. So he nodded in defeat.

I snuggled a little closer to Luke and said, "There are lots of eligible women who would love to go to the movies. You should come to church with your mother on Sunday. There's no better place to meet people."

He nodded and shuffled off. As much as I hated the thought that I'd hurt his feelings, I hoped he'd feel awkward around me and therefore avoid me. One Baxley bothering me was plenty.

Once Robby was gone I turned back to Luke. "Luke," I tried again. But before I could get any further we heard the sounds of gunfire outside.

Luke's eyes locked with mine for a split second. Then he whispered, "Keep everyone inside," before slipping out through the front door.

The sun had set, but it wasn't dark yet. I watched as he disappeared around the side of the library toward the parking lot. Then I turned to face the crowd that was silent for the first time since the party began.

I pasted on my there's-nothing-to-worry-about smile and said, "Everyone just keep eating and enjoying yourselves. We're planning a little fireworks display, but it sounds like they're having trouble getting it set up. It might be dangerous, so I'm going to have to ask you all to stay inside while I check on things."

I found my mother's face in the crowd. "Mother, if you'll please stand here and guard the door."

My mother rushed over to me. "If it's not safe outside, you need to stay in here too."

I always feel guilty when I disobey my mother, especially when I know she's right. So I gave her a quick hug and then hurried outside, following the direction Luke had taken.

CHAPTER ELEVEN

I peeked around the corner of the library warily at first. I intended to scope out the situation before I announced my presence. But what I saw made me throw caution to the wind. Sloan was lying on the ground by the U-Haul truck with two tiny bullet holes in his chest. A gun was on the ground close to his limp fingers.

Agent Norman was standing over him, holding a gun in both trembling hands. A red gash marred the black fabric on the sleeve of his T-shirt.

Mark Iverson, Cade, and Luke were standing behind Agent Norman in a haphazard semicircle.

As I came around the corner I heard Mark say, "Agent Norman, put your weapon down."

Based on the insistence of his tone I felt sure this was not the first time Mark had made this request.

Agent Norman let his arm drop to his side but did not release the gun. Even though all three men in unison said, "No, Kennedy!" I ran from the safety of the library's brick wall and kneeled beside Sloan.

His beautiful black hair was spread out around his head like an inky halo. In the fading light he looked pale, and he was ominously still. Whimpering, I gathered Sloan's head onto my lap and cradled him like a baby. "No," I whispered. "You can't die."

"He tried to kill me!" Agent Norman was yelling. "When we got out to the truck, I said I'd drive and asked him for the keys. He pulled his gun and tried to take the truck. I guess he's the rogue agent. He's been working for the drug dealers all along. He was going to take them this stuff so they could make more fertilizer and ship it to South

America." He looked up, appealing to us. "I didn't want to kill him, but I had no choice!"

"Has someone called an ambulance?" I demanded.

They all ignored me.

The sheriff stepped out of the shadows from the neighboring building. "I was standing here the whole time, Agent." His tone was cold and harsh. "Do you want to change your story?"

Agent Norman brought his weapon up again and swung it back and forth between the men. Apparently he didn't see me as any threat because he had his back to me. "I'm going to get in that truck and drive out of here," he said. "And she's going with me." He waved the gun vaguely in my direction.

He was close to me, so close that I was pretty sure I could reach out and grab his leg. I didn't think I could knock him down from my somewhat awkward position on the ground, but if I could distract him long enough for one of the men to gain an advantage, it could mean the difference between catching the killer or not. I leaned forward, but the weight of Sloan's head and shoulders held me pinned in place.

"All of you move that way," Agent Norman directed to the left with his gun.

Mark, Cade, Luke, and the sheriff all obeyed.

"It was you all along," Mark said. "You did destroy Sloan's report and steal his computer. Because something in that report incriminated you."

"I've been working on this too long now to let some lazy, disorganized undercover agent ruin it for me," Agent Norman growled. "Or an old drunk either."

"JD," I whispered. That rotten, no-good, dishonest FBI agent had killed poor JD. I reached toward him again, but if anything Sloan seemed to have gotten heavier and I couldn't budge.

"I'm willing to let you take the truck," Mark said. "But not Kennedy. She stays here."

Agent Norman's laugh sounded desperate and dangerous. "You'll shoot me the first chance you get if I don't have a hostage."

All the men in near-unison said, "Take me."

I was already about to cry since Sloan was either dead or dying. Then to see these men offer their lives for me was very emotional. But

Agent Norman ruined the moment by grabbing a handful of my hair. Sloan's weight had me pinned to the ground, so when Agent Norman jerked I didn't move, but I screamed and tears of pain sprang into my eyes.

While I was writhing, a hand came out of nowhere and sliced Agent Norman at the ankles, felling him with one blow. Cade and Luke tackled him simultaneously. Then Luke held him while Cade secured the handcuffs.

I frowned, looking around for the person who had knocked down Agent Norman. Then I realized that Sloan's eyes were open and he was grinning at me.

"Thank goodness for Kevlar."

I didn't know it was possible to be so happy and so mad at the same time. I pounded my fist on his vest-protected chest. "But you took off your vest at the bottling plant!"

"I made a show of taking it off so Agent Norman would think I was unprotected," Sloan explained. "Then I put on another one when he wasn't watching."

Miracle stepped out of the shadows where the sheriff had been earlier. She held up a camera and said, "I've got it all on tape."

I looked around and realized that the whole thing had been staged. "This was a setup *too*!" I demanded. "And I wasn't in on it either?"

"I'm sorry, Kennedy," Mark apologized profusely. "But since we were dealing with an FBI agent we knew we needed a confession to get a conviction. And we couldn't risk Agent Norman catching on—so we didn't tell anyone. Even you."

"We really wanted to get Agent Norman," Sloan said. "It was more important than anything, even hurting your feelings."

The sheriff jerked Agent Norman to his feet. "Now what to do with you?"

Miracle looked at Mark. "I'm not sure what the protocol is."

"You'd better ask the Special Agent in Charge and see how he wants us to handle it," Mark told her. "I warned him earlier today that he might be receiving a call."

While Miracle stepped a few feet away and dialed a number on her cell phone, Sloan sat up with a wince.

"Ouch!" he whimpered.

"Didn't your bulletproof vest protect you from the gunshots?" I asked in concern.

"It kept the bullets from killing me," Sloan confirmed. "But my chest still hurts like . . . well, it hurts. Right where you hit me."

"I'm so sorry!" I cried.

He grinned again. "How about we just forgive each other?"

I knew he had tricked me, but I nodded. "You're forgiven if I am."

At this moment Miss Ida Jean came running around the corner of the library. "When are the fireworks going to be ready?"

Cade stepped between her and the rest of us, blocking her view. "There's been a little problem with the fireworks," he adlibbed smoothly. Sometimes being a good liar comes in handy. "In fact, we're going to have to cancel the show for tonight."

Miss Ida Jean sounded disappointed. "Oh, that's a shame."

"Let's get you back inside." Cade took her by the arm and led her to the front door.

Mark gave Sloan a hand and once he was standing, helped him remove his T-shirt and the damaged vest. Sloan stood bare-chested in the twilight. His dark hair was blowing back from the chiseled features of his face. He was a magnificent sight, and if all the residents of Midway hadn't been inside the library, he would have created one of the biggest scenes the town had ever witnessed.

Luke walked over and peered at the two little dots the bullets had left on Sloan's skin. "They broke the skin so you'll need to put some antibiotic ointment on them. And you might want to get an X-ray to be sure you didn't crack a rib. But I think you'll be fine."

Apparently Sloan respected Luke's battle experience because he just nodded and pulled his T-shirt back on gingerly.

"How did you know your supervisor was really the rogue agent?" I asked.

"He had easy access to my report and files," Sloan said. "Someone else could have taken them, but he was the most obvious suspect."

"And then he suggested this wimpy sting where all we got was some fertilizer and a few low-level thugs," Cade added. "We knew that plan was designed to protect the formula and the more important criminals."

"He had things worked out pretty well," Mark said. "Until Miss George Ann noticed that her wood was missing from her barn."

I groaned. "Does this mean that Miss George Ann gets partial credit for solving the case?"

Mark nodded with a smile. "I don't see how we can deny her."

"You could just chalk it up to bad luck," Sloan taunted Agent Norman. "Or you could say that everybody gets what's coming to them, eventually."

Norman sneered at Sloan. "I have friends in high places, and your little video won't stand up in court. I will *never* be convicted."

Sloan moved closer and hissed, "Yeah well I have friends in low places and after one word from me you won't *live* long enough to come to trial."

Agent Norman paled.

"That's enough, Agent Sloan," the sheriff said. Then he turned to Cade. "Let's take him over to the jail and keep him there until the FBI folks in Atlanta figure out where he's going for a more permanent stay."

"I'd be delighted to show this smart city guy around our little country jail." Cade was grinning as he grabbed Agent Norman by the handcuffed arms and pulled him toward the sheriff's department.

Once they were gone I turned to Mark and Sloan. "So JD found out what they were doing and Agent Norman killed him?"

"That's the way we figure it," Sloan concurred.

Mark said, "The kids were tricked into participating in Norman's fertilizer project and were then coerced into staying with the program."

"They did get paid," I pointed out.

"But once you get involved with these guys they won't let you out," Mark said. "So I still expect the kids to get off pretty easy."

I narrowed my eyes at Sloan, "You won't really tell anyone to hurt Agent Norman in prison, will you?"

Sloan scowled. "I'm still thinking about that one."

Miracle returned to our group. "We're to bring Norman and the truck of fertilizer supplies to Atlanta tonight. Sloan, are you up for a little drive?"

He rubbed the sore spots on his chest. "I guess I'll have to be."

Miracle called the sheriff and had him bring Agent Norman back. It was decided that the U-Haul truck wasn't secure enough to transport a prisoner. So the sheriff and Deputy Cross volunteered follow behind the truck in a squad car, all the way to Atlanta, with Agent Norman handcuffed in the backseat.

While the others were securing Agent Norman, Sloan put one of his hands on each of my shoulders and shook me gently. "You're a brave girl," he said, "but let me give you some advice. Never try to grab at a crazed gunman. Leave the heroics to us professionals."

I frowned at him. "You knew I was trying to trip Agent Norman, and you purposely held me down!"

"Of course I did. The last thing we needed was you messing up our carefully laid plans!"

I felt a little silly until he moved his hands onto my back and gave me a quick hug. "Don't worry about it. And be watching for me. I'll come see you sometime."

"Just be sure you use the door," I muttered.

His laughter was still ringing in my ears after they had left for Atlanta.

"I'm going home," Mark said. "And this time I mean it!"

Cade sighed. "The sheriff left me with the job of figuring out how to write all this up in a sensible report."

"Good luck with that," Mark commiserated. But he didn't offer his assistance.

Cade walked across the street toward the sheriff's department. That left me and Luke alone again, finally. I knew I had much to explain. I began with, "Luke . . ."

Then my mother came charging around the corner of the library. "What on earth is going on out here?" she demanded. "Ida Jean says that you had fireworks planned but you never mentioned them to me."

"Sorry, Mother. I forgot."

"And now she says they aren't working, and we don't know whether to go on with the auction or wait for you to fix the fireworks or what?" she looked around suspiciously.

"The fireworks are over for tonight," I said wearily. "Let's just have the auction so we can all go home."

***

When we got back inside, the crowd was milling round quietly. In the adult research section two tables had been cleared of food and about a hundred rectangles of barn wood approximately 12×6 were spread out neatly. I moved closer and saw that the little gold label attached to each plaque said, "In memory of Jarrard Dupree, library patron."

Tears blurred my eyes so I couldn't see that my mother had walked up to stand beside me, but I knew she was there. And in that moment I loved her more than ever before. "This is a miracle," I said. "You only had a few minutes after I got back with the wood."

"I got the Haggerty Print Shop to make the labels in advance. After you dropped off the wood, Daddy cut it up with his table saw. Then we borrowed your truck to bring the pieces here.

"All the church ladies who weren't serving food stuck on labels and we got it done. Which reminds me . . . Daddy said to tell you your truck's parked out back and the keys are in the floorboard."

I nodded absently, still astonished by what my friends and family had accomplished.

Miss Eugenia hobbled up and whispered, "I want a full accounting of what happened outside."

"I've been sworn to secrecy by an FBI agent," I whispered back. "So unless Mark will give you the details, you'll have to wait until the morning paper comes out."

"Mark never tells me anything," she muttered. "But I guess I can wait on the paper." Then she turned to face the crowd. "Let the auction begin! I bid a hundred dollars for the first plaque."

I smiled and said, "Sold!"

She picked up a plaque and walked back to her seat.

It took us just under an hour to sell all of the plaques. Miss Eugenia's was the most expensive, and the cheapest one sold for ten dollars. All in all it was a very successful night. I was still basking in the glow of JD's glory when Miss George Ann came up, demanding her cut.

"This will have to be handled properly," I told her. "I'll double-check the total in the morning and write you an official library check."

She eyed the old cigar box where my mother had placed the money when people paid for their plaques. "Why can't you just give me cash?"

I figured she was trying to avoid paying taxes on the paltry sum she'd "earned." So I took great pleasure in telling her that this would not be possible. She left in a huff, which only made it better.

"Kennedy," Mother said after Miss George Ann was gone. "You should be ashamed."

"I'm not," I replied firmly. "I'm following the letter of the law, and I believe I've done my duty to someone Grandmother Killingsworth didn't even like in the first place."

Mother laughed. "I'd say you have."

We started cleaning up, and Miss Ida Jean said she'd like to stay and help but her bursitis had started to bother her.

My mother—who had been on her feet for days making Robby's party into a success—smiled sweetly at Miss Ida Jean and said, "You go on home and rest. We'll take care of all this."

Miss Ida Jean nodded as if this was perfectly reasonable. Then she turned to me. "And the idea about the fireworks was a nice one, Kennedy, but next time you need to make sure you know how to operate them so your guests aren't disappointed."

I was too tired to even get mad. "Yes, ma'am."

Luke helped take out bags of garbage, sweep up cake crumbs, and load borrowed chairs into the van from the Baptist church. When we had the library restored to order, I hugged my mother and sisters and all the church ladies. I expressed more appreciation in a few minutes than I probably had in my whole life. One by one everyone left until finally it was just me and Luke.

I took a step toward him, anxious to explain away the hurt in his eyes and reassure him about my feelings. I said, "Luke . . ."

And then the library door swung open again. I turned to see my mother and Heaven standing there looking at us.

"The judge gave Heaven permission to stay with her parents tonight," Mother explained. "As long as Luke is there to make sure she's properly supervised."

My shoulders slumped in defeat. I would not get a chance to talk to Luke alone after all. Heaven had claimed him. I'd been beaten by an eight-year-old.

"I'll text you," Luke promised, but he didn't say it with feeling.

After they were gone, Mother patted my cheek and said, "Come by the house for breakfast tomorrow so we can talk."

I nodded, mostly because I couldn't refuse my mother anything after all she'd done for me recently and partly because after my awful day I was desperately in need of comfort food. We walked out to the parking lot together. Cade was crossing the street to his squad car and politely came over to speak to us.

When my mother drove away I was left alone with Cade. He seemed to be in a mellow mood. He wasn't texting or acting like he was desperate to get away. So I decided to take advantage of the moment.

"You and Luke worked together pretty well taking down that armed FBI agent tonight."

Cade scoffed. "Either one of us could have handled that wimp by ourselves."

He was admitting that Luke was physically capable—another good sign. "I had a talk with Luke awhile back, about the past and the things that happened between you."

Cade froze, all congeniality disappearing instantly. "Why did he have to go and dredge all that stuff up," he growled.

"Because it's time to bury the hatchet," I said. "This same tiny . . . (a lot of other adjectives came to mind like rundown and backward, but as I've mentioned, Cade has a short attention span so I kept it simple) town is home to all of us so we're going to have to get along."

Cade cut his eyes over at me. "Really, that's how you feel?"

I nodded. "I'm not condoning what you did, but . . . you were young and stupid—"

"And drunk," he added.

Luke hadn't mentioned that part, but I didn't find it hard to believe. Alcohol had also been involved when he took Missy Lamar to the drive-in.

"I never liked Scoggins," Cade admitted.

I saw this for what it was—an explanation of unforgivable behavior. So I nodded again.

"He was one of those cocky kids. He gave you a look like he thought he was better than you—even though he was nothing! He was poor. He was a nobody. He wasn't even clean!"

"Cade," I warned.

He took a deep breath. "We hadn't seen each other in a while and he offered to buy me a drink. I'd already had a few and so I was willing to take a drink from anybody—even a Scoggins."

I frowned—apparently there was a lot of the story that Luke didn't share with me.

"Then he started bragging about how he had gotten into the Marines and he was leaving for basic training the next day. I saw that look in his eyes again—the one that said I'm a Marine and you're just a sheriff's deputy. I'm going to see places you'll never see. I'm better than you! And it reminded me of all the reasons I didn't like him."

Cade ran his fingers through his hair to calm himself. Then he continued. "But I didn't let on. We sat there and drank together like buddies. After he'd had a few he let it slip that he'd always had a thing for you and how he was going to look you up when he came home a somebody, maybe even a hero!" Cade laughed harshly. "Like a Scoggins could ever be more than nothing."

I was even more confused. "Cade, what are you talking about?"

Cade said the rest all in a big rush, like he had to get it out. "He went on to basic training and the next week I saw you at that church barbecue. And I realized that Scoggins was right—you were mighty cute. So . . ."

The full horror of what Cade was saying washed over me. I forced my lips to form the words. "You married me just because Luke expressed an interest in me?"

"Is that what he said?" Cade demanded, angry now. "He accused me of that when he came home from his first tour in Iraq, and I told him it was a lie. I might have gone over to talk to you for the first time just to make him mad. And I'll admit I made sure he got the word that we were dating. I knew that would wipe the smug grin off his face."

"Oh, Cade." Just when I think he can't possibly hurt me any more, he finds a way.

"But I didn't marry you because of Scoggins!" Cade claimed. "I loved you. I still love you. We just aren't soul mates."

I let that last remark pass because I was afraid if I thought about it too much I might kill him. "I didn't know."

Cade frowned. "What do you mean? You said he told you!"

I was amazingly calm considering another one of my naive fantasies had been shattered. "He told me about high school, how you made fun of him for trying to play football and eventually made him drop out of school altogether. I had no idea you married me just to spite him."

He held out his hand to me. "Kennedy," he tried. "Like I said, it might have started out that way, but . . ."

"I can't be near you right now," I said. "I have to get away so I can think."

"Please, Kennedy," he pleaded.

"I'm not mad at you, Cade. And eventually I'll forgive you. But this is new to me and, well, you're going to have to give me time."

I walked to my truck and climbed inside. As I pulled away from the parking lot, I saw Cade standing there looking so sad and dejected. I remembered how happy and relaxed he'd been when we first started our conversation, and I was almost sorry for him. Almost.

***

The moon was high in the clear spring sky when I turned onto the road that led through the woods to the Scoggins Salvage Yard. The trees that used to scrape the sides of my car had been cut back, and the potholes that had threatened to ruin my tires had been filled with gravel.

When I pulled into the clearing I could see changes there as well. The tires that had been scattered over several acres were now piled into one huge steel-belted mountain. Gravel had been poured to designate the driving areas and some grass seed had been planted in a first attempt at a lawn. Both houses had new roofs and had been painted.

It was still a salvage yard and necessarily had parts and pieces of vehicles lying around, but improvements were everywhere, and I knew that they could all be attributed to one person. Luke. Who would not allow himself to be limited by his name or his past.

I didn't see him sitting in a chair on the porch of his father's house until I was climbing the steps. Then he spoke from the shadows. "Now this is a surprise."

I turned to face him. "I should have called, but I was afraid you'd try and talk me out of coming and I just—I couldn't wait. I had to talk to you."

He nodded, although his expression didn't seem welcoming, and my heart began to ache.

"I'll get you a chair," he said. He stood and walked toward the front door.

I stopped him by putting both of my hands on his chest. "Will you just hold me for a minute?"

I expected him to wrap his arms around me, giving me the comfort I needed, even if things between us were unsettled, even if he thought I might love another man. And that's exactly what he did. I pressed my cheek against the crisp fabric of his shirt and wept. He stroked my hair until I stopped crying. Then he pulled my face back with a finger on my chin.

"It's okay, Kennedy," he said softly. "I understand. Sloan seems like an okay guy, and if you'll be happy with him . . ."

I frowned. "I won't be happy with Sloan! He's just a friend. He came to me because he was in trouble and he didn't think anyone would look for him at my place. He slept in Mr. Sheffield's office, and I told him I'd shoot him if he came upstairs."

Luke's eyes widened.

"He didn't believe me either, and I probably wouldn't have really shot him, but the point is he didn't even try. It's not like that with us."

Luke's features relaxed a little. He wasn't smiling yet, but he wasn't frowning anymore.

I grabbed a fistful of shirt fabric in each hand. "You'd give me up so easily? Without a fight?"

"I'd do almost anything to make you happy," Luke said. "Even give you up if that's what you wanted."

I rested my face on his chest again. "I was talking to Cade tonight—trying to get a promise from him that he would never fight with you again, and he inadvertently told me all about what he did. Not just the high school stuff, but how he asked me out in the first place to hurt you."

Luke tangled his fingers in my hair and I could hear his heart pounding in my ear. "Those were dark days," he admitted. "I planned Cade's murder more times than I could count while I was in Iraq. I'm not proud of my feelings—but I'm being honest. I hated him and I almost couldn't live with the knowledge that he had married you. The only thing that kept me from going AWOL and coming back here to tell you was the sure knowledge that you wouldn't have wanted me over him."

It was true and I was ashamed. "I wasn't ready for you yet."

He pressed a kiss to the top of my head. "It was bad enough when I found out you had married him, but then when I heard about that whole thing at the drive-in with Missy Lamar and the divorce . . . I felt so responsible. It was like I had personally caused you all that pain."

"We'll let Cade take responsibility for my pain. And I was responsible for my own choices."

He didn't respond, which I knew meant he didn't agree, but he didn't want to argue.

"Why didn't you tell me?"

"I would have—eventually," he said. "But not until things were settled, one way or another. I didn't want that knowledge to push you toward Cade or away from him. I wanted you to make your decisions based on how you felt."

I've always been a little leery of the whole concept of a higher power. But I'll admit that at that moment I started to believe. For if there could be a man this wonderful, maybe there was a God as well.

"I love you," I whispered.

"I love you too," he said. "I have since the third grade."

I wanted to cry again but swallowed my tears. "I'm sorry it's taken me so long to catch up with you."

"I'm just glad you made it," he said. "And I don't want you to feel pressured. There's no rush. We'll just let things work themselves out."

I smiled. "We'll take our time, but it wouldn't hurt to at least start making mental plans for a small, tasteful wedding and a romantic honeymoon."

"You work on the wedding," he said. "I'll handle the honeymoon. I've been mentally planning that for years."

KILLINGSWORTHS' DECORATION DAY PICNIC

Grandma Killingsworth's Fried Chicken

6 boneless breasts
1/2 tsp Lawry's seasoned salt
1 C buttermilk
1 tsp salt
1 tsp pepper
1 1/2 C all-purpose flour
Vegetable oil

Wash chicken and put in a Ziplock bag. Pour in buttermilk and refrigerate for at least 3 hours (overnight if possible).

Heat oil in a large, deep pot. In a separate Ziplock bag, combine 1 1/2 cups flour, 1 tsp salt, 1/2 tsp Lawry's seasoned salt, and 1 tsp pepper. Shake well. Test oil by dropping a tiny pinch of flour into it. If the flour sizzles and floats, the oil is ready. Drop the chicken pieces into the flour mixture one at a time and shake until each piece is completely coated. Then drop into the oil. Cook for 5–10 minutes until chicken is golden brown (and usually will float to the top). Do not overcook. When chicken is done, place pieces on a plate lined with paper towels to absorb the excess oil until time to serve. Oil can be cooled, strained, and stored for the next time. Serves 6.

NOTE—After you take the chicken out of the oil, cut one piece to be sure it is fully cooked. If it is not, you can put the chicken in the microwave for a minute or two to complete the cooking process without burning your crust.

Iris's Pulled Pork Sandwiches

Large pork loin roast (about 5–6 pounds)
1 tsp liquid smoke
2 TBSP pork rub
1 tsp garlic salt
Favorite barbecue sauce (Iris uses Big Bob Gibson's—available on www.bigbobgibsonbbq.com/)

Preheat oven to 275 degrees Fahrenheit. Place roast in a large roasting pan. Score it to give the seasonings more surface area. Start with the liquid smoke. Sprinkle 1 tsp along the top of the meat and massage it in. Then repeat this process with the pork rub and garlic salt. Cover tightly with foil and bake for 3 hours. At the end of 3 hours take the roast out and pour off some of the fat (not all—but most of it). Then use a fork to see if the meat will separate easily. If it will, your roast is done. If not, it needs to cook a little longer. Return it to the oven for 30 minutes. If it still seems stiff, return it for 15-minute intervals until it falls apart. Serves approximately 10 hungry people, and you'll probably have leftovers that can be frozen.

When roast is finished cooking, allow it to "rest" for 30 minutes. Then mix in your favorite barbecue sauce and serve on buns.

***

Decoration Day Baked Beans

2 large cans of Bush's Original Baked Beans
1 small bottle Heinz Ketchup
2 tsp chili powder
1 C corn syrup (Karo)
2 TBSP Worcestershire sauce
5 slices of bacon

Preheat oven to 300 degrees Fahrenheit. Mix all ingredients except the bacon together and pour into a large casserole pan. Fry the bacon slightly and then put it on top. Cook for 2 hours.

Deb's Linguine Salad

1 box of linguine noodles, prepared according to package directions
1 small bottle of Zesty Italian salad dressing
1 6-oz. can green pitted olives (without the pimento, if you can find them, drained)
1 6-oz. can medium pitted black olives (drained)
1 C shredded cheese (cheddar or parmesan)
1 tsp garlic salt
Pepper to taste

Mix all ingredients together in a large bowl and allow to sit in the refrigerator for at least an hour before serving. Serves 8–10 people.

***

Paige's Potato Salad

5 lbs of red potatoes
1 small bell pepper (diced)
1 small onion (red or yellow) diced
1 medium jar sliced pimentos
1/8 tsp pepper
1 1/2 tsp celery salt
1 tsp poppy seeds
1 1/2 to 2 C Hellmann's Mayonnaise
1/4 C mustard
1 C sweet pickle relish

Mix all ingredients well. Refrigerate before serving. Serves 8–10 people.

Strawberry Jell-O Salad

1 C thin pretzels (crushed)
3/4 C melted margarine
1 large box strawberry Jell-O
1 8-oz pkg cream cheese
1 small Cool Whip
3 TBSP sugar
2 C boiling water
2 10-oz pkg frozen strawberries

Mix margarine, pretzels, and sugar in 9×13 pan. Bake at 400 degrees Fahrenheit for 7 minutes. Cool. Dissolve Jell-O in water. Add strawberries and chill until partially gelled (about the consistency of preserves). Blend cream cheese and Cool Whip. Spread over pretzel crust. Pour Jell-O over cream cheese later and chill for several hours. Serves 8–10 people.

***

Aunt Docia Wood's Glorified Brownies

1 C melted butter
4 large eggs
1 tsp vanilla extract
1 1/2 C all-purpose flour
Pecan halves (optional)
1/2 C cocoa
2 C sugar
1/2 tsp salt
Large marshmallows

Preheat oven to 300 degrees Fahrenheit. Lightly grease a cookie sheet. Combine melted butter with cocoa, then add eggs, sugar, vanilla, and salt. Mix well. Add flour and mix just until moistened. Pour into pan and cook for 20 minutes.

Take pan out of the oven and line up marshmallows so that there will be one on top of each brownie when it is cut (usually 4 across and 6 down). Put pan back in the oven for about 5 minutes until they puff up. Remove the pan and press each marshmallow down with the back of a spoon. Then cover the brownies with the frosting.

Frosting

1/4 cup butter, melted
1/4 cup cocoa
1 TBSP milk (as needed)
2 C powdered sugar

Combine butter and cocoa with about a TBSP of milk. Add 2 cups of powdered sugar. Add more milk or more sugar as necessary until it is a pouring consistency.

    Top each marshmallow (which is now covered by frosting) with one pecan half. Allow to cool completely before cutting and serving.

ABOUT THE AUTHOR

BETSY BRANNON GREEN currently lives in Bessemer, Alabama, which is a suburb of Birmingham. She has been married to her husband, Butch, for thirty-one wonderful years, and they have eight children, one daughter-in-law, three sons-in-law, and five grandchildren. She is the Mia Maid Adviser in the Bessemer Ward and works for Hueytown Elementary School. She loves to read, when she can find the time, and watch sporting events—especially if they involve her children. Although born in Salt Lake City, Betsy has spent most of her life in the South. Her writing and her life have been strongly influenced by the town of Headland, Alabama, and the many generous gracious people who live there. Her first book, *Hearts in Hiding,* was published in 2001, followed by *Never Look Back* (2002), *Until Proven Guilty* (2002), *Don't Close Your Eyes* (2003), *Above Suspicion* (2003), *Foul Play* (2004), *Silenced* (2004), *Copycat* (2005), *Poison* (2005), *Double Cross* (2006), *Christmas in Haggerty* (2006), *Backtrack* (2007), *Hazardous Duty* (2007), *Above and Beyond* (2008), *The Spirit of Christmas* (2008), *Code of Honor* (2009), and *Murder by the Book* (2009).